MATA NAVEENA

A Peace Corps Writers Book

An imprint of Peace Corps Worldwide

Printed in the United States of America

by Peace Corps writers of Oakland, California.

No part of this book may be used or reproduced in any manner

whatsoever without written permission except in the case of

brief quotations contained in critical articles or reviews.

For more information, contact peacecorpsworldwide@gmail.com.

Peace Corps Writers and the Peace Corps colophon are trademarks of PeaceCorps-

Worldwide.org.

ISBN-13:978-1-935925-58-3

Library of Congress Control Number: XXXXXXXXX

First Peace Corps Writers Edition, September 2015

To all the people who helped make this book a reality,

especially my parents Richard and Wilma, my sister Gayle Rabinovitz,

Yashoda Singh, Trevor Welker, Donna Cavedon, Najibur Rahman and his children Amir

and Maria, Ed Lynch, Vijay Kumar Bhagat, and Hank Cerasoli.

Mata Naveena

by

Will Michelet

TABLE OF CONTENTS

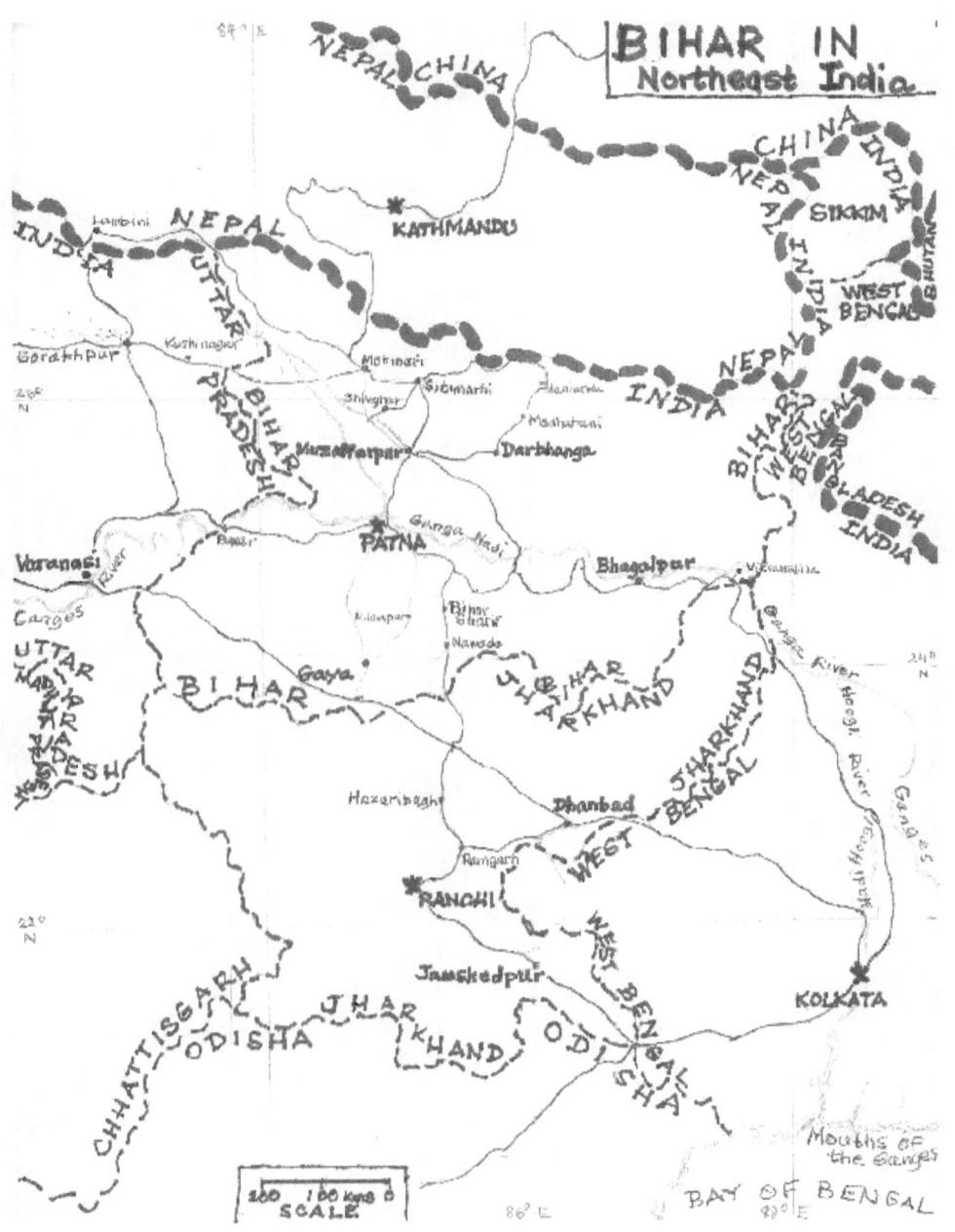

SPRING

Chapter One

The electricity was building in the night air, and when the initial faint rumble of thunder came, the Chaudrys and their children were drawn to the verandah to watch the storm develop. Far off to the right, a long string of lightning crackled down the dark sky almost to the horizon. In the north where the gods resided in the mountains, there was a delayed thunderclap that rolled through the unseen foothills till it caused the house to tremble, and Aravind, dressed in spotless white *kurta* and *paijama* that sharply contrasted with his deeply bronzed face, slipped a protective arm around his lighter-skinned wife Neela as they gasped together in wonder. When the clouds opened to pour an ever more intense spate of raindrops, he uttered, "Oh, joy, the monsoon has come at last," and she cried out, laughing as the drops began to splatter on her face, "and if it had waited much longer, the paddy would have been lost."

They and their son Kumar and daughter Lakshmi, whose small blue *sari* was a lighter hue than that of the garment worn by her mother, stood there together, the storm coming to bathe them on the open porch as it pounded its life-giving force between the pillars. The ensuing chill did not dampen the excitement even of Neela and Aravind as their bodies clung to each other in gratefulness for this gift from the heavens....

In the meantime, their younger daughter Shashi had whimpered when she heard the first grumble of thunder in the distance, and she, in a clean but dinghy red skirt and rose blouse, jumped with her parents and siblings, her eyes fearfully scanning the windows of the sitting room. As her mother and father and older brother and sister moved toward the verandah, the sky behind her exploded with a burst of light, and she spun around to see a jagged thunderbolt zigzag toward the earth far outside the last window behind her. Instinctively she headed to her room and raced to the door of her closet inside it and paused a moment there till the first full clap of thunder shook the walls.

Without a thought, then, she pushed on into the dark enclosure and pulled the closet door shut to quiet the crackling and thundering of the rising storm. But even as she wound the soft cloth of her hanging dresses around her ears, she could not stop the rasping and rumbling in the sky or the pounding on the roof, and she stood there shivering and twisting the clothes around her head like a bandage. She could neither shut out the awful battle of the night storm outside her home nor slow her body from shaking with sobs as she wailed into the inky blackness around her....

*   *   *

Saturday morning Shashi's mother greeted her sister and Shashi at the door of the Chaudry house in a dowdy gray housecoat over her nightdress, just as Aunt Ranibala, adorned in a rich red *sari* wrap, left to walk back across Maniarwa to her own house. Neela then turned angrily to her daughter and jerked her into the front room. 'What kind of a ruckus are you causing over at Lal's house?' she demanded. 'Ranibala was considerate enough to offer to watch you the whole weekend, you know!'

"I know, Mataji," Shashi said. "But Uncle Lal scared me, coming in my room like that after I was asleep."

"You be quiet about that! He's my older brother. He was just coming in to kiss you goodnight."

"But he stayed a long ti—"

"Oh, you and your imagination, Shashi! He's my older brother, your Uncle Lal. He probably had to work late at the creamery and hadn't been able to get home in time to –"

"That isn't true, Ma," Shashi cried. "He got home right after I got there. He ate dinner with u–"

"Shush your mouth, Shashi!" Neela led her from the front room into the kitchen and lowered her voice. "I won't have you causing trouble between my only brother and me." She paused a moment. "It's probably just your imagination that anything happened, but if it did, you can be sure I'll take care of it." She glanced at the hearth then continued, "Anyway, you'll be rewarded in your next life if you stay quiet about this." She sat her daughter down hard on the floor there and walked on over toward the stove. 'I'm going to have some *chai,* and we're going to talk this out.'

"Can I have a cup of milk, Ma?" Shashi asked. "I'm hungry."

"Well, you didn't expect your uncle and aunt to feed you after what you said, did you?" Neela asked as she put a kettle on the fire. "You can't just make up any of your stories when you're over there, *beti.*"

"I didn't make anything up, Ma!" Shashi started to sob. "I was scared my *mama* was going to start touching me agai—"

'I told you to shut your mouth about that!" Her mother's dark eyes flashed over at her and froze her to the ground. "I can't be looking after you every minute of every day, Shashi. You're almost eight years old."

"But, Ma, I don't like that." She wrinkled up her nose so her Amma'd feel sorry for her. 'If Mami Bala knew—"

"I told you there's nothing to know!" Neela took a step in Shashi's direction, glared at her, and stamped her foot. 'Bala herself told me nothing like you say ever happened." Her mother turned back to take the kettle off the fire. "And even if it did, I told you, you'll be better born in your next life."

Bala didn't know because Lal was always careful to make sure she didn't see or even suspect a thing. "That's why I cried out last night, Mata. I'd heard Bala go out to the field before Uncle Lal came into my room. When he wouldn't stop, I heard her come back inside, so I cri—"

"I don't want to hear any more about this, Shashi," her mother said and put her hands over her ears. Then she saw the kettle was steaming and picked it up to pour the tea into her glass. "And if you stop crying about this, I'll heat up some milk for you."

Shashi knew it would be bad to go on telling her mother about what happened. Mother got so tired by Fridays, especially in the summer when Shashi wasn't in school like now that she'd always ask Bala if her daughter could go over there for the weekend. She knew Bala didnn't have any girls of her own and would always say yes. "Okay, Ma," I said. I watched her lift the lid of the jar where she kept the sweets. Maybe she's going to give me a *jelabi* too. Besides maybe I did imagine those bad things Lal has been doing to me, and even if I didn't, I'd get rewarded in my next life if I don't say anything about it.

She did bring me a *jelabi* along with the glass of *dudh* she poured out for me, and she sat down across from me. "You know, sweetest, Mata gets tired after answering your questions all day long." I picked the *jelabi* off the saucer on which she always put my glass and took a nibble out of it like she showed me. Ma reached over to pat my other hand and said, "Sometimes you have to give your mother a rest."

"I know, Ma," I said, putting my *jelabi* back on the side of the saucer like I was supposed to while I carefully took a sip of the warm milk.

"So you've got to be a little daughter for Aunt Bala too. I didn't exactly expect the gods to give you to me so long after your brother and sister." She looked at me meaningfully like I was both supposed to realize she really didn't want me and actually supposed to think the gods gave babies to people. "So you're going to have to be careful not to upset *Mama* Lal. Your Ma needs the help of her older brother with raising you..."

I loved *jelabis*, but this one started to feel sour in my stomach. "I understand, Ma," I said. "I understand," I repeated and nodded my head so she understood I did.

*   *   *

It had been some time since Gauri and any of her family had visited the Chaudry home in Maniarwa. As a dutiful daughter, Gauri had made periodic trips to visit her father and stepmother where they lived in the center of town in the house in which her sister Neela and she had grown into maturity. And Neela and her family had stopped by Gauri's home in Darbhanga, where her husband Ranyan had worked in the District Collector's Office from shortly before the birth of her oldest child. But for Gauri to visit and take food at her younger sister's house on the north end of Maniarwa, this was the first time.

Neela had seized upon the occasion of the day after Gauri's 45th birthday, when they would be in Maniarwa and their father and his wife might watch her children for the evening, to finally invite Gauri and her husband over for dinner. It would provide the sisters an opportunity to become better reacquainted after the many years since Gauri had left the family home here. So while Neela's husband Aravind and their son Kumar showed Ranyan the Chaudry family garden on the very edge of Maniarwa, Neela and Gauri put the finishing touches on the vegetable curry that would be the centerpiece of the second celebration of the older sister's birthday. While this was happening, Neela's older daughter Lakshmi attended to the rice and *chapatis*, and little Shashi moved from cook to cook interrogating them about their culinary techniques.

"So have you had good rains this summer in Darbhanga?" Neela asked her sister while Shashi was bothering Lakshmi on the other side of the fire. "Aravind just can't stop talking about the size of the cauliflower and squash in our garden with the monsoon we've had in Maniarwa this year."

"You know, I'm not as close to the fields in the District Headquarters as you are here," Gauri said as she finished peeling a potato and dropping it in the pan of boiling water on the front corner of the fire. "Ranyan sold off our field when he was promoted to Assistant Collector just before Anil was born. But with the modest prices I've had to pay at the municipal market for produce these last few months, I'm going to guess the rain has been pretty good."

"Mata, how come Aunt Gauri doesn't know how much rain she's had?" Shashi asked as she started around the fire to the other side. She knew that her auntie's deep red *sari* with black trim must have cost a pretty penny. "Doesn't the rain fall on her house in Darbhanga too?"

"Of course it does, *beti*, but that's not what your *mausi* meant," Neela said while she looked over at the yellow-green curry simmering in a pan on the edge of the fire. "Why don't you help Lakshmi make the *chapatis* while she's watching the rice?"

"Thanks, Ma," Lakshmi said, laughing. "I haven't got any more time for answering her questions than you do."

In the meanwhile, the men were walking the last side of the Chaudry plot. "You can see these cauliflowers need the shade this row of banyan trees gives them from the afternoon sun," Aravind, wearing his white field shirt and *dhoti*, said, nodding toward the boughs' dense foliage to their west. "Have you ever seen bigger heads than these babies have grown this year?"

"Oh, c'mon, Pitaji," Kumar, whose loose pants and *kamiz* showed less stains than those of his father, said from behind the men. "Our field's no better than all the other ones out here on this side of the village."

"I don't know," Ranyan, whose sear-sucker suit seemed out of place in the village, said. "Your plants do appear well cared for." He looked back over his shoulder at the field as they re-entered the lane that would lead them back to the Chaudry house now that they had completed their circuit of the plot.

"And we're not even getting the best of the crop," Aravind said, hurrying to keep abreast of his brother-in-law as he picked up the pace home. "The British have pushed the taxes so high, we wouldn't be able to feed our children decently if we didn't grow much of our own food."

"Oh, they're not that bad, Aravind," Ranyan said. "If it weren't for the railroad they built all the way into Nepal, you wouldn't have the chance to buy your children readymade clothes for school." And the three men, all about five and a half feet in height, continued toward home....

Less than an hour later, most of the family was wiping their plates clean with the last morsels of their *chapatis*. Shashi, seated between her mother and sister, had long ago finished eating the main dish. "Are we gonna have any sweets, Amma?" she asked quietly enough that she hoped her father wouldn't hear. "I'm still hungry."

"So why don't you have some more of this delicious curry?" her Uncle Ranyan said, picking up the pan in front of him and offering it through Neela to his young niece. "Your mother worked hard all afternoon to make this meal, and all you want is something you could buy for *paise* in the market."

"My Ma made some *mithai* for dessert too," Shashi said, her deep-set, mutable eyes dancing. "I saw her hide it in the pantry early this morning."

Before Ranyan could respond, Papa changed the subject. "Don't you think Neela's done well with the meal without using salt, Ranyan?" He pointed his head at the nearly empty pan of curry, which just a few minutes earlier had been overflowing its sides. "Ever since Gandhiji made his March to the sea in Gujarat, we've practically learned to do without the flavor of salt."

"I think it's the best idea Gandhi's had yet," Kumar joined the discussion. "The British have no right to tell us we can't produce our own salt."

"Maybe so," Ranyan said. "But I'll tell you I'm happy I didn't resign my post at the Collector's Office ten years ago when he announced that strategy as a part of our non-cooperation with them. If I had, I don't know what I'd be doing now."

"I guess I'm glad I didn't quit the Railways too," Aravind said, nodding his head in agreement after thinking about it a moment. "We weren't supposed to have the little one," he whispered, winking at his wife, and directed his chin to her other side where Shashi was chattering to her sister. "Otherwise I'm not sure we could have made it when she came alon—"

"I know you didn't want me." Shashi snapped her head around and interrupted her father. "But Lakshmi told me that at least the goddess Sita must have."

"Shashi must have one of those new-fangled hearing aids," Aravind said to no one in particular, chuckling to himself and nodding toward his youngest daughter. "I'll tell you nothing gets by this one."

"Well, if you ask me, she has no respect," Ranyan said. "She doesn't know when to keep her mouth shut."

"Oh yes I do," she said. "Ma told me to be quiet about what Uncle Lal did to m– "

"Shashi!" My mother elbowed me hard. "Shush about that!" she said quietly.

"Ma, that hurt," Shashi cried. "I didn't mean to s—"

"*Chup rahoo, beti!*"

"Leave her alone, Ma," Lakshmi said from behind me. "She's just a little girl."

"But a very naughty little girl!" Uncle Ranyan contributed.

"She is not!" Lakshmi argued back. "She didn't know what she was saying…or doing."

"You keep out of this, Lakshmi,' Mata said. "Ranyan's your uncle."

"I don't care," Lakshmi said, getting up with tears in her eyes. "Shashi's a pretty good little girl."

Uncle Ranyan looked at Pa. "What do you think, Ari?"

When Dada didn't say anything, *Mausa* Ranyan went on, "What kind of daughters are you raising anyway, Aravind?"

"Very fine young ladies," Papa said slowly. "And to tell you the truth, Ranyan, I'm not very proud of myself for staying on with the railway after Gandhi urged us to quit government service.' He looked around the table, holding our eyes an instant each one of us. "My kids are big enough now that I just might do it yet,' he said, 'even if we have to struggle."

"Pa," Lakshmi said, "are you sure?"

"I am," he said deliberately.

"I'll help you in the field after school," Kumar said. "If I hurry, I can get back from school in Madhubani at least an hour before the sun goes down most of the year."

Papa looked at Mata. "What about you, Neela? Will you support me on this?"

"I don't know, Aravind." Mata shook her head. "It's going to be hard."

'"What do you think, Shashi?" Dada looked at me.

I switched my eyes from his to Ma's. She was glaring at me. "I don't know, Dada." I bowed my head so I didn't have to keep looking at them.

"'You'll be a fool to resign the Railways, Ari," Ranyan said. "It's none of my business, but your life here will go way down if you leave the government."

"Maybe not," Kumar said. "If everyone does what Gandhiji says, the British will have to leave India sooner or later."

"And where are we going to do then?" Mata asked sadly. Then she turned to me. "You see what you've started now, Shashi?"

*   *   *

The British had built Madhubani East High School just a few years before, and Shashi was happy her parents had decided to send her there instead of the secondary school at Khajauli, where she would not only have to walk to and fro from classes each day but also would have been instructed principally in Maithili by the town Brahmins. Besides Uncle Lal taught science at Khajauli, and she had dreaded becoming his pupil even if she had just imagined he had bothered her when she was young.

In Maniarwa, it was just a five-minute walk to the train for Madhubani and even less than that from the Mangalbani Station there to the high school. My train usually gets here at least an hour before my classes begin and I have to wait more than an hour after school lets out to get home, she thought as the custodian appeared to let her into Miss Banerjee's room as he did each morning this semester. But this way if I have my homework done. I have good light to read before the teacher arrives, and then I can play on the field-hockey team when classes are over.

"*Namaskar*, Hadi *babu*," she said to the custodian as he came around the hall and selected the proper key for the door. English was her favorite class, and Miss Banerjee more than lived up to the reputation of Bengalis for skill at the language. "*Aap kaisee hai?*"

"*Sub thik hai.*" Mr. Hadi said, looking up at the clock on the other end of the hall. "You got here especially early today, didn't you, Shashi?"

"The train made it into Mangalbani nine minutes early. I came right here," she said, closing her <u>Wuthering Heights</u> but keeping her forefinger on her place as she followed Hadi into the room. "I'm supposed to give a report on this book today, but I've still got 17 pages to read. So it's great you're here a little early too, so I should be able to finish it before class." Hadi, like most Muslims in North Bihar, she knew, was much more educated than his position would indicate, but she had learned in Dalton's Indian History class last year, the British still preferred the Hindus because the Mughal rule that only ended a century and a half ago was too fresh in their memory. Hadi was wearing a simple, white skullcap and green, plaid *lungi* today, but the stitching on his *kurta* still showed that his family has money. "Thanks. *Bahut shukriya*"

She could feel Hadi watching her as he stood at the door while she continued on to her desk. I like to wear a *salwar kameez* instead of a sari – that way I don't have to change for the train home after hockey – but I hope he can't see by the way it hangs on my hips that they aren't even.

I quickly take my seat, but when I look up, I see him still smiling at me like Aunt Bala's youngest son Chandra would whenever I'd come out for breakfast after staying at Lal's house during the summers way back when. "I swear, Shashi," Hadi said, shaking his head. "You walk more like a woman every day."

She felt the blood rise to her face and was happy her friend Jyoti was also coming early this morning, so she could explain to her why Catherine was so obsessed with Heathcliff. I wish she could help me with a little algebra in exchange, but I'm quicker at that than she is too.

As luck would have it, Jyoti opened the door just as Hadi started to say something else, and she could see his fair skin started to color too before he went on out through the door before her friend came through it. "Hi, Jyoti," I said. "I'm glad you're here early. I haven't finished the book ye—"

"I haven't either," she said.

"Good. Let's read some before we talk about it," I said, opening the book to where I left off.

"Shashi," Jyoti said, sitting down next to me. "I still have sixty pages to go." She took off her pink shawl to reveal an expensive yellow *salwar* and *pantaloons* that made me embarrassed for my old brown set. "I'll never get done with it before Miss Banerjee gets here. Can't we talk about the book now?"

"I guess," I said, finishing the paragraph and laying the book spine up on my desk. Jyoti wasn't that pretty, but she was much lighter than me. Maybe that was why Judge Subha adopted her. She wasn't very smart either, but Dada always said brains don't usually end up counting for much in the caste system either. "So what do you want to know about Emily Brontë's gem?"

"I don't exactly understand why Cathy is so taken with Heathcliff," she said. "After she recognized the practicalities of the situation and married Edgar, why can't she forget him?"

"Catherine and Heathcliff were soul mates." I paused to see if she understood, but no light came on behind her eyes. "She only married Edgar so she could help Heathcliff regain his rightful status after her brother was able to take it away from him when their father died. *Tum samajhta hai?*"

She nodded but then asked quickly, "But what's so great about Heathcliff anyway? I know he's supposed to be handsome, but that's not everything, is it?"

"It's a lot." Myself, I don't understand how Catherine could have sex with Edgar, much less want to have children with him when she didn't love him. Not only was Edgar boring, but he was pale and puny on top of it. "Edgar was a dandy who had the finest clothes," I said, "but he couldn't begin to wear them like Heathcliff wore his even after Hindley made Heathcliff dress like a servant."

"I don't know, girlfriend," Jyoti said, shaking her head. "Bhopa Jindegi says he loves me, and he dresses well for a *kayastha*. But I'd never marry him even if he is good-looking. My *pita* said the only reason they adopted me is that I was a *kshatriya* like him and that I'd darn well better marry a *kshatriya* or a *brahmin* if I want a decent dowry."

Not me, I thought. Dada said I should tell him who I like when it's time to get married, and then he'll talk with the boy's parents to see if something can be arranged. "I wouldn't like it if my father told me that," I said. "My mother probably agrees with your father, but I doubt Dada's going to listen to her when the time comes." She paused and pulled <u>Wuthering Heights</u> toward her from the end of the desk. "But this doesn't really have much to do with the book, does it? What else do you want to know about it?"

"Yesterday Shrimati Banerjee told us Heathcliff might have that disease that the British call 'monomania'," Jyoti said. "Isn't that another good reason why Cathy didn't want to marry him? Couldn't their children end up with that too?"

"I don't know if those things are inherited." I hope not, I thought for the first time, because Mata doesn't seem to care about anyone but herself. "Besides," I said, "monomania isn't necessarily a bad thing to have. It just means you won't settle for less than what you want." For one thing, I said to myself, I'm never going to be touched by someone I don't love. "Why is that a bad way to be?" I asked Jyoti.

"I don't know, Shashi. Miss Banerjee seemed to think it was."

"She's a Bengali, Jyoti. You can tell by her name." They always seem to think they're better than us, I didn't say. "They don't have the same values we Biharis do. They're so practical they don't even expect to love their husbands. They're just looking to marry someone who can provide good food to their children."

"That's not important to you?" she asked, looking at me like I was from another planet.

"I want more than that, Jyoti. I want to love my husband as much as I do my children."

"What is love anyway?" she said.

I thought for a second. "It's where you want to jump on your husband's funeral pyre even if the British have made it against the law."

"You'd really do that?" she opened her eyes widely and asked just as the door opened and Miss Banerjee came in.

I'm glad I didn't have to answer her. I knew that's what I want to believe I'd do, but I didn't really want to think about it anymore....

*   *   *

No one from either my father's or mother's families had ever gone beyond secondary school before, Shashi was thinking as she and her best friend Sangeeta Singh rode in their best saris up Ashok Raj Path toward their senior-class meeting. Coming out of the new high school in Madhubani, she had received a government grant which had covered most of her expenses at Patna College in the Bankipur section of the Bihari capital, and although she had to work twenty hours a week as an assistant warden at the girls hostel near Patna Market, it had enabled her to sail right through toward a B.A. with a double major in English and Education and with A's in just about every class she took. And still, she smiled to herself as she slid forward on the seat as the rickshaw neared the corner of the campus auditorium, I've had plenty of time for a good amount of fun. "So what exactly is this meeting for again, Sangeeta?" she asked her companion. "Are we at last going to get a schedule of the events for graduation week?"

"They're going to cover graduation for sure," her friend answered. "But I think the main emphasis of the speakers is going to be about the question of how we as seniors should balance our obligations to the effort against the Axis in the World War the British have entered and to the 'Quit India' drive of the Congress Party."

Inside the auditorium, it seemed the entire senior class of nearly a thousand was there, and the expectant hum the crowd produced made any conversation between the two friends impossible. A youngish-looking student in a white *khadi* shirt and dark trousers recognized Sangeeta and led them to an open space on the central aisle not far from the speakers' platform. Once he deposited the two girls there, he continued on to the dais where a half-dozen people were testing the sound system.

In minutes, the student who had guided them to their place in the audience, began speaking into the megaphone. "Welcome, classmates, to the first meeting of the class of 1943." The crowd, which had hushed for his words, reciprocated the greeting with a groundswell of cheering. "We members of the Class Steering Committee," the speaker continued, then paused a moment to acknowledge with his free hand the pair of students on either side of him, "have asked you here today so we can decide what to do about a number of important decisions we have to make."

A murmur swept through the audience again, and as it was dampening down, a male voice just ahead of the girls called out, "First of all, the decision about where we're going to hold our party after the graduation ceremony, I hope", and his voice dissolved into some laughter and the cheers of Shashi and others around the crowd.

"Yes, that too," the speaker responded, chuckling, "but hold your horses. Right now we've got something more important to take up," The crowd quieted again and leaned forward onto to their toes to hear better. "My name is Rajiv Gupta, and I'm the chairman of the Young Congressi Club for Patna College among other things," the audience stirred slightly once more for a moment, "and my friends and I thought that we as the Class of '43 should take a position on Gandhiji's Quit-India campaign."

Again the murmuring increased, and Shashi noticed that the student furthest to Rajiv's left, beyond the tall, good-looking man next to him, was a woman in a light-blue sari. So she turned to her friend and clasped her arm. "Sangeeta, you see that girl on the far side," she said quietly before the speaker began again. "She's in my Indian History class. She's a Bengali and she talks all the time."

'Now all of you know, I'm sure, that the British have had Gandhi and all the Congress leaders in the Poona prison for almost a year," Rajiv went on, and the crowd stirred again, "because the Party said that it will not cooperate in the war against the Axis until the British grant us our independence here in India." The audience broke into a cheer and applauded.

When the auditorium quieted down again, Rajiv resumed, "I'm sure you realize the issue is a complicated one. Jawaharlal Nehru himself has said that the racism the Nazis openly espouse is one of the major things were are fighting against in the rule of the Raj. The British tell us every day they don't believe that we Indians are ready to govern ourselves yet." Here the people booed and hissed for maybe a half minute.

"But that's not the only reason the Congress is fighting," Rajiv said. "We're fighting against imperialism too," and the audience grumbled a moment more and then waited for him to elaborate, "and there can be no doubt that it was an Imperial decision when Britain declared war back in 1939. Britain never asked a single Indian when it was decided that we were going to fight Germany, and now Japan here in Asia, and I don't think we can accept this." Now the crowd began to clap, and it soon rose to a sustained roar.

'That's what I think,' Rajiv continued. 'But the rest of my friends up here may have other views.' He looked to his right and then to the other side. 'If any of you want to weigh in as to whether we should cooperate with the British war effort, please come on over,' he said and extended the megaphone from one side to the other.

The woman in the blue sari on the far left approached and took the amplifier from Gupta to a surprised and subdued response from the gallery. "My name is Indira Ray, and I'm, of course, the secretary of the Steering Committee." She laughed, and the audience joined her. "I'm going to tell you right off that not only do I think we shouldn't support the British in their war till they give us our country back. But I also think we should support the India National Army – the INA – which is mobilizing with the Japanese right now on our eastern border," the crowd started to stir again, "and may soon be inside India to liberate us from the yoke of the Raj. I'm here to tell you that that at this very minute Subhas Chandra Bose is at the head of a force of brown men who will shortly be entering our country for the specific purpose of driving the British out of it!" The people now broke into pandemonium.

While the cheering went on, Indira handed the megaphone back to Rajiv, and he looked around the stage to see if there was anyone else who wanted to speak. After a minute of indecision, the tall man between the two, who had been assessing the crowd carefully, came forward to take the amplifier. "Hello," he said, nervously dipping his head. "My name's Mohan Verma, and I'm the Second Vice-President of the Steering Committee." He smiled, and there was a smattering of applause from the onlookers, who had finally quieted down. "I guess I just realized I'm of another opinion about the matter at hand." Instantly the crowd perked up their ears to hear what he would say.

"Undoubtedly, the reason why this question of whether to support the British war effort has been brought to a head is the fact that as we speak Subhas Chandra Bose is in Tokyo, presumably throwing in his lot with the Japanese war machine as it prepares to invade our country." The crowd was roiled again by the statement.

"We are asked to believe that Japan will help us liberate our country from the British out of the goodness of its heart, because it is offended by the European colonialism that denies us the right to rule ourselves." Verma paused here while the audience mulled his words. Shashi closely watched the tall young man as he gathered himself for his next salvo. "We would be fools to believe the Axis intends us Indians any good. Bose himself has reverted to Japan from Germany where he has lived the last several years, because he was repulsed by its racial policies and convinced that Hitler wanted to use his Azad Hind, his Free India shadow government, for propaganda purposes." The crowd listened now attentively to each word. "Ultimately, I submit, Bose wasn't convinced that the Nazi Germany he hoped to see invade our country with his Indian National Army wouldn't end up enslaving us more than the British Raj ever thought of doing…"

Here the crowd began to raise a cheer, and Verma shouted above it, "That's the reason Bose decided to throw his lot in with Japan, which, of course, is at least Asian and brown like us.' The crowd's concurrence lifted a decibel or two. "But what's Japan's track record, or Mr. Bose's for that matter? The fact is that the INA was founded in Singapore by Mohan Singh just a half year ago to be the vanguard of the force that would topple the British here. But Singh himself came to see that it became merely a pawn for the Japanese, who intended to drain Indian resources for the Axis cause that the British never even knew existed." The crowd roared again, and Shashi smiled in approval at Sangeeta as she joined the tumult.

"So what did Mr. Singh get for his trouble of mobilizing and training a half *lakh* of Indian troops for the Japanese? He's back in Burma in a Japanese prisoner-of-war camp, and we all know what these camps are like. *No*, the Japanese are no liberators, and neither is our respected Mr. Bose, this Netaji!" At the mention of this erstwhile national hero again, the people around Shashi moderated their jubilation, but she clapped harder and shouted, "*Jai Hind!*"

"Look, I'm no supporter of the British, and I laud Mr. Bose for suggesting back in '39 that we should not preclude the use of force to regain Indian freedom. But to join ranks with the Fascists against the Allies would be like going from the frying pan into the fire." Here Mohan paused again, and while the audience tentatively applauded him, Shashi leaned over to whisper in her friend's ear, "This Verma can speak. That's for sure!"

"You better watch out, Shash," Sangeeta said. "Your Rahul would be jealous if he saw how you're behaving!"

"If any of you believe like me that we need a little socialist redistribution here in India when we do become independent – and that's one of the reasons I was attracted to Bose in the first place – it's a little hard to fathom how he could so quickly jettison the Soviets for the Nazis," Mohan continued, "especially after Hitler's sneak attack on the Russians with whom he had just negotiated a non-aggression treaty. I know I don't trust Hitler. Do you?" And the crowd's resounding *"No!"* grew to a crescendo.

"The bottom line, ladies and gentlemen, is whether the massive task of decolonization here can reasonably be undertaken in the middle of World War II. I say it cannot," he shouted. "The time and the resources it will take to get our own independent government off to the start it deserves would make it impossible to marshal the resources to defeat the Japanese war machine here."

The crowd around the girls started to stomp their feet as well as clap, and they joined them while Shashi yelled to her friend, "This man can reason, Gita!" She battered her hands together joyfully. "I'd follow him anywhere," and Sangeeta nodded vigorously in agreement as she shouted encouragement to the speaker.

"Look," Mohan moved toward a conclusion, "what the British did with the famine in Bengal is awful. But at least they've admitted their error." The crowd agreed. "I say if they'll promise us independence within two years after we win this war against this Axis incarnation of evil, the British won't double cross us like Hitler would. The world wouldn't let them back out of a commitment to leave India, and the British are too smart to even think about trying to."

From the crowd's reaction, it was clear that the momentum had shifted to Mohan. "This is the best course," he said. "Gandhiji has shown that it's what he supports, and that's good enough for me. Let's dig in our heels and do what we have to to defeat the Axis. Let's get the violence out of our system by directing it against the Germans and the Japanese here in South

Asia. When we defeat them, we can go back to being the peaceful people we are and bring forth our independent nation through Gandhi's *satyagraha*. We will be better for it and so will our new India."

Mohan lowered the mike and joined the crowd while it began to sing, *"Jaana, gaana, maana..."* It was clear he had carried the day, and Shashi and Sangeeta followed their fellow students in a triumphant procession that jubilantly circled the hall and exited to the green that led down to the river in the spring sunshine.

A quarter hour later they found Rahul and his friends in the middle of the small *maidan*. Sangeeta's roommate and several other senior women gathered around them as soon as Rajiv Gupta appeared with the hero of the day, the final speaker Mohan Verma. Shashi spotted him immediately, and their eyes caught each other's momentarily as she was edging away from Rahul, one of the few underclassmen at the gathering. Sangeeta, who knew Mohan from her economics class, followed her friend's drift across the periphery of the group and offered to introduce her to him.

Mohan, talking to Rajiv, left the other side of the group as the girls detached from its main body and came to a stop a few steps closer to the river bank. "Hey, Sangeeta," Mohan said. "I thought I saw you inside. You going down to the river?"

"Not really," she said. "We just needed a little breathing room after that crowd inside."

"Who's your friend?" Mohan asked, moving his eyes over to Shashi. "I've seen you around at school, but we've never met."

"Shashi Chaudry," Sangeeta said. "She's my best friend." She took a hold of her companion's arm and presented her. "Shashi, this is Mohan Verma and his friend Rajiv Gupta." She laughed. "But I guess you know their names from their speeches inside."

"How could I miss them," Shashi said, smiling first at Rajiv, then Mohan. "I especially liked the last one."

"You and everyone else," Rajiv said, looking from Shashi to Mohan. "This guy never ceases to amaze me."

"What do you mean?" Sangeeta asked.

"I mean I expected him to urge that we not cooperate with the war effort," Rajiv said. "Mohan's always been a big Bose follower."

"So?" Sangeeta asked. "What do you think of Bose now?"

"I think Mohan's convinced me," Rajiv said after a moment. "I think that he's right that our first task now is winning this war."

"I agree," Shashi said, looking up at Mohan even though at five foot five she was tall for a Bihari woman, while Sangeeta squared up with his friend. "We can't really make the transition to independence till this war is over. We're threatened as much by Japan as England is by Germany."

"I couldn't have said it better myself." Mohan smiled at her in a way that put her at ease, then paused a beat before asking, "So I take it you're going to graduate this spring too?"

"I hope so. I've been working at it long enough."

"How long is that, Miss Chaudry?"

"Well," Shashi began as she felt the blood rising to her cheeks, "only three and a half years actually."

"Where are you from?"

"Darbhanga."

"The town?"

"Nearby," she said, vaguely annoyed that he had asked her exact birthplace. This Mohan must be at least five ten, she thought, and he was lighter-skinned than she too. "A little village name Maniarwa not far from the Nepal border."

"Right in the heart of Mithila," he said "Up toward where Rama first saw Sita, you mean?"

"Almost." She paused. "Actually it's the other way around. Sita saw him first." She felt herself coloring again. "Where are you from, Mr. Verma?"

"Bhagalpur. You know a couple of hours downriver from here."

"I know the place," she said, looking up at him once more. "What are you going to do when you graduate?"

"I'm not sure. I've got majors in history and business."

"You couldn't make up your mind, huh?"

Now she could see his color rise slightly. "I'm keeping my options open," he said, smiling.

"Between politics and what?"

"Why do you say that?"

"Well," she started, "for one thing, you give a pretty persuasive speech, Mr. Verma."

His eyes searched hers for a moment. "Thanks … but actually I think I'd rather work for myself," he said. "I'd like to open up some kind of commercial venture after the war."

"In Bhagalpur?"

"No," he said. "Around here. I like Patna, and I expect there'll be a lot of opportunity here when independence comes." Their eyes caught and held each other's again. "But enough about me. What do you want to do?"

"I'm sure I'll teach," she said. "There aren't many other jobs a woman in India is being prepared for, even at Patna College."

"What about getting married?"

She smiled at him fleetingly but dropped her eyes and said nothing.

"No, no," he said, shaking his head so the forelocks of his fine, dark hair fell, and he brushed them back. "I didn't mean that. I've seen you around with that guy over there." He nodded at Rahul who was standing with his friends on the other side of the larger circle and watching them. "You know, studying together in the library, walking by the river. I even saw the two of you at a film at Excelsior once."

"Yeah, he's kind of my boyfriend," she said, smiling but then quickly grasped his forearm. "But don't tell my parents."

"Are you going to marry him?"

She thought a minute then shook her head. "No, it's not like that … I don't think." She looked up at him. "What about you? Do you have someone back in Bhagalpur?"

"Nobody serious," he said. "I've got my mind on other things right now …, Miss Chaudry."

"I can see that …, Mohan," she said, smiling at him. "I can see that."

"Well," he said, hesitating, "I hope to see you again, Shashi."

"I do too, Mohan…."

Chapter Two

After graduation, Shashi got a teaching job in her home District, at Mainiagachhi near the junction of the railway lines to Madhubani and Darbhanga. As a result she was able to see much more of her family than when she had been in college, especially during her first year of teaching when Rahul had been finishing his degree at Patna College. When he graduated the next year and returned to his family home in Hajipur to take a job in the Subdivisional Engineer's Office there, he began to come up to visit her in Mainiagachhi once a month, but on every other weekend, Shashi still rode the train up to Maniarwa to see her parents, who were having none too easy a time since her father had begun supporting the household by working the family plot.

Shashi had helped out her parents as much as she could from her meager salary as a beginning teacher, and her mother never let her father forget that if he had not left the railways, their youngest child would have been able to save the train fares to visit them and so be able to contribute more to their household. But on one trip to Maniarwa Shashi made in the late spring the second year she taught at Mainiagachhi, she was happy to find her Aunt Gauri drinking tea with her mother outside her parents' home when she arrived late Friday evening for the weekend. Shashi knew her *mausi* had taken to making her family calls at Maniarwa without Ranyan but did not realize she was still coming over to see her sister Neela on those visits.

"*Kaisi hai, Mausiji?*" she said as she hugged the aunt she had not seen for several years. "What a wonderful surprise to find you here too."

"*Dhanyavad, bhatiji,*" Gauri said. "Your mother told me this morning at your grandparents' house you were coming tonight, and I wanted to be sure not to miss you."

"Well, I'm glad you didn't," Shashi said. *"Tum kaisi hai, Mataji?* Where's Dada?"

"Oh, he's out working in the field as usual," her mother said. "Not that Gandhi would come over and help him. I heard that the Mahatma has been back to Champaran several times to work with the indigo farmers since he's been out of prison, but do you think he could come over to help our *kisan* here in Darbhanga," she added sarcastically. "It's only a few hours away on the Northern Express, you know."

"Oh, Neela," Shashi's father called out of the darkness behind his daughter. "Will you leave poor Gandhiji alone," he said, coming into the light of the fire on which the kettle sat. "He's got his hands full now that the World War is nearly over and we have to get ready for independence. His health's not that good, you know."

"Dad," Shashi cried with joy, rushing to hug him. "How can you be still working the fields without light?"

"I don't," Aravind said while greeting the other women. "I have a torch," he said, indicating the sturdy bough wrapped in charred cloth at its end that he carried along with his hoe, "but I really start getting ready to come home with the last of daylight." He turned back to Shashi after embracing his wife. "But how's my *teacher* doing this week?"

"Bahut achaa, Pita," Shashi said. "I'm really getting the hang of working with 14 and 15 year-olds. This week I introduced Shakespeare to my classes, and most of the students seem to love it. So much so I'm thinking of having them put on 'Romeo and Juliet' at the end of the school year."

"Isn't that play too hard for them, Shashi?" Gauri asked. "I remember when Anil's class did 'Midsummer Night's Dream' his last year of secondary school, but they were older than 15 and it was a comedy. Isn't 'Romeo and Juliet' about a tragic love affair?"

"It's the saddest love story, *Mausi*," Shashi said. "But my kids really want to do it. It'll be the first time any school in the District has ever presented it."

"I suppose you didn't have anything to do with them wanting to do it?" her father said. "How'd they even know what 'Romeo and Juliet' was about?"

"I told them about it yesterday," Shashi said. "And this morning I had them read the best parts of the play. After that, they were really excited about it."

"Are they going to have enough time to memorize all the lines before the end of school?" her mother asked.

"If students want to do something enough, I've learned they can do anything," Shashi said. "When these kids are ready for college, I want the ones who go to do better than I did."

Her mother looked at her a minute. "Well, right now," she said, "let's sit down and eat something. I have to think you're all hungry, and I've got a delicious *sabzi* curry inside."

A few minutes later while they were eating, Gauri looked over at her brother-in-law and asked, "Tell me, Aravind, when you're putting in those long hours in the field, do you sometimes wish you still worked for the government?"

"Not in the least," he said. "We have a country to build here, *Sali*. First, we have to win this war against the Japanese, and then we have to be able to feed every Indian decently when we're free of the British."

"Well, at least we stopped Bose in Nagaland," Shashi said, "and now the Japanese Empire is about to collapse. Pretty soon we'll be able to concentrate again on taking back our country."

"That's what I mean, *beti*. We made the right choice," he said. "Back when Germany and Japan first formed the Axis, Gandhi said we had a tough fight ahead of us, but it was one we had to make if we wanted a country we could be proud of. When he saw that Bose hated the British so much he could no longer think straight, he knew that we couldn't follow him into an alliance with the Japanese."

Aravind paused a moment and when no one picked up the thought, continued, "Gandhiji's a special person. He's not perfect, but he hasn't been wrong about anything important yet. With Nehru making the practical day-to-day decisions and Gandhi providing the principled spiritual guidance, I'm sure Bhagwan will see us through to the best result possible."

When the curry and *roti* were gone, Shashi started to collect the banana leaves to feed the goats. "Not so fast, *beti*," her mother said, holding up her hand to halt her. "When I knew Gauri and you were both going to be here tonight, I made a little surprise for us," she said getting up to retrieve a basket whose cover she removed as she set it between them. "I know how much you love *halva*."

"Oh, Ma, you shouldn't have," Shashi said, kissing her mother's cheek before she reached for the basket.

"I know I shouldn't have, but we have to celebrate sometimes. And I can't think of a better occasion to celebrate than you two visiting here at the same time."

"It's too bad Lakshmi…or Bala couldn't have come," Shashi said.

"Lakshmi's got her hands full," her mother said. "With three small kids to take care of, she was too tired to come. But Bala," she said, looking straight at her younger daughter, "I'm not about to feed her after all the problems she's caused between my only brother and me."

"Oh, sweetheart, you've got to get over that," her husband said. "You and Ranibala used to be inseparable."

"*Used* to be," Neela said, turning to Gauri. "But now that I've got my sister back, I'll never forgive Bala for the trouble she's brought to our household."

Silence followed this remark.

"You know, Neela," Gauri finally said. "We should plan a trip back up to our old home in Phulhar. Just for us women. We should go and see Uncle Mano and collect flowers at the Baag Taraag." She looked at her sister, who nodded approval. "It's where Sita Devi first saw her true love, and I don't think Shashi's ever been there." She paused and laughed. "Maybe she'll find her Rama there if we go."

"Oh, *Mausi*," Shashi protested. "Maybe I'm not ready to fall in love."

"That's right, Gauri," Aravind said. "My daughter's busy becoming the best teacher in all of Mithila. She doesn't have time to fall in love yet."

"But I have time to see the Baag Taraag,' Shashi said. "I've always wanted to go there...."

*   *   *

Rahul was still reasonably devoted to Shashi after he finally finished Patna College, and when he started working back in Hajipur, he soon began coming over to Mainiagachhi to see her at least a weekend every month. But Shashi came to realize he liked *toddy* and whiskey a bit too much for her taste, so toward the middle of her third year teaching in Mainiagachhi, she was more than anxious for the journey Gauri had finally arranged to Phulhar for the four women and even called Rahul off for that weekend when it came up on one of his planned visits to see her.

So she met her aunt at Sakri Junction as they caught the train that would carry them north to Manairwa. There they would pick up Shashi's mother and sister for the rest of the journey to their ancestral town of Phulhar, where the last brother of her maternal grandmother still lived.

The ten kilometers or so from Maniarwa the ladies covered by a horse-drawn *tonga* over some of the richest and most densely populated farmland in Bihar. Midday on Sunday the ladies would return to Maniarwa on foot keeping to the shade of the banyan trees that grew along much of the route between the two towns, but this evening it was just too dangerous for them to travel other than with a man, who not only could protect them but could show them the way and get them to their great uncle's home at a reasonable hour.

Since the journey was being undertaken in the month of Chadra in the middle of spring, they set out from Maniarwa at least an hour before sunset in a double-seated *tonga* guided by Ganesh Kameshwar, an old friend of Aravind whose field had been adjacent to the Chaudry family plot for decades. As they got onto the country lane heading toward Narath and headed into a glorious western sky enhanced by the evening fires that were becoming more and more visible as they proceeded, Neela, who sat on one side of Ganesh, said, "It's so good of you to take us, *sribhai*, but I absolutely insist you let us pay you something for your trouble. Our Uncle Mano will feed you at Phulhar, but you won't get back home until well past midnight, I suspect."

"*Nahii*, Srimati Chaudry," Ganesh said. "How many times have you given me *chai* and *chapattis* in the field at night when you were feeding Aravind? Carrying you on this journey to Phulhar is the least I can do to repay you."

The road was good for the first three-quarters of an hour until it reached the aggregation of villages around Narath just before it reached the highway to Jaynagar near its junction with the Basopatti Road. The expedition traveled mostly in silence while the dusk allowed the women to appreciate the fine fields that stretched out on either side beyond the trees that grew alongside the road, but when they entered the narrow lanes curving through the villagers' homes, Lakshmi asked her sister how her third year teaching at Mainiagachhi was proceeding.

"The kids are still sweet," she answered. "But I must admit I'm resting a bit on the reputation I've already established as being as enthusiastic teacher. I still like what I'm doing … but I don't know. I might be ready for a change pretty soon."

"You mean getting married?" Lakshmi said. "Are you and Rahul talking about tying the knot?"

"Not really. He'd like to…, but not me. I'm looking for something more."

"I know you've been trying each other out," her sister said, smiling. "I wish Hari and I had before we got married."

"You seem to have done alright," I said. "Aren't you about ready to have another child?"

"No, I'm done," she said. "Three's enough. I only meant that it took us quite a while to get used to each other after we got married."

"Rahul and I are plenty used to each other," I said after I thought about it. "Probably *too* used to each other." I searched my sister's eyes as we leaned forward. "But how about you, *didi*? Are you happy?"

"Everything's alright," she said after a moment. "I love my children, and Hari's a good man. But I'm not smart like you, Shashi. This is as good as life is going to get for me."

"You're probably lucky, Lakshmi. I'm never satisfied. I don't know if I'll ever be happy...."

They reached Phulhar about an hour into the full darkness of night. Their Uncle Mano was waiting for them and came out on the verandah when the *tonga* clattered to a stop in front of his house. "At last, you've arrived," he said, his arms outspread as he approached Gauri to greet her first. "It's been way too long since you've been here."

"We thought you'd come down and visit us in Darbhanga, Mano," she said, hugging her great uncle. "Ranyan and I have plenty of room now that all of the children are gone."

"Oh, I don't go anywhere anymore, *bhati*," he said, sweeping his arm around as he stepped back. "I've got everything I need here in this little *basti*."

"You remember my sister Neela, don't you?" Gauri said. "She came with me the time before the last time I visited you up here."

"Of course," and they hugged too.

"And these are my daughters," my mother said. "Lakshmi"

"I remember. She's as pretty as ever."

"And this is my youngest, Shashi. She's never been here before."

"Well, we'll just have to show her what she's been missing in her home village," Mano said, hugging me but only after he noticed I had no *bindi* between my eyes. "This is the place of the 'first sight,' you know, the Baag Taraag where Sita first caught sight of her Ram…."

The next morning they set out early to the field where Ram so many centuries before had been collecting flowers on a fine spring day just as Sita was passing on her way to receive the blessings of her *devi* Parvati. When they got to the field, Mano explained that the Girijasthan Temple they were approaching overlooked the meadow where Ram and his brother Lakshman had been gathering marigolds to take to her father Janaka in the nearby seat of his Kingdom of Mithila.

"The setting here is little changed from that time," he explained as he pointed to the huts in the distance that commemorated the spot the brothers had been picking out their offering. "Sita had been coming every day by the Kalyaneshwar Gate from the palace in Janakpur just over the border. Every day she traveled these ten or so miles to ask her goddess Girija, who is local incarnation of Shiva's wife Parvati, if Sita might be released from the promise of her marriage to an older man the King of Mithila had made."

Shashi gazed out on the Baag Taraag, and a man emerged from the largest of the huts with a book under his arm and walked toward them for a moment. Somewhere she had seen this man before, but she could not place him. He was tall, swarthy, and uncommonly handsome, and she could almost hear his voice, she thought, as he turned off the path to walk through the flowers. "On the day of the 'first sight' Sita rushed on to plead to Girija with greater urgency," Mano continued. "She had fallen in love with the man she had seen in the meadow, and she implored the goddess to be released from her father's vow."

She watched the man stoop and smell the beautiful gold blossoms at his feet. She knew who he reminded her of. It is that Mohan, who spoke against allying with the Japanese, she was almost sure. "So Girija granted Sita a way to have her wish fulfilled," her uncle said. *"Sun Siya satya ashish hamari; Pujahi manokamna tumari.* If you pray to be released at the nearby temple in Manaharpur, you shall be." Shashi watched the man below rise and walk off into the trees. "Sita went to Manaharpur," Mano went on, smiling serenely, "and all know Girija's prescription worked ... for the benefit of all Hindustan."

"Can we go there, *Mamaji?*" Shashi said, watching the breeze ruffle the leaves of the trees into which Mohan had disappeared. "I would love to see the place where the 'first sight' came to fruition."

"Of course," he said, starting down from the Girijasthan. "I was going to take you there anyway. We can easily walk there from here along this way."

"But surely we must walk through the meadow first," Shashi said

"As you wish."

So Mano led them through the Baag Taraag, and at the place Shashi had seen the man bend over to pick a flower, she stopped too and inhaled the unearthly fragrance. It filled her being, and they went on toward Kalikpur.

Soon up ahead in the village of Bardepur, they saw a rounded cupola with several megaphones wired around the spire. "That is the Mahadev Mandir," Mano said, pointing to the whitewashed temple. "We think it is at the same place as the old Manokamnasthan."

A forlorn *pandit* in a saffron *nathaa* and *dhoti* and black oxfords.stood in front "Hello," he said shyly. "You have come a long way to have your wish fulfilled." Why does he seem to be talking to me, Shashi wondered.

"As a matter of fact, we have," Gauri answered. "I have come from the District Headquarters. I have been to the Baag Taraag before, but until today I didn't even know of this place."

"Yes, this is the place where Parvati grants the wishes of women," the priest said, his eyes on Shashi rather than her aunt. Why does he continue to look at me? "Is it you, *srimati*," he asked, turning to Gauri now, "who wants the fulfillment of your heart's desire?"

"No, of course not," she said, dropping her eyes. "I have long been married and am a grandmother several times over." She moved her eyes to me. "It is she, my *bhanji*. Her name is Shashi. She is the only one of us who is not married."

"And how can that be?" the *pandit* said, appraising me. "By my father's name Verma, she is certainly old enough to be married." He gazed into Shashi's eyes, which she felt turning darker. "And I daresay pretty enough to be married too."

"Thank you, Panditji Verma," she said, looking at his eyes but having to drop her own. "I am not sure I am ready yet to have children."

"You're going to have to get ready soon," Verma said. "So many of our boys are now off to Burma and Africa and even Italy fighting in the Great War. It is the last time we Indians will fight for the British, but as the Mahatma said, we had to do it." Shashi lifted her eyes to Vermaji again, and his locked upon hers. "Many of these boys will die, but those who come back will need good wives. And children, not only for themselves but for the thousands who will not return...."

*   *   *

A year and a half later, Shashi had left her post at Mainiagachhi and just completed her first year's contract teaching at Bhagalpur, known throughout Bihar for the special value its people put on their children's education. The journey from Rahul's home in Hajipur to Bhagalpur, being much more time-consuming, Rahul had never visited her there, and, in fact, it had been weeks since Shashi had answered his last letter.

World War II had been over for nearly two years, and finally the last of the Indian men who had fought against the Axis and survived had been demobilized and returned to their homes. In early 1947, Mountbatten had been sent out from England to negotiate the British withdrawal from India, and after the awful communal riots in late '46 around the country's Partition, Gandhi had come to accept the sad reality of India being divided into Hindustan and the new nation of Pakistan on its eastern and western borders, where the majority of the inhabitants were Muslim.

When the school year was over in 1947, Shashi returned to Maniarwa to visit her family and stayed on for several weeks in relative cool until the monsoons came, but before returning to Bhagalpur, she had gone to see Rahul in Hajipur. The visit there had not gone well. While Shashi and he were still drawn to each other, Rahul's father had opened negotiations with a Brahmin family in Chhapra, and Rahul told her that if she would not marry him now, he would no longer be able to resist his parent's pressure to marry the Chhapra girl, whom he had met late in the month of May and liked.

Rahul had told Shashi nothing of these negotiations, which seemed deceitful to her. Besides she had no desire to settle in Hajipur, which though just across the Ganges from Patna, was still five hours away from the capital by steamer and seemed a miserable provincial town to her, nor had she any wish to become the wife of the local magistrate there, which Rahul hoped to someday eventually become. So she refused his offer, but as freethinking as she thought herself to be, she finally came back to Bhagalpur a little wanly and definitely feeling older.

Fortunately, her good friend from college, Sangeeta, whose father had secured his daughter a teaching job in Patna, had agreed to visit Shashi for Bhagalpur's Vish-hari Puja, which represented its biggest festival of the year on July 20th in 1947. Shashi had found lodging with a Narayan family in the Nathnagar quarter of the city for her first year in the area, and she had become part of the family through her tutoring of the children in English. So Mrs. Narayan was more than happy to move her kids around to free up a room Sangeeta could share with Shashi for her visit to Bhagalpur. The whole arrangement was particularly convenient, because the Shankh Kund, the steep granite hill at the bottom of which the Snake Queen Festival was celebrated, was about equidistant between the Narayan home and the Ganga it overlooked.

It was so close, in fact, that the Sunday morning after Sangeeta arrived, the young women decided to walk over the side of what was now called Mandara Hill, following the footsteps of Lord Vishnu himself to the picturesque site where the snake charmers would be offering milk to the Nag and his queen within sight of the city's original port on the Ganges canal there. The old harbor had been there at least since the time it had been the embarkation point for the Chinese monk Hsuang-tsang when he carried back to his homeland the copies of the Buddhist scriptures he had copied at the nearby universities of Nalanda and Vikramshila in the seventh century. It was at this same point Hindu pilgrims had landed for centuries while taking pilgrimages to reach the place on the Shankh Kund where the Panchjanya conch shell referred to in the *Mahabharata* had been discovered. And just down the river from this great hill, where the serpent Vasuki had agreed to be the rope which would churn the ocean to procure the nectar of the gods that would make the Earth, the ancient city of "good luck" or Bhagdatpuram had grown up on the banks.

"See, Sangeeta, there is the snake where he coiled in the first soil," Shashi said, pointing to a swirl imprinted in the granite they were walking past, and then looking on ahead down to the splendid panorama before them. "Can you imagine the thousands of years this mountain has given Indians this beautiful view of their sacred Ganges River?"

"Almost from the beginning of time if you believe in this sort of tale," said Sangeeta. "I don't." She stopped and looked at her friend a moment. "Do you?"

Shashi started to descend the slope again, and Sangeeta caught up with her. "I don't know. It's improbable but ... but it's a lovely story for kids at least. I don't really think about whether it's literally true or not."

They continued on down the hill, into the area where the crowds were starting to gather and the snake charmers were beginning to set up their operations in silence. "Do you want to have your own children, Shash?" Sangeeta finally asked. "Are you coming into that time of life at last?"

"I guess so," Shashi said. They passed into an area where there weren't many people around. "You know, I love teaching, and I love the kids, Geet," she continued, "but ... I don't know if I can teach forever.'

They approached a place where the terrain flattened out and families were gathering around an open space.

"Yeah, I know what you mean," her friend said, coming to a stop behind a man and a woman with two small children who were spreading a blanket upon which to sit. "Both my parents – but especially my father – are starting to ask me if I'm ready to get married."

"Are you?"

"I guess," Sangeeta said, shrugging. "What else is there to do?"

At this point, a band could be heard approaching from the direction of the canal, and soon the girls saw its horns and drums were drawing a chain of followers as it made its way toward them. When it passed them and entered into the open space, the crowd the band had brought with it had formed into a long procession winding and twisting behind it like the giant serpent of the mountain. Most of the people in the joyous parade were small children attended by their parents, and toward the end of the tail Shashi saw the Narayans with their three youngest, who swept in front of Sangeeta and her to begin the first of several circuits of the impromptu clearing.

When the song ended, the Narayan kids raced to the corner of the square where the facsimile of the cobra queen's head had been set up, and Shashi and Sangeeta went after them to say hello. There the kids sprinkled *kaldi-kumkum* powder over Mansa's crown and paid obeisance to her with offerings of milk and honey, and soon the teachers were also participating in the fun.

"This will bring good luck in your marriage, girls," Mrs. Narayan told them, when all their nourishment had been offered, and the women settled back to watch the children continue their celebration with Mansa.

"Let's hope that it does," a deep, male voice concurred from behind them, and Shashi spun around to see a familiar face smiling down upon her. "I thought I recognized you two," he said. "What are you doing here at our Vish-hari Puja worship?"

"Oh, Mohan," the youngest Narayan girl Jasmine cried, and she rushed past Shashi to hug the man around his legs as her parents moved around him to greet his parents with whom he had come. "You've gotten home in time for Bhagalpur's special day."

"I wouldn't miss it for the world," said the man Shashi recognized as the one she thought she had seen at the Baag Taraag, while he now held out the little girl at arm's length, lifted and twirled her around. "I had a feeling we'd run into you here, Jammy," he said to the girl.

"Mohan was only released from his Army supply detail in Bombay three days ago," Mrs. Verma explained to her old friends the Narayans. "But he phoned and told us he would try and get train connections to arrive here for the festival. We just this very minute came from the station after picking him up."

"It's been years since I've been at a Vish-hari," Mohan indicated as he put Jasmine down. "But I had no idea I'd run into you two here," he said, turning to Shashi and her friend. "What in the world are you doing at Bhagalpur's on Queen Serpent's Day?"

"Shashi's been boarding with us for the last year," Mrs. Narayan volunteered. "She's teaching English at Nathnagar Secon—"

"And Sangeeta just came to spend a weekend with me before school started again," Shashi completed the sentence.

"And we used to live next door to the Vermas downtown," Mrs. Narayan finished the introductions, pointing her head toward Jasmine. "All my kids just love Mohan."

"And my son just got demobilized from the war effort." Mr. Verma said. "But how do you two know him?" he asked the girls, glancing at Mohan.

"We all graduated from Patna College together," his son said. "I met Shashi and Sangeeta at our senior meeting just before our last classes there."

"It's not exactly like that," Shashi corrected him as she looked at Mr. Verma. "Actually we were there when your son gave a speech that convinced our class to support the British war effort against the Japane—"

"I heard all about that," Mr. Verma said, glancing at his son. "But I guess he turned out to be right," he added, smiling. "The British are nearing the completion of their withdrawal from India as we speak, and we're getting our independence in less than a month."

"Your son has a good sense about things," Shashi said. "I don't know him very well, but he seems to have a pretty good idea about what tomorrow's going to bring."

"Now isn't that interesting," Mohan observed, smiling as he nodded at his father. "We were just discussing that."

"They sure were," Mrs. Verma stepped forward and said. "Parvan wants Mohan to take over his silk business here in Bhagalpur, and the subject occupied most of our ride over here. Mohan's not so sure he wouldn't have better opportunities in Patna."

"It's his life," Shashi offered. "He—"

"He's been away from Bihar the better part of four years," Mr. Verma completed her thought. "He doesn't know how much Bhagalpur has changed."

"How much has it changed?" Mohan asked "As I understand it, no sooner than Gandhi got things calmed down between the Hindus and Muslims in Bengal last year, there was an attack on the Muslim community right here. This sort of thing has been happening in Bhagalpur since I can remember."

"It's not as though the Muslims didn't have anything to do with it," Mr. Verma said. "They're the ones who—"

"Do you have to start arguing already?" Mrs. Verma said to them, then turning to Srimati Narayan. "It's just like when we lived next to each other in Asandpur, isn't it?"

"You're right, Mom," Mohan said, taking the arms of his two classmates. "A puja's no time for arguing." He looked at his father and Mr. Narayan. "Why don't you all get re-acquainted while I show these young ladies around my hometown?"

"What a nice idea," Shashi said quietly enough so only Mohan could hear as the three of them began to step away. "Sangeeta's leaving for Patna tomorrow morning, and I'm sure you can show her the sights of Bhagalpur today better than I can."

"I do know everything there is to see in this town," he said, "despite what my father says."

"How long are you going to be here in Bhagalpur, Mohan?" Sangeeta asked as the three friends moved off from the others down toward the canal.

"At least till Independence Day," he answered.

"Great. Maybe then I'll have someone to celebrate it with," Shashi murmured again. "Besides I don't have to start teaching again till August twentieth. Maybe you can show me some of the places around here like Vikramshila that I've never seen before."

*   *   *

Several days after Sangeeta left, Mohan did take Shashi to visit the ruins of the Buddhist University of Vikramshila. His father had one of the few private cars in Bhagalpur, a Land Rover he had picked up for a song from the last British District Collector before he returned to England, and Mohan was able to borrow it for the two-hour drive east along the Ganges.

The initial part of the journey was on the *pacca* highway toward Bengal and closely followed the main east-west railway line all the way to the village of Anadpur, which was about a mile inland from Kahalgaon Station near the bank of the river. The pair left Bhagalpur before nine in the morning and reached the point where the dirt track departed for the last 11 kms to the ruins in little more than an hour. It would take them that much time again to reach Antichak village just below a promontory in the Ganga, around which it made its great bend to the south for its journey to the Bay of Bengal. The Vikramshila site itself began on the northern edge of Antichak and stretched almost to the river.

Mohan, who had visited the site one summer while he was going to Patna College, had spoken little during their time on the highway as he concentrated on making good time through the morning traffic on it. When they turned left at Anadpur's only intersection, he pointed to a tea stall on the corner and said, "We can have a cup of *chai* here, Shashi, if you want. I apologize for not offering one earlier, but I just didn't think of it."

"*Kooi baat nahii*, Mohan," she said. "I really don't need anything now."

"It may be our last chance for good and clean food, not to say anything about the dust from here on to Vikramshila. This is the last blacktop we'll see till we get back here."

"But I brought along some *chana* and *chapattis*," she said, lifting the strap of her cloth bag that was resting on the floorboard. "It's the least I could do, and I think I have plenty for both of us."

"Fine with me," he said as he reaccelerated, and the vehicle bounced over a bump in the road at the end of Anadpur. "But I'd bring your bag up to the seat if I were you..The rest of the way to Vikramshila will be rough like this."

"Good idea."

They didn't talk much as the Land Rover labored over the *kacca* road for the better part of the next hour. Initially the track passed over flat land through fields of pulse and mostly paddy on either side, but the way was deeply runneled from the recent rains as it wound through a couple of *bastis*. Slightly before quarter to eleven, they climbed a slight rise beyond a grove of eucalyptus trees, and from the top of it, they could see several small hills between the water of the river reflecting the sun as it curled around the point sticking out into it up ahead. Before the point, a larger village stretched out on both sides of the track and beyond a mostly brown area between the village and the Ganges the adjacent fields were set off by rows of neem and banyan trees that extended all the way to the riverbank.

"There's Antichak," Mohan said, "and Vikramshila on its far edge. It's hard to imagine this was one of India's principal learning centers a thousand years ago, isn't it?"

"What happened?" Shashi said. "I understand this place was built when Nalanda University up by Patna started to deteriorate, and pretty soon there were at least a thousand monks studying here under hundreds of professors teaching a whole array of subjects."

"Bhaktiyar Khilji closed the university down about seven and half centuries ago," he said. "Vikramshila had a lot of sculptures of Buddhist gods, and you know the Afghanis after they adopted Islam were so literal about it they weren't going to leave any of sculptures standing when they got here."

"So they leveled the university like Muslims did everywhere they went?"

"That's not really true in India," Mohan said. "When the Mughals finally took over Bihar, they left the temple at Bodh Gaya alone, and we Hindus here were allowed to keep worshipping at most of our temples."

"What happened to all the people at the university here?"

"Most of them went back to where they came from, I suppose. Maybe the descendants of some of them still live here in Antichak."

They passed through the heart of the village and stopped the Land Rover on its far end next to the ruins. Mohan helped her down from the car, and she looked into the faces of the curious peasant children who had followed them to see who had come to visit Vikramshila. She remembered that mostly Tibetans studied here, but she didn't see any Mongoloid features in these kids that approached them.

The two of them clambered over a broken part of the ruins' perimeter wall, and Mohan pointed across the complex to its quarter facing the river. "There's the main entrance," he said.

"The man who took our family around when I came here before said the university looked out on the river. When visitors arrived during the period the university was open, they usually came by boat on the Ganga."

Shashi took his hand as they stepped through the broken pieces of masonry on the ground. She could see two straight walls perhaps three meters apart extending a great distance toward the river where they met the remains of a perpendicular wall. "What's this?" she said, looking toward an open area inside the parallel walls. "It looks like a huge courtyard enclosed by these long buildings which seem to form a square around it."

"These four long buildings are supposed to be the monastery where the student monks lived," he said as they walked along the nearest of the walls. "Between these parallel lines are the cells where they slept. Inside is a verandah where they could walk and relax or study during the daylight hours."

Shashi nodded in understanding. "What's that big mound beyond the monastery?" she asked as they approached what she knew to be Vikramshila's main *stupa.*

"That's the main temple," he said. "It's where the monks would go to pray and to worship the Buddha."

"Let's go inside," she said. "I heard — I mean I wonder if there're still any statues left inside."

They climbed up on a terrace elevated around the *stupa* about a meter off the ground and walked along the main part of the building hand in hand where they could see some perfectly proportioned carvings of figures in the undamaged parts of the wall. When they came upon a stairway, they picked their way up it to a higher terrace and then on to a doorway into the still mostly roofed enclosure.

Inside they could see by the light admitted through the sections of the curved ceiling that had collapsed a huge stucco statue of Lord Buddha, seated in the lotus position. They silently walked around to its front which was largely in shadow. It as though they had gone back a millennium in time.

She shuddered and nestled into his shoulder. When he protectively sheltered her from the damp cold with his arm, she lifted her face to him, and he was drawn to her waiting lips.

They kissed long and ardently. Suddenly she withdrew her hands from the back of his neck and moved away. As she stepped back, her right hand softly brushed over and lingered an instant on his private parts.

He started to pull her to him again, but she held up her palm against his chest to stop him. "Not here," she whispered. "It's sacrilegious to do it in this place."

"But where…?"

"The library," she answered quickly, pulling him across the chamber. "To the font of learning."

Somehow she led them back to a covered rectangular building attached to a corner of the monastery. Inside it was warmer yet not stifling.

They kissed again, and she began to unbutton his shirt. When he took over disrobing himself, she began to unwind her sari, and as he stepped out of his pants, she laid the cloth upon the smooth dirt floor.

Soon she was guiding him into herself….

Later she lay in his arms while his heavy breathing gradually dissipated. "It's like a miracle, isn't it, my love," she finally said. "From this can come another being…."

*   *   *

During the next three weeks, Shashi and Mohan got along so well that before Independence Day, they were spending most of their nights together in a hotel in Bhagalpur's Adampur quarter. August 15, 1947 was not a day of celebration for them, however. Two days earlier, Shashi had received notice that the renewal of her teaching contract at Nathnagar Secondary had been rescinded, and she was out of a job.

Fortunately her official record and credentials were excellent, and Sangeeta's father had been able to arrange an interview for her at St. Martha's School in the Anglo-Indian community of Danapur west of Patna. The secondary school English teacher there had been having a difficult pregnancy and was unable to take up her duties for the coming academic year, and Shashi stood a good enough chance of getting the job that she decided to move her belongings to the Patna area rather than return home to her native Darbhanga District north of the river. Mohan, who had already been thinking of relocating to the Patna area himself, offered to escort her to the Bihar capital, and before their Sunday morning train, they put Shashi's things in storage at the station. For Mrs. Verma had invited the two of them to a Saturday evening supper from her kitchen at their Asanandpur home.

Parvan was none too happy about the invitation as Mohan learned when he walked in the front door without knocking a bit before the appointed time. Shashi had refused to follow him in unannounced and was waiting outside the front door.

"Parvan, do you mean to tell me that you were responsible for getting Mohan's friend fired from the Nathnagar School?" Mohan heard his mother demand of his father just as he entered the front sitting room.

"I don't know whether I got her fired or not, but I know she's no good for our son," Parvan said "All I did was to tell the school board that she was staying with Mohan last Monday at the Paradise Hotel in Asampur. An hour before, I had seen them go in there together and embrace behind a second-floor window a minute later. What kind of a woman does that?" he asked. "She got herself fired, Sara."

"You realize that if Mohan finds out about this," she said, "he'll be furious. You've been hoping he'd decide to work with you in the silk shop, but now you can be sure he won't."

"He's not going to find out, Saraswati," Parvan said. "How's he—"

"I have found out, Dad," Mohan said from the doorway to the kitchen. "From the words out of your own mouth."

"How'd you …," Parvan cried, spinning around to face him. "You mean you just walked in here without—"

"You told me yourself it was still my home, Father. It was the first thing you said when I got back from the war."

"Did *she* hear?" Mr. Verma said, shifting slightly so he could see if there was anyone behind his son.

"No, Dada, don't worry," Mohan answered. "Shashi said we should have knocked before coming in," he said, glancing back at the front door. "So she insisted on waiting outside until you two came to bring her inside."

"I knew she was a well-brought up girl when I met her," Mohan's mother said, glaring at her husband. "So I, for one, have no objection to her becoming part of our family."

"Well, *I* do!" Parvan said. "If she's been spending the night with you already, who knows how many other men she's known?"

"Right now, she's here for dinner," Mohan said. "And you'd better be decent to her, Pitaji," he added, as he started back toward the front door….

Shashi came into the kitchen behind Mohan so chastened at losing her job it wasn't clear to the others she hadn't heard the argument between them. "Ma," Mohan began introducing her, "you remember Shashi Chaudry, don't you? We met her at the Vish-hari Puja in Champnagar."

"Of course," Mrs. Verma said, setting down the spoon with which she was stirring the curry sauce, and come toward Shashi. "The Narayans –your landlords—introduced us at Mandara Hill." She knows why I got fired, Shashi realized, but she's genuinely trying to be warm. "I'm so glad you could have dinner with us before you lea—"

"Dada, this is Shashi," Mohan interrupted her to present her to his father.

"Yes, I remember her too," Mr. Verma said. He too was trying to be decent, but she could tell he didn't want her there. "Our son ended up showing you and your friend some of the sights of Bhagalpur that day if I remember right."

"He did." She lifted her eyes, but when they met his she wanted to drop them again. "He took us to the Snake Temple and Tilka Manghi University that afternoon." With her eyes, Shashi appealed for help from Mohan, who was now standing behind his father. "And what else did you show us, Mohan? I don't recall where else the three of us went."

"The Jain temple by the canal," he said. "And then the Gudwara and the Maulanchuck of Khanquah Shahbazia downtown."

"Of course he wouldn't have shown you any of our *mandir*," his father said. "It's almost like Mohan is ashamed of being Hindu."

"Oh, he showed me plenty of *mandir* after that," Shashi said. "The Ventkateswara in Nagachia and Budha Nath Temp—"

"I'm sure he has," Mr. Verma said. He knows why the school district let me go too, Shashi realized, and he's looking at me like I'm a *vesya*. "You too have been spending so much time together, I've hardly seen my son since you met him."

I could feel my face getting hot. But I love Mohan. I have to defend us. "The first time I actually met your son, Mr. Verma, was just before our graduation from Patna College. He had given a wonderful speech that day that convinced the senior class not to ally with the Japane—"

"You already told me about that," Mr. Verma said. "Myself, I think we should have followed Netaji. He was from Bengal. You know."

"So is my father," Mohan said as Mr. Verma puffed out his chest. "At least, he's part Bengali."

"What do you mean by that?" his father charged, then turned his eyes toward me. "You know I became friends with Tagore when he was here writing *Gitanjali*."

"He wrote *part* of *Gitanjali* while he was here in Bhagalpur, Parvan," Mrs. Verma said, then turned back to the stove. "Anyway, everything's just about ready to eat. Why don't you sit down while I get it on the table?" she said, nodding toward a dark wooden *mez* in the corner with four wooden chairs. "Why don't you two young people sit over there on the back side, and Parvan and I will sit over here across from you, so I can get out if anyone needs anything more."

"Can't I help you carry things now, Mrs. Verma?"

"No, no. It'll just take me a minute. You sit down, Shashi," she said but looked at Mohan, who brought over the rice in a brown bowl and a basket of *chapattis*. Mrs. Verma carried the light-green curry in a pan that she set on a wicker hot pad and a small dish of *lal mirc* chutney. "Mohan has to put chile on everything," she explained when she saw me looking in the dish. "It must be the Nepali blood I passed on to him."

"Oh, you are an Indian, Saraswati," Mr. Verma said with a flip of his hand. "We're *Brahmins*" He looked at me as his wife spooned curry over the rice I had put on my ceramic plate. "What caste are you, Miss Chaudry?"

"*Daaad*," Mohan tried to object.

"Parvan, how rude!" Mrs. Verma said. "You've just met Shashi."

"No better time to find out," he said, quickly turning back to me.

"My father's a Yadav," I answered. "My mother's Kayastha. Her grandparents were cowherds, though her father was a teacher in a village school."

I could tell Mr. Verma didn't approve of marriage across caste lines, but conscious of his wife staring at him, he didn't say anything.

"So what did you think of the Independence Day celebration in Delhi yesterday, Mom?" Mohan said to change the subject. "Did you listen to Nehru's speech?"

"That man can certainly turn a phrase," his father said. "'A tryst with destiny' is a wonderfully poetic way of describing our position in history now."

"Myself, I like what's behind the poetic phrases," Mrs. Verma said. "That we are now stepping out of the old into the new. It is indeed a new day today, the first day of independent India after nearly three centuries of British rule."

"And five hundred years of Muslim rule before that," Parvan added. "We Indians haven't really been free for almost a thousand years."

I could tell Mohan didn't appreciate this remark. "Isn't it unbelievable that Gandhi isn't even in Delhi for the occasion?" he said. "The very soul that brought us freedom wasn't able to be there to see our own tri-colour hoisted over the Red Fort."

"It was a good thing he went down to Calcutta," Mr. Verma said. "The Bengali Muslims have been causing havoc there for a year. Ever since Jinnah's Direct Action Day. Personally I'm happy that scoundrel and his Muslim League aren't going to be part of India," he said before continuing. "Frankly we'd be better off if all the Muslims went to Pakistan."

"It isn't just Muslims who caused the problem, Dada," Mohan said. "And it wasn't just in Bengal and Punjab either. I understand thousands of Muslims were killed right here in Bihar after the Bengal riots, many of them right here in Bhagalpur."

"Like I told you, that's been blown way out of proportion," Mr. Verma said. "There were a few Hindu demonstrations against the Muslim killings in Noakhali, but the bloodshed here was minimal compared to the mass murders of Hindus in Bengal."

"Parvan, how can you say that?" Mrs. Verma said, covering her eyes. "It was awful downtown here last year. Women and children were burned alive in their homes. I never imagined we Bhagalpur Hindus could be so cruel."

"It shouldn't have surprised you, Mata," Mohan said. "Everyone says it happened here back in the Twenties and the again in '36. The only explanation I can think of is that the Hindus here are jealous of the Muslims because they put Bhagalpur on the map with their silk work."

"I don't know what's wrong with you, Mohan!" I had seen Mr. Verma getting ready to explode and slam the table. "Don't you have any loyalty to your own? I've been keeping at least a score of Muslim families in food by employing them down at the store and mill."

"Yeah, after you learned the silk business from those Muslims," Mohan cried, "and then took advantage of their fear after the communal riots here when I was starting secondary school."

"You get out of here!' Mr. Verma screamed, jumping to his feet. Then he turned his fury on me, swinging his arm out to point at the door. "And take your tramp girlfriend with you!" At that moment I finally understood he was behind my Principal coming to the hotel Monday night. "I don't ever want to see either of you in this house again!"

"Parvan, what are you saying?" Mrs. Verma began weeping.

"I'm saying that from this day on, I only have one son," Mr. Verma said. "Vishnu would never have said something like this to his own father." I could see from his reaction that Mohan had hit pretty close to the truth about the history of the family silk business. "I've given you more advantages than I ever did Vishnu yet he's always shown respect to me. He would never have brought my car back from Vikramshila looking the way you did when I let you borrow it."

"Fine," Mohan said quietly, standing up. "All you ever wanted from me was someone to do your bidding, someone to take over your business and be paying you for it for the rest of your life." He took my hand and gently helped me up and led me away from the table. "Well, find someone else, Pitaji. I'll make more money on my own than you ever dreamed of."

"That's a laugh," his father sneered after us as we retreated through the front room. "Everything you know about actually making a living I've taught you. In a year from now, you'll be back here begging on my doorstep."

"Never," Mohan said, stepping over the threshold. "I'll never come back here...."

SUMMER

Chapter Three

When spring was just around the corner in 1949, Shashi was beginning to yearn for something more permanent than the day or two Mohan and she could spend together on the weekend in Patna's downtown section of Bankipur. She almost always arrived at their room in the Dak Bungalow midway between the station and Gandhi Maidan before Mohan was able to come down from Patna City, where he was now the manager for his schoolmate Najib Khan of Bihar Tire. She had missed only two or three Four-fifteens in from Danapur in the two years she'd been teaching English and history in the secondary school there, while Mohan never finished his work for the company before half past six on Fridays whether he was working in breakdown at the shop where he had started with the company or doing sales calls at the petrol pumps on the bypass or at the government workshops near the Secretariat.

But though Shashi always became impatient for him to take her in his arms after their long work-weeks apart, she was also reassured in her certainty that he was working hard to improve himself and would surely become a good provider without having to return to his father's silk enterprise downriver. A year ago Mohan had come up to Maniarwa to visit her parents for Saraswati Puja, and the two of them had finally at his mother's insistence gone back to Bhagalpur last Diwali and had a tolerably good time. Shashi had slept in Mohan's sister Kamli's old room and become quite good friends with his other sister Mangala and the wife of his older brother Vishnu over the long weekend, but she still felt uncomfortable around Mr. Verma, especially after Mohan and he had their inevitable argument about his future.

So today Shashi was reasonably happy when she saw Mohan get down from a rickshaw in front of the verandah of the room where she had been awaiting him in the cool night air. While he paid the *rickshaw waalah*, she hurried out to greet him on the lawn between their room and Dak Bungalow Road. "Oh, Mohan," she said, embracing in the dusk's enveloping shadow, "these weeks apart are getting longer and longer."

Some distance from the nearest source of light, he kissed her ardently and then said, "For me too, *mithas*, I've been constantly thinking about what you'd be wearing all day."

"I don't know how long I can go on living like this," she said, leading him back onto the verandah. "Mataji asked me in her letter again this week if we are getting married," she lied as they passed into their room. "I don't know what to say to her…."

Several hours later they were walking on the breakwater along Digha Diara. It was a clear night, and the light of the waxing moon reflected on the Ganga like a carnival ground awakened for the evening.

"So, *mera sahad*, I have some exciting news for you," Mohan said as he moved his arm from around her shoulders to take her hand as he stepped down onto the sand at a point where a slight beach formed before the water. "Najib has asked me to open a shop for him in Muzaffarpur. There is no company serving the tire needs of North Bihar, and it is all but certain that Nehru will soon begin to build a bridge across the river near Lakhisarai. When's it's completed, our Bihar Tire store will be in a great position to capitalize on the increased traffic."

"What a great opportunity," Shashi said, walking on the sand. "And a tribute to all your hard work." I paused. "Do you want to do it?"

"That's what I want to talk to you about," he said. "Do you think I should?"

"It would mean we'd see each other even less than we do now," I said, "unless...," hoping he would fill in the blank with a way to avoid that.

"Unless you move up to Muzaffarpur too. You'd be much closer to your family, you know."

"*Kyaa chatai hai?*" I asked brightly, realizing I'd been teaching almost six years now.

"I mean with your record you could easily get a job teaching in Muzaffarpur. Najib says it's going to become a big city."

I was hard not to let my disappointment in his reply show. Here on this beautiful, moonlit night down by the river he seemed to be proposing that we continue our liaison without a mention of marriage. "What about what happened in Bhagalpur? Surely that will come up," I said. "The only reason it didn't in Danapur was because of the influence of Sangeeta's father."

"I don't think the people at Nathagar School will say anything. When they allowed you to resign before you left there, they promised that the subject of our relationship would never see the light of day."

"I know," I began as we came to a rest by the water and I looked up at him. "But how will we ever know if they do say something." I prayed to my Sita Devi that he'd see my point as he usually did. "Besides I should be thinking of having my own children soon. I'm almost 28"

"You're probably right." He appeared to be thinking hard. I willed him to feel guilty about me losing my job in Bhagalpur because of him. "And I don't want to be responsible for ruining your teaching career."

"Of course you don't have to be responsible for me!" I said quickly. "I can just stay at Danapur. They love me there."

"Or maybe we should just get married," he said. I couldn't believe it came this easily. "I can't imagine that I could ever love anyone as much as I love you," he continued, facing me and putting his arms around me. I looked down, and he dropped to his knee, keeping a hold of my right hand. "So will you marry me, Shashi?" he asked nervously, or was there a bit of irony in his tone? "I love you, and I want you to be the mother of my children." He paused. "I want to spend the rest of my life with you."

"Oh, how romantic," I said, giggling a little and looking up at the moon. "But seriously, sweetheart, I also want to spend the rest of my life with you, so I accept." I laughed and fixed my eyes on his. "I mean, yes, I will," I added and pulled him up and threw my arms around his neck to kiss him, slipping my tongue into his mouth to remind him of what he was getting. "You're the most handsome and finest man I've ever met, and I love you and don't want to ever let you go," I said, and I grasped him even harder to me for dear life….

"Well, it's settled then," he said, finally disengaging from our kiss. "We'll get married here in Patna before we move to Muzaffarpur."

"Oh, Mohan," I protested, separating myself from him. "A girl gets married only once in her life. I want my father to give me away in Maniarwa. I want to have a proper wedding there."

"I don't know if I'll have the time to do that, sweetheart," he said, taking my hand and stepping back across the sand toward the breakwater. "Besides, can we really ask your parents to put on a wedding for us? Your father said he's just beginning to make a decent living for them from his field."

"We'll make the time, Mohan," I said, proceeding slightly slower than he was. "And the money too, if that's what you're worried about. Anyway my parents owe me a wedding."

He pulled me on a few steps before he spoke again. "Alright, Shashi," he said, and I immediately dropped my resistance and followed him to the wall. "We'll figure out a way to bring in the new India with our wedding."

"You won't regret it, darling," I said as he helped me back up onto the breakwater. "I'll help you as much as I can," I continued while we started to walk on it in hand in hand, "with the wedding and with everything else in our lives. And I'll make beautiful children for you too."

I'm quite sure he picked up the pace back to the bungalow with that.

*   *   *

Shashi insisted on the whole shebang for the wedding, and where Aravind couldn't cover their plans with what he was making from his tiny family plot, Mohan silently stepped in to pick up the balance. Shashi was more worldly than her husband to be, and at this planning stage for their marriage, there was little he would not do for her.

They settled on late June for the nuptials, by which time they had found a honeymoon cottage in Muzaffarpur where Mohan was getting close to opening Bihar Tire's second store. But it was still an issue between the betrothed whether they would return there directly after the ceremony or take any form of what the British had called a honeymoon proper.

The Chaudrys had borrowed every tablecloth in the village to accommodate the wedding party, and on the longest of them all, the bride, groom, the parents of each of them, their living grandparents, and favorite sibling along with spouse sat in front of the door to the family home.

"So, Aravind," Gauri asked her *bahnoi*, who sat across from her between her sister and the bride, "how do you feel, having married off your youngest at last? I was beginning to wonder if she'd ever have children."

"I'm a little surprised she's starting on that as soon as she is," Aravind said, glancing over at Shashi. "She's always been one to do exactly the opposite of what she's expected to do."

"So, honey," Neela contributed, "you're saying Shashi is doing the unexpected by getting married?"

"Mom, I heard what you said," Shashi said from the other side of her father. "Did it ever occur to you that I just might have fallen in love for the first time? Mohan's a pretty unique man, you know."

"Can you say that a little louder?" Mohan leaned in from her other side, laughing. "Nobody ever tells me that at the shop I go to every day to make a living."

"You must have heard it when you were in the army, though," his grandfather Ghosh said from across the setting. "Otherwise the British would never have given you that Victoria Cross."

"I think they'd just prepared too many medals, Grandpa," Mohan said. "I only saw action in one battle all the time I was in Malaya, and the only thing I did in it was to come out alive."

"You see what I mean?" Shashi said, taking his arm and laughing herself. "He's not the type who flaunts his valor, even if his modesty is a little insufferable at times." She looked at her maternal grandfather Kapur opposite her husband, who guffawed as though his favorite granddaughter had said the funniest thing he'd ever heard. She knew him well, since he had moved to Maniarwa after his first wife died in Phulhar. He does look like he has Muslim blood, she thought, even if one could never tell by the way he acts. He's always trying to please people like a bride on her wedding night. It's as though he's afraid someone will finally realize he doesn't really believe in our gods if they get to looking at him too closely. "Are you having a good time, grandfather?" she asked him.

"I couldn't be better," Grandpa Kapur answered. "I can tell you married a good man," he said, looking directly across into Mohan's eyes. "He's kind, I think, but he still gets the job done."

"That's for sure," I agreed, pretending to laugh. "He's already told me we're going to Varanasi for a honeymoon, but we have to come back after one night because the shop in Muzaffarpur can't do without him any longer."

"On Monday afternoon we're getting our initial stock of tires to open," Mohan said by way of explanation. "I have to make sure they're all inventoried properly and ready for sale on our grand opening next Friday." I could tell I'd struck a nerve. "I want to make sure we get off to a good start at the new store," he added.

"Well, that's what a good husband does," my father said from behind me. I turned to see him nodding with approval at Mohan, and I felt a pang of jealousy. "He makes sure he's providing a good living for his family."

"Yeah, that's what Mohan does alright," his father Mr. Verma said from behind him. "He's conscientious about providing for everyone but his *own* family."

"Hush up, Parvan," his wife quietly shushed him from her side. "I don't want you starting anything to ruin Mohan's day."

"I was just making an observation, dear," Mr. Verma said. "We Bengalis are taught to say what we think."

"And so are we Biharis," said my sister Lakshmi from her seat across from him. "And I think my sister's pretty lucky, Mr. Verm—"

"You're just like her," Mr. Verma said, glancing over at me. "You don't behave like a woman's supposed—"

"Dad, I told you I didn't want you saying anything to ruin this day if I invited you," Mohan said, raising his voice and glaring at his father. Then he turned to me as he started to get up. "If we're going to make it to Benares tonight, sweetheart, we better get going."

I saw both of our fathers nodding in agreement when I stood up. But I knew we had not heard the last of this dust-up, for I was pretty certain Mr. Verma would never give us anything for our lives except discord....

        *   *   *

Our first child Gopal Mohan Verma was born March 14, 1952, almost exactly one year and nine months after our night in Varanasi. I figure it took the first year after our honeymoon to clear out my ovaries of the birth control I had practiced since my relationship with Rahul began my first year at Patna College. Even so, the birth was long and difficult, and after my water broke and Mohan took me to the hospital, the ordeal of the actual delivery and the child's initial cry did not occur until the mid-afternoon of the following day. Gopal was a dour, disciplined baby from the instant he squalled out his first breath, and I was almost afraid of him when we came home from the hospital two days later and concern for him started to rule our little flat on Motijheel Road in the center of Muzaffarpur.

Although he never said it, I know Mohan was proud our first-born was a boy, and I took great care to see that the little package in which we had invested so much was properly cared for. His birth had not been easy, as I was small and well past term when my water finally did break.

By this time, Mohan had made Najib's Bihar Tire store in Muzaffarpur well-known and trusted throughout North Bihar. In addition to his guaranteed wage of Rs 350 a month, Naju had given him a 5% commission on everything over fifteen thousand rupees of inventory he sold each month, and I was happy that the arrangement provided us with relief from the financial worries with which I had lived my entire life. But I still didn't see why he had to put in such long hours at the store – after all he had several well-paid assistants there by then – even if he was the one ultimately responsible for it as he always told me. So, not long after Gopal and I came home from the hospital, Jyoti came over from Madhubani and helped me for several weeks, but she couldn't really understand why Mohan had to stay so late at work either.

My mother would never have put up with it. When she got it in her head that Dad seemed too friendly with Srimati Naranga, whose hut he passed to get to the family plot, she made life so miserable for him that he never came home later than he had said he would no matter what he had to do in the field.

But before I could really test that idea out with Mohan, I was pregnant again with Shiva Kumar. Shiva's birth had been much shorter and easier than Gopal's, but Mohan and I had to return to rhythm and condoms if we didn't want our lives to be ruled by our fertility.

We kept our second child in our marital chamber for about three months before we sent him out to sleep with his older brother in the sitting room off the kitchen. Shiva's nighttime whimpering, though, was sufficiently bothersome that we soon began to look for a bigger place to live.

Fortunately, Mohan's commissions from the store were growing rapidly by then, and we took one side of a two-story house right on the Burhi Gandak not far from the grounds that would become the Muzaffarpur Institute of Technology. Downstairs we had a little front room along with a kitchen *cum* a spacious area for eating, while two small bedrooms on the first floor allowed each family member a modicum of privacy.

When I got pregnant with our third child several years later, though, Mohan had grown the tire business in North Bihar enough that we immediately began looking for more living space. So when our oldest daughter Tara Lakshmi was born Nov. 21, 1955, we rented a small house with three rooms we could use for sleeping opposite the health-services compound north of the city. Not long after we moved there, Mohan came across a used, light blue Hindustan Baby coupe for a bargain from the owner of some lorries transporting produce from throughout the district to Sonpur Ghat. After that, his trip to the store in central Muzaffarpur never presented much of a problem.

Shiva was by then a handsome boy of nearly three clamoring to join Gopal in a nursery school I sent him during the days, but Tara was the most beautiful little bundle of femininity I'd ever seen. Her eyes were hazel, almost the clear blue of my mother's family, and as she grew she became so fair I was sure that when the time came she might even fetch a Brahmin in marriage. As each day closed in the early months of 1956, Mohan and I basked in our little girl's loveliness, while the boys pretty much entertained themselves in their own room after supper for several hours before the lanterns were extinguished for the night.

Then, without warning, we received a rude announcement that shocked us out of our idyllic domestic life.

One cold dusk in late February, Mohan came home earlier than usual with a somber mien that reflected in his entire being. It was just after we had heard the news that Nehru's government would separate Gujarat out of the province of Bombay, the remaining part of which would be named Maharashtra for the Marati language spoken there.

"What's wrong, darling?" I asked the moment my husband walked in the door, I had heard the car door close outside and had seen him coming toward the house through the front window as I usually did every time the kids were driving me crazy. Today Gopal had been especially obstinate, insisting on teasing Shiva into a frenzy that had the effect of provoking a constant wailing out of Tara that I knew their father simply would not tolerate. But there was something else already agitating Mohan that I would have to elicit before I could call on his disciplinary powers.

"You look like Prasand's brother Govind just took up the last hour of your time dancing around the real reason he won't pay his tire bill," I joked, "which is the well-known fact that his older brother Rajendra is still the President of India even if he is now too old to do anything for anybody anymore."

"If only it was that simple, sweetheart," Mohan said, "I could pry a sufficient amount out of that pompous bastard to add enough to our kitty so we'd have enough to pay Najib the price he said he would sell me the store for. But it's a bigger problem than that."

"What'd that little idiot do?" I asked. I'd never say it to Mohan -- Najib's been his best friend since they were in Patna's St. Xavier's together – but I knew we should have never trusted a Muslim. They may not believe in charging interest, but I knew he'd find a way to go back on his promise of not selling us the store. "He didn't have another heart attack, did he?"

"No," Mohan said, putting the fingers of his right hand to his mouth and looking up to the heavens. "Thank god for that. But he's afraid he's going to."

"So what'd he do?"

"He's agreed to sell the entire business to Madras Rubber," Mohan said." That's why he wanted to come here and have lunch with me today. He said he wanted to tell me face to face."

"When's this sale supposed to take place?" I asked.

"The transfer's supposed to be final by the end of this fiscal year. June 30th."

"That's a couple of months away," I said. "Can't we get the rest of the Muzaffarpur store price together before then and buy it from him."

"I asked him about that," Mohan said. "But the North Bihar operation is the main reason Madras Rubber wants to buy Bihar Tire. The Muzaffarpur store is the most profitable part of the business."

"So we've worked hard the last six or seven years, and he gets all the benefit of it?" I said. "I told you we should have insisted on a written contract from him before we moved up here. He couldn't have made a go of the Muzaffarpur store without you."

Mohan didn't say anything for a minute. "It's not as though Najib planned to have a heart attack," he said slowly. "Not at his age."

"Yes, but we would have been protected if you had gotten his promise to sell you the Muzaffarpur store in writing," I said.

Mohan was silent for a moment. "You know I couldn't ask him for that," he finally replied quietly. "Not only was Najib my oldest friend, but he might not have given me this opportunity up here if I'd asked for a written contract back then." He paused. "And it was a great opportunity to prove myself."

"So what good has this great opportunity done for us at his point?" I asked. "You've been late every night getting home for the last five years for nothing."

"That's not really true, Shash. These years up here have taught me how to succeed in business and given me the confidence I can do it anywhere. Besides Bihar Tire has supported us and the kids in pretty good style while we've been up here." He halted a moment. "Besides, we do have a pretty good nest egg saved up to move on to something new.

"But that's a big risk," I said. "Now I see why Ambedkar isn't so crazy about Muslims."

"This has nothing to do with Muslims," he said as Tara started screaming again upstairs. "And anyway it's less of a risk to start a business now than it was right after independence when we came up here."

"Just a minute Mohan," I said. "Let me go and bring Tara down here for her nap. The boys are making her cry again."

He said, nodding and heading for the kitchen, "Go ahead. I'll make us some tea."

"No, I'll be right back," I said, starting up the stairway. "You rock the baby for a change, and I'll make the tea. You know my tea is always better than yours."

"Then I'll come upstairs with you," he said, following me up. "You get the baby ready to come down, and I'll settle those boys down."

He did so in short order. Discipline was not my forte when I was teaching, and these kids come from my own body. And I wasn't about to be as strict with them as my mother was with me. Besides I didn't ever want to go back to teaching, and the children liking me more than they did Mohan was my job security as a housewife.

Downstairs, Tara quieted right down too. She loved for her father to hold her, and by the time I came back into the front room with the tea, she was smiling and cooing up into his face as he walked back and forth while rocking her in his arms. For a moment I felt a twinge of jealousy – she never seemed so happy with me even when I nursed her – but then I remembered how crazy I got when she cried. "Well, look at the little princess," I said. "You've captured her heart again just like you do mine."

"She is my first daughter," he said. "I love the boys, but she's special and something a little different."

"You mean…," I wanted to give Tara a little sister too, "we can have another."

"I didn't exactly say that," Mohan said, smiling. "Right now we've got other things to focus on."

"We do?" I asked, fluttering my eyes shyly the way I could tell he liked. "Since you're so sure you can make a go of a new business, why not another child now?"

"True …."

"Just don't team up with the Muslims again."

"What do you mean by that?"

"I'm a woman, Mohan. Your idol Ambedkar's not so fond of the way Muslims treat their women."

"And we're Hindus, babe, and Ambedkar's not so fond of the way we treat our disadvantaged castes either," my husband said. "In fact, he just announced he's going to convert to Buddhism in October. If it wasn't so hard to get to the Nagpur area where he's going to do it, I'd go down and join him at the ceremony. He's invited everyone who wants to come, you know."

That's not really calculated to attract a lot of customers for a new business here in Muzaffarpur, I thought, but instead I said, "Never mind the Muslims, then. You're not really looking for a partner in this new enterprise, are you?"

"Not really. For what I'm thinking about, one man in management is all I'll need for now." Tara gently burped in secure contentment.

"What are you thinking about, Mohan?"

"Well, one thing is lychees. There's no other place in India that has soil as good for Sahi lychees as Muzaffarpur, and hardly anyone's growing them around here now," he said, smiling. "And you know what the bodhisvattas say about Sahis for spiritual power."

"No, I don't," I said. "But what do you know about growing fruit?"

"Not much," he admitted, "but you could help me. You come from a long line of cultivators here in North Bihar after all."

"My mother was a *kayastha*, remember," I said. And what kind of life is that going to be for our children? A lot of work, and they'll probably be as poor as I was growing up. "You think you'll be satisfied doing that, honey?' I asked instead.

"I'd be working outside," he said, thinking. "I don't see any problem with being happy growing lychee trees. But the problem is getting ahold of enough land around here to make the endeavor worthwhile. It's probably the most crowded part of Bihar and the most traditional. And the zamindars are producing so many sons in this area, I don't know if I could even rent enough land at a decent rate to make a profit on a lychee business."

"So what's your backup plan?"

"I want to do a little more investigation into it before I tell you," he said, smiling again. "The one thing I can tell you now, though, is that we'll probably have to move back to Patna to do it effectively."

I tried not to show him how happy that would make me. "That's a shame," I said. "I was just getting used to living here in the provinces." Used to it but not liking it any better, I said to myself. Here in Muzaffarpur everyone knows what everyone else is doing. The other problem is there's nothing to do. Patna's at least got enough movie houses so you can always find a seat when you want to see a film. And the Ganga's always there to go down to when you want, not far from the Gandhi Maidan in Bankipur, which is the nicest garden I've ever seen.

"You understand we're going to have to make some changes, Shashi, don't you?" Mohan said.

"Of course." I nodded in agreement. But I don't want to have to start teaching again to live in Patna, I thought, even though everything's more expensive there. I don't see how we'll be able to swing it unless Mohan clears as much from his new enterprise as he did from Bihar Tire, as I don't do well with anxiety....

Chapter Four

By the time the transfer of Bihar Tire actually came to pass, I had talked Mohan into renting a house with an option to buy in the Rajendra Nagar Colony near the bypass from the railway station to Patna City. Initially he had thought we should have gotten into something more modest till his new venture in burial plots proved itself. But I was definitely pregnant again by the time we had to decide, and that fact alone gave him a shot of confidence as it always did.

Rajendra Nagar was payback to me for Mohan's new enterprise in graveyard plots being even more intimately tied up with Muslims than his working for Najib in Bihar Tire. His friend had actually been the one to point out to him Muslims' dire need for cemetery land because of Islam's requirement that a body be committed to the earth within a day of death. Though Mohan actually made his first property deal for a Christian family I had met while teaching at Danapur, the Muslim community in our state was more than ten times bigger than the Christian.

But, first and foremost, our house on Road Number 7 would have more than enough room for four children. To begin with, Mohan set up his makeshift graveyard-properties office there with a desk and chair, file cabinet, and 2-line phone in a corner of the ground level. I helped him with the typing and the calls when he was scouting out land purchases for cemeteries or when I saw on our phone in the sitting room that he was on the business line.

We immediately got the boys enrolled in school – Gopal was in his second year in the primary school up toward the station at St. Joseph's, and we had enough money saved from the Muzaffarpur days to send Shiva to a nursery. Tara more than occupied me when the boys weren't at home. But Mohan had to travel the entire state. The one thing he had insisted upon was that we live in easy range of the railway station, though he seldom failed to get back home to sleep. When he did have to stay over somewhere, however, my mornings were frantic, getting the boys off for the day, keeping Tara out of mischief around the house, fielding the business calls which seemed to increase every day we lived in Rajendra Nagar, and handling the growing discomfort of my latest pregnancy.

As my due date for our fourth child came near, I began to see the onset of the nervous problems that would plague the rest of my fertile years. Increasingly I needed someone's late afternoon help to take care of the boys when they came home, but more and more Mohan's business consumed him through the early evening hours. One night toward the beginning of our first cold season back in Patna, the situation came to a head when the phone rang while I was cooking dinner and Shiva was teasing Tara and got her particularly riled up almost to the point of hysteria. Finally I moved the pot off the fire and raced to grab and hold her with one arm before picking up the phone.

"Honey," announced Mohan's familiar voice, "I just wanted to tell you to go ahead and eat. I'm not going to able to—"

"Mohan, you're not going to be late again tonight, are you?"

"I'm sorry to say I am. The Imam over here in Sharif can't see me for another half—"

"So you're not even going to come home for dinner?"

"I'll get there as soon as I can, but this man is really importan—"

"And we're not?" I cried. "I'm making *murgi masala*. Your favorite."

"I'm sorry, honey, but the Imam said more than a dozen families in his mosque want to buy plots for their famil—"

"I really need you to settle the boys down, Mohan!" I interrupted, my voice starting to crack. "They've got Tara wailing, and she's driving me crazy!"

"Yeah, I can hear her—"

"You better get here soon, Mohan!" I yelled and slammed the phone down.

It was a good hour and a half before he finally arrived. Tara was impossible, and the chicken was overdone by the time I got it into the curry sauce. Gopal let the rice go mushy when I asked him to help, and Shiva made Tara cry even louder when I asked him to keep her occupied while I finished cooking supper.

When Mohan came in the back door, I was weeping at the table because everything was so chaotic. He came over to comfort me, and I blasted him.

"Why can't you get a job with regular hours, Mohan?" I cried, pushing his arm away. "My father was never late for dinner."

"You were the youngest child, Shashi," he said. "By the time you came along, the other kids were raised, and he'd left the railroad."

"No he hadn't!"

"Anyway, I've still got five mouths to feed."

"It's your own fault, Mohan!"

"C'mon, hon—"

"Don't *honey* me. I can't stand this, Mohan!"

He didn't say anything.

Finally, I said, "You're the one who wanted to have children."

"And you didn't, Shashi?"

"*No*," I said "Not so many."

Silence.

"I'm the one who said three is enough," he finally said

"I'm not taking any of those new pills, Mohan. You know what Panditji says."

"You're going to have to accept the good with the bad then, honey."

"I need your help with these kids, Mohan," I wailed.

"And I'm helping you all I can," he said. "The only way I can make enough money now to pay the bills is in this properties business. You've got to be patient."

"I am patient," I cried. "But I can't stand this." I made as if to pull out my hair.

He ignored the gesture. "Give me a little time, honey," he said quietly. "After I get a reputation as someone who can deliver the goods, things will be easier."

"I hope so…."

         *   *   *

After Reva was born, things got worse, not better. Mohan stopped calling when he was going to be late because he said he didn't have the energy to go through two arguments at the end of a long day. Though the baby was the cutest little thing, she was always hungry, and by the time Mohan got home so late he couldn't eat with the rest of us, Reva had sucked me out of every bit of patience I had.

I was getting more and more resentful of him, and one night he didn't get home until all the kids were asleep. He had gotten back after nine o'clock before, but as I waited for him in the chaos, I got angrier and angrier.

The first thing I came to realize is that the main reason I wanted kids in the first place was that was the only way I could get my mother to love me. I would never tell anyone else that, but it was the truth. Mataji had said having children was the only unqualifiedly good thing she had ever done in her life, even if she didn't want me by the time I came along. I think she started talking about the grandchildren I'd give her as soon as I had my period for the first time.

She said grandchildren was the reason for that bleeding – something about our babies being proportionally so much bigger than the chicks or puppies born in our yard -- and there was certainly nothing else good about it. It was so dirty and messy. I was so ashamed I was happy to sleep with the chickens under the little coop outside up against the house. The cramps in my belly were agonizingly painful too – except for actually bearing a child I don't know that I've ever experienced anything so uncomfortable and embarrassing in my life.

My first childbirth, of course, was the worst. I have always been short and slender, so my body was not prepared to carry such a burden much less bring a life into the world. Gopal was a normal-sized baby, but even carrying him my body gained almost half its weight again by the time he was ready to be born…. *My* chatis *ached, I couldn't sleep well, and I was always tired. And I was always hungry, eating not only for myself but the creature growing inside of me. In the mornings especially, I often could keep nothing down, with an awful sour feeling in my belly that climbed up my pipes to my throat and finally spilled out to give me a moment's respite though I knew I would again have to try to keep something else down or neither I nor the baby would survive the ordeal.*

And then one day this bloated bubble inside of me, perpetually kicking and rolling , finally burst, and water came pouring out of me – how embarrassing and humiliating that Mohan had to see me like this. And then that ride in the rickshaw to the hospital where I could feel every pebble or bump on the road. I was screaming so awfully that the whole of Muzaffarpur would know I wanted to die….

I'm ashamed to admit but the next thing I remember is when I woke up I don't know how much later and that ugly little thing was pulling on my nipple and I could feel another fluid come through it and out into his mouth as he sucked it and it felt so good compared to what I had just been through that though it hurt, it almost felt sexy lying there and being sucked dry….

I didn't hear his first cry of life or feel when the mid-wife cut the cord between us or remember the afterbirth sliding out…. When I did come to, I felt so much lighter and better. I knew I was not supposed to even remember how awful it had been ….

But I did remember…. And I still wonder whether all that pain could possibly justify the agony of that birth?

And that was just the beginning….

There were four angry mouths demanding that I feed them, mouths wide open crying and hollering at me for more and more and more. It seemed like I was being pinched and pestered and pushed and pulled on every minute. But it didn't compare to the pain of having Mohan slipping away from me.

I looked at the clock, and it was now after eleven. And I wondered if that is all I had to look forward to in this life, another moment that would be worse than the last thing I had suffered through that still lived inside of me....

*   *   *

Shashi never saw coming the surprise Mohan had arranged for her one Sunday morning at the end of the cold season. Though they now had their beautiful younger daughter Reva to complement Tara and their boys, he had somehow inveigled Sangeeta and her fiancé Sukhay to watch all four kids for the better part of the day while he took Shashi off alone into the countryside. As an inducement to their babysitters, he had made a fine brunch of *alu* and *chapatiis* to go with *lassis* and *rasgullas* he had picked up from the nearby vendor of sweets.

Mohan wasn't much of a cook, but he had been puttering in the kitchen late the night before and then again from the crack of dawn on Sunday by the time their friends arrived unexpectedly at about nine-thirty.

"There you are, right on time," Shashi could hear Mohan greet them at the front door. He had insisted on her staying in bed for the tea and toast he had brought to her earlier, but by now she was dressed and reading and able to quickly join them in the kitchen.

"I expected those darling boys and Tara to open the door for us," Sangeeta was saying as she came in from the front room. "Where are they anyway?"

"Playing quietly in their rooms for a change," Shashi said, laughing. "When Mohan's at home, *ghee* wouldn't melt in their mouths. I don't know how he does it, but I'm not going to quarrel with success."

"Fathers usually seem to have that touch," Sangeeta said as she embraced her old friend before glancing back at Sukhay who was talking with Mohan. "I'm hoping my fiancé learns the secret from your husband."

"You can be certain I'm learning everything from him I can," Sukhay said as he looked over at the table set in the corner. "Including how to make Sunday morning breakfast for my wife after we have kids."

"I'm as impressed as you," Shashi said. My man still surprises me, she realized. Not only is he handsome, smart, and a good provider, but he's still very considerate. I know I'm lucky, but he'll never know I recognize it. "Don't get the idea he does this every week," she said with a laugh. "Before today I didn't have any idea he could make *chapattis* to tell you the truth."

"This guy can do everything," Sukhay, who owned a kitchen store in Patna Market, said as he put his arm around the shoulder of his friend. Mohan and he had only met a few times, but they seemed to genuinely like each other. "How he set it up for me to borrow his buddy Najib's Ambassador coupe for the day *I* have no idea."

"My motivation was not that we're going to use it for our bike ride in the countryside," Mohan said, chuckling. "But we need a way to get our bikes out of the city while you two watch the kids," he added, motioning for the others to sit down while he headed for the stove. "Shashi, can you go and call the older kids from upstairs before you sit down? We can't ask Sangeeta and Sukhay to feed them more than once while we're gone...."

Well before eleven, Mohan was securing the bicycles into the boot of the car parked out front. When he came in to get Shashi for their outing, he took from the counter several tiffins and a thermos and put them in a picnic basket to take along. In another quarter hour, they turned off the bypass onto the Gaya road at Pahari village, and soon the car was cruising through the lovely Gangetic Plain, which was already showing the tender green of the first paddy planting of the year. Shashi snuggled up to her husband, and shortly they were belting out the words to "Nain tumhare mazedar."

They drove along to Islampur, where Mohan filled the car at a petrol pump whose owner he knew. After he parked it next to his friend's house in the back and made sure the owner's 14-year old son would keep watch of the vehicle, he unloaded the bikes, tied the picnic basket on his back, and they set off pedaling. Not far south of the town, he turned off the highway and went down a dirt track toward the Mohana River, on whose banks Vishnu was reputed to have sojourned so long ago. At a beautiful spot in a mango grove, they stopped to look at the water gently rippling by below.

"Mohan, how did you know the way out here?" Shashi asked as she pulled her bike up next to his. "I didn't see a single sign the entire way."

"I've been planning this picnic for some time now, sweetheart," he said. "I've been selling some gravesites around Islampur, so I've been asking my customers about places to take a bike ride in the area. The river's really lovely here, isn't it?"

"It surely is."

"Well, let's ride on ahead alongside it. The scenery gets even nicer up the way."

Just after Halasganj came into sight up ahead, Mohan stopped, put down his kickstand, and began to untie the basket. Shashi heard a cow moo and locked into the rolling pasture to her right being grazed by about a score of goats and cows of various colors.

Hand in hand they made the slight descent to the river's edge. Mohan set the basket on a rock about a meter above the water, and they went down to the bank to take off their *chappals* and dip their feet in the murmuring current.

Seated on the bank, he put his arm around her as they breathed in the country air in the dappled shade provided by a rosewood tree. After some minutes, he asked her if she was hungry.

"I must admit that I am," she said. "I haven't had so much exercise in months. I could eat a goat."

"Let's get to it then," he said, rising and reaching for the basket. He handed it to her and climbed to untie the blanket bound behind the seat on her bike, then spreading it on a grassy basin next to the rock. She opened the basket and laid out the tiffins, *chapattis*, thermos, and two clay cups....

As they ended their picnic, Shashi licked the last of his chicken *masala* off her fingers after she had finished the final *chappati*. "You know, darling, this is about the best *murgi* I've ever had," she said. "Now that I know you can cook too, I don't think I'll ever let you go."

"Who said I can cook?" he joked. "I got the recipe from my mother yesterday morning before you got up and just followed her directions."

"But your thoughtfulness ... I was about ready to accept the fact that you were like all Indian men, that a wife is nothing more to you than the mother of his children."

"You don't understand, Shash, that I wanted you and only *you* to be the mother of our children."

"Forget the children for a moment, Mo. It's just the two of us here today."

"I know… Isn't this spot beautiful?" he said. "I knew you'd like it."

"It's perfect…, but any place would be with you."

"For me too," he said.

They looked at the citadel of black rocks atop the hill across the river. It was like another country.

"You know," he said, "that is the hill from which Vishnu vanquished the *adivasis* of this area."

"Thank god he did," she said. "This place is too beautiful for them." She looked into his troubled eyes as he turned to her. "It was meant only for us."

After a while, he looked at his watch. "It's almost three," he said. "We're going to have to get going. I told Sukhay we'd be back by five."

"Do we have to?"

"Sadly, yes, my love," he said, standing up.

And this day I dutifully followed him to our bicycles to begin our journey back home….

*   *   *

It was nearly seven by the time Mohan got out of Danapur on the bus. He had been in the town east of Patna for a mid-afternoon appointment with Fr. O'Donovan, who had agreed to introduce him to a large Anglo-Indian family in the cantonment which had decided to secure a final resting place for their descendants. Mohan had also been looking for a reasonably priced used car to replace the one he had to sell in Muzaffarpur to help finance the move to Patna, and the priest had also arranged for him to see a vehicle that fit his budget when its owner Dennis Haywood had returned home from his office in the city that evening.

Mohan had liked his old Ford, but Haywood had wanted more than he could pay for it at this point. So Mohan had offered the asking price, the second half of which he proposed to secure by a lien that he would pay off within half a year. Mr. Haywood had requested a week to think about the offer. Thus, when Mohan jumped onto the riverside bus bound for Ashok Raj Path just as it was leaving Danapur, he found an open seat by the window and leaned back contentedly at his day's work well done.

By the time the bus pulled into the bus stand on the Gandhi Maidan, Mohan had just about enough time to sling his briefcase around his neck and jog across the park to the Kit Kat and meet Najib for a beer at the appointed eight o'clock hour. He anticipated their old college friend Arash Nariman would also be there, and since he had not seen him in the fourteen years since they'd graduated, he did not want to be late for what he expected to be a delightful reunion.

As he burst through the door into the fan-cooled barroom, he immediately spotted Naj at the near end of the bar with a man he never would have guessed to be his old chum Aru, who had been a trim football forward the last time he had seen him. This gentleman was stocky, almost stout, and in contrast to Najib's leisure suit and his own beige cotton shirt and dark trousers, wore a tie and tweed jacket. Though Arash turned toward Mohan with a familiar twinkle in his eye, Mohan first grasped his former employer's outstretched hand and shook it, saying, "I bet you thought I was going to be late, Naj, didn't you?"

"It crossed my mind, knowing you had to take the bus from Danapur," Najib said. "You remember Arash, don't you?" he added quickly, turning to the well-dressed man alongside him.

"Of course I do," Mohan answered turning to his old college friend. "How could I forget that twinkle in your eye? Good to see you again, Aru," he said, hugging his burly buddy. "How long has it been anyway?"

"Almost fifteen years, I figure," Arash said as he stepped back from his friend's embrace. "I remember you were headed off to report to the conscription office in Bhagalpur – you always knew how to make a guy feel guilty – and I was going up to Allahabad to continue my studies."

"It appears that you finished them quite well," Mohan said. "I understand you're a professor or something now."

"That's exactly what I am," Arash said, smiling. "But actually I just scraped by in Allahabad like I did in Patna College. My parents have all kinds of friends in high places, and just as I got my doctorate in history, Benares Hindu University needed a Parsi on its faculty, and I'm still there."

"Come on, Aru," Najib said, gently elbowing his old pal. "No false modesty among friends. You couldn't have gotten that job unless you were good."

"What'll you have, Mo?" Aru said, chuckling and nodding to the barkeep, who had come over to stand before them behind the bar. "Naj already hit me up for one."

"A Golden Eagle, what else?" Mo said. "Remember that last time we got loaded before graduating and ran into those *adivasi* women from Orissa...."

All the gang at Patna College always knew that Aru's parents, both physicians at Kurji Hospital, had adopted their son as a small boy, but he had never let on before he had any interest in finding out who his birth parents were. That precise quest, however, is what he now told Mohan and Najib had consumed much of his energy over the last decade or so. Finally, last year he had tracked his birth father to the town of Surat on the Gujarat coast, but by the time Arash was able to get over there to meet him, the man had died. But when Mohan learned that Arash had eventually met his birth mother in Bombay during that same trip, there was no way he could not take the opportunity to have dinner with his friends next door at the Kwality Restaurant. By then, he could think of nothing else but hearing from Aru the details of his reunion with his birth-mother.

"So how did your mother end up in Bombay in the first place?" he asked after giving his order for his favorite liver and onions to go with his third beer. "And how did you ever find her anyway?"

"Before I went over to Bombay side then, I had learned from my adoptive parents how they got me," Aru said. "They weren't particularly happy that I was determined to find my birth parents, but when I insisted, they gave me the particulars of how the adoption had taken place."

"Of course they would," Najib said. "Everyone knew that your adoptive parents were open and wonderful people. They always made me feel so welcome when I'd visit you at home when we were in school."

"Me too," Mohan agreed. "I really liked Maneck and Dina. They were so straightforward they made me feel they actually liked me too." No one said anything. "So what did they tell you about the adoption, Aru?"

"My parents were still quite devout Parsis, you may remember," Aru said as he drank from the glass of water that had been provided to go with his dinner. "They were very committed to continuing the survival of Zoroastrianism, so when they realized they could not have children themselves, they decided they wanted to adopt a Parsi child if they could."

"How did they ever end up in Patna themselves?" Najib said. "I don't think there're too many Zoroastrians around here."

"Jobs," Aru said. "They had both finished their internships in Bombay – almost all the Parsis live there now, you know – and they were interested in trying someplace new. Kurji needed well-trained doctors then and offered a better deal than anywhere else. Then, surprise, surprise, they really liked it here."

"Patna is one of the secret treasures of India," Mohan commented.

"Getting back to my search for my birth parents, though," Aru said, swallowing the last spoonful of his soup, "in order to find a Parsi orphan my adoptive parents had to go to their old temple in Surat where they grew up – the Parsis originally settled on the Gujarat coast when they came from Persia, you know. The *atharvan* in Surat told them about a married Parsi trader there with five children who had gotten his secretary pregnant a few years back and had placed the child in a foster home." Arash looked at his friends and smiled wanly. "I was that little boy, and the trader and his secretary were that romantic couple who brought me into this world."

"So where were you when they got you?" Mohan asked.

"I was living with a Parsi foster family in Porbandar. With a cotton manufacturer who already had eight kids of his own. So he was more than happy to give me up to a young set of Parsi physicians who couldn't have children of their own."

"So your old priest in Surat gave you your real father's name and address?" Najib said.

"It wasn't quite that simple," Aru said. "By the time I got to Surat, my birth father was dead, like I said. His widow was living with a son nearby, though, and the son remembered and told me my birth mother's name. His father apparently had set her up with an income and a place to live in Bombay after she gave me up."

"You'd become quite the private investigator, Aru," Mohan said.

"Now here's the interesting part," Aru leaned forward and said. "My birth father had taken my stepbrother into the fire temple near Malabar Hill in Bombay when he was still quite young. Afterwards they went to the Mahalaxmi Race Track, which was nearby. At Window 7, my stepbrother said they met a lady named Indira Baxter, who seemed to know not only his father but everyone else at the track. Before they left, he said his father gave her some money."

"Ah, the plot thickens," Najib said.

"Indeed," Aru said, looking through them to the back of the restaurant. "So I went down to Bombay and started asking for an Indira Baxter at the Mahalaxmi Track. Right away a guy I met at betting Window 7 showed me to a cottage just across the way from the stables." He paused and focused back on his friends. "Sure enough, this Indira Baxter, the lady who came to the door there, turned out to be my birth mother...."

After a moment of silence, Najib looked at his watch. "God, it's after eleven," he said. "I've got to get home.

Mohan, however, seemed transfixed by the story.

"From the outside, it was a cute little bungalow," Aru continued. "Inside there were racing forms and movie magazines scattered all over the place. Dirty dishes in the sink and dust everywhere else."

"What was this Indira like?" Mohan asked.

"Frumpy and overweight, what else," Aru said. "Her son George – she had married an English banker who had stayed on in Bombay with HBIC after the British left – had just moved back in with her after his divorce. Neither of them seemed that excited about meeting me."

"Did you talk to them a long time?"

"I was ready to go a half hour after I got there," Aru said. "Then she asked about my parents in Patna, and when she found out they were doctors, she became friendlier, asking me what I was going to do after I got tired of teaching."

"What'd you say?" Mohan said

Aru squirmed in his seat and looked at his watch. "Let's save it for next time, Mo," he said, yawning. "I've got a UP History class to teach tomorrow afternoon and a very early train back to Benares in the morning. I'm going to have to fill you in on the rest of the story when we get together again. Besides, it's still unfolding," he said, laughing. "Indira has now taken to calling me every time she has a bad day."

"What's your wife think about that?" Mohan asked him. "Shashi wouldn't like it a bit if my mother called me more than a couple times a year." He shook his head and smiled. "It's like she's afraid I'll remember how well my mother took care of me before I left home."

"Well, Hitosa – that's my wife's name – doesn't have to worry about that," he said with a chuckle. "I didn't even know Indira existed until last year."

"How about you, Naj?" Mohan turned to his former boss and still best friend. "Is Mira so jealous of you with your own mother living just down the street?"

"Not at all," Najib said. "In fact, Mira's over there visiting Mom all the time. She says she likes my mother better than hers."

"How long you been married, Aru?" Mohan said, turning back to him. "Wives seem to get a little more possessive with time."

"I hope not," Arash said. "Hitosa and I have been married for only three years."

"You have any kids?"

"Not yet," Aru said. "Hitosa still loves teaching, and I want to get a little better established at the university before we start our family."

"Mo didn't want to wait for that, did ya?" Naj teased, nudging his pal and smiling. "Pretty soon he's going to be able to field a family football team."

"Naj said you have four kids already," Aru said. "How many more are you going to have?"

"We've had it. Four's enough to put on this planet," Mohan said. "That's if I can keep Shashi off of me."

"Don't blame it on her," Najib said. "There is such a thing as birth control, you know."

"Yeah, if I could trust her to do it," Mohan said. "Shash says she loves being a mother, and she's a good one. And she just can't help getting pregnant."

"You could use condoms, Mo," Aru said.

"Well, condoms aren't foolproof either," he said. "Besides she doesn't really like me to use a rub—"

"It's your fault as much as hers then."

"Maybe." Mo looked down. "Sometimes it just doesn't feel right to stop and put one on."

"What are you talking about?"

"C'mon, you guys," Mohan said, slapping the table. "I don't feel like going into the details if you don't get the picture." He looked at his hands, then turned his wrist. "Aieee," he exclaimed, waving at the waiter standing by the cash register. "I have to get going. Shashi's going to kill me…."

*   *   *

This was the first time Mohan hasn't gotten home by midnight, Shashi fumed in the easy chair which she had turned to face the front door. I haven't even tried to get the kids to sleep – I want him to see how insatiable they are, what is like for me when he is out there having a jolly, good time selling his cemetery plots to all those dirty *Musselmans*..

There was a burst of laughing and thumping from the boys upstairs as they thundered around their room above her, and then Tara hollered at them from next door, "Can't you be mawr kwite! I wanna go to sleep," she cried. And then, of course, Reva began bawling, "Aaaaah, aaaaaah, aaaaaaah."

Shashi got up and went to the foot of the stairs. "You boys just wait till your father gets home," she screamed. "If you don't quiet down right now, I'll have him take the belt to you the minute he gets here!"

Probably, more than this threat, the sound of a motor rickshaw coming to a stop in front of the house calmed Gopal and Shiva down. Shashi turned from the stairs and raced to the window, pulling back the curtain to make certain it was Mohan. She thought she saw him stumble as he stepped down to the street. Quickly, she snapped off the light in the front room and went back to her chair to wait for him to come in.

As soon as he opened the door, she could smell the alcohol. "This is a fine time to be getting home," Shashi said casually. "Your dinner is ruined, and I couldn't get the kids to bed."

"That's okay," he said. "I ate with Naj—"

"I knew it! That Najib just can't stand it that you're happily married."

"Naj loves you, Shashi. And the kids t—"

"Where'd you eat?"

"At the Kwality."

"So you were at the Kit Kat too," she lifted her voice to say. "I can smell that awful Golden Eagle all the way from here."

"You'll never guess who we met there, honey," he started.

"Some dancing girls from Calcutta?"

"C'mon, Shashi." He knelt down next to her. "Arash was in town," he said. "You remember him from the College, don't you?"

"Of course, I remember him. He was after me before you even knew me," she lied. "I should have let him catch m—"

Mohan tried to take my hand. "C'mon, sweetheart—"

"Don't you *sweetheart* me!" she cried, pulling her hand away. "I don't have to stay married to you, you know."

He overlooked her threat. "Why are the lights on upstairs?" he asked instead as he stood up.

"I told you! I couldn't get the kids to bed."

"Well, I'll fix that." He headed for the stairs.

"Don't you dare go up there smelling like that, Mohan."

"Daddy," Gopal called down from the top of the stairs. "You're so loud down there we can't sleep."

"You little liar," she screamed, charging over to the foot of the stairs to look at him. "Shiva and you were wrestling a minute ago."

"We were not," Gopal, said, retreating toward his room.

"So why was your light on, then?" Mohan asked, starting up the stairs.

"I just turned it on when you and Mom started yellin—"

"Don't you start making up stories too, Gopal," Mohan said, taking two steps at a time now. "Your mother told me you won't go to bed."

"That's not true, Daddy," Shiva said, appearing beside his brother now. "She told us we could stay up till you got home."

Mohan stopped at the top of the stairs and turned back toward her. "Is that true, Shashi?" he demanded. "These boys have school tomorrow."

She burst out crying and fled into the kitchen....

*   *   *

From the time Shashi learned to read in primary school, books had been the elixir by which she could escape when dark clouds covered her horizon, she realized several nights after the blowup with Mohan. When she was a student they were her work as well as a make-believe world that relieved any pain or drudgery that entered her life all the way through college.

Then, while teaching school, she became addicted to Hindi movies supplemented by the novels that made her a better purveyor of literature in English to young Indian students. But the stories in them provided her with a sort of cocoon – short-term in the case of the films but lasting up to a month while she was making her way through a novel. They became a parallel reality for her to the humdrum of those years when her relationship with Rahul was so unsatisfactory. Narayan and Rao, Dickens and Austen, the Brontes, even Premchand in Hindi not only made her impervious to the long nights alone but also gave her the hope to believe that something more satisfying for her lay ahead. Then, when Prince Charming finally came into her life in the person of Mohan, she pretty much forgot about books, she admitted to herself as she opened up *Nectar in the Sieve* to the place she had left off, because she didn't need the strength or hope they gave her anymore. She had it in the flesh then, and she didn't need their alternative reality anymore.

Now they each read their own books separately at the same time, but it wasn't with the same urgency with which she used to do it before they got married. From her easy chair, she looked over at Mohan stretched out on their bed when a faint rasp in his throat interrupted the deep breathing into which he had fallen when his latest Christie mystery had dropped from his hands as he drifted off to sleep. He had come home exhausted after a grueling trip to attend to the booming cemetery market in Muzaffarpur. He still had to cover most of the state even though he had an assistant handling the Patna area and running the office he'd opened in Patna Market, to which he had had to return to prepare things for the next day on his way home from Mahendru Ghat.

After supper, while the boys went up to their room to do their homework and Tara helped her with the dishes after she had put her sister down, Mohan had gone into their room to relax with *Murder on the Nile*. When she looked in on him as Tara headed upstairs for the company of her dolls, Mohan was sitting in their new lounge chair, but he happily relinquished it to me and retreated to the bed to finish the chapter he had just started.

For some time, they read on companionably in silence, before her thoughts returned to their problems. She had taken up reading to the children again when Gopal reached the age of comprehension, but it was with a different motivation than her own pleasure. She wanted the children to be good readers like she was, and, indeed, they did all become addicted to books like she had been and become wonderful students. But because she still was not reading for her own pleasure anymore, she made Mohan and, to a lesser extent, the kids her complete precccupation.

It's what a wife and mother was supposed to do, but it placed too great of a responsibility on the rest of the family. It was not fair to them…or her.

"Mom," Shiva called quietly from the hall while tapping on the door to their room. "Can you read Tara and me to sleep," he continued as he opened the door a crack and peeked in. "Gopu still has to do his Hindi and geography, but he's offered to come down to the front room to finish his homework if you'll read to us on my bed. Besides, Tee told me to tell you she won't be able to get to sleep without hearing you read for a while."

"Of course, darling," she said quietly as she got up and headed toward the door. "What do you want me to read?"

"How about that *Little Prince* book you told us about," he said. "Tara's the one who actually suggested it."

Shashi went back into their bedroom to retrieve the book, while Shiva climbed the stairs to alert Gopal and Tara that she was coming up. Before following Shiva upstairs, she slipped off Mohan's sandals and his new reading glasses and laid them aside.

On her way up the stairs, she met Gopal coming down with his school books. "Thanks, Gopu," she said. "It's nice of you to agree to finish your homework down here."

"No problem, Mom," he said. "It's been a long time since you read any of us to sleep. I remember how I used to love it."

"Are you sure you don't want to join us?" she asked him.

"I wish I could," he said, shaking his head as he continued past her, "but I've still got a lot of work to do for tomorrow's classes."

As she finished climbing the stairs, she realized she was still almost afraid of her earnest oldest child. She had been so fearful she would do something wrong with him as her first-born, she had never even tried to discipline him when he didn't do what he was told, so she guessed she was lucky he was as good a boy as he was. She had read to him before he went to school as she also did for the others, but she didn't know how to talk to him much otherwise so he was such a stranger to her. The teachers always said he was bright and learned easily, but she still didn't know Gopal and doubted that he would ever be anything other than somewhat distant from her.

When she walked through the open door of the boys' room, Shiva was already laying on one side of his bed waiting for her, but Tara was still fidgeting as she stood next to the bed.

"Can Reva come too, Mom?" she asked. "She's still awake, and I was only two years old when you first read to me."

"Okay, honey," she smiled at her and said. "But don't get her all excited bringing her in here. She has to go to sleep soon." Shashi was proud that Tara wanted her little sister to start reading early like she had done herself. Already Tara could pretty much follow children's books in both Hindi and English, even though she wouldn't start school until next year.

Tara dashed out of the room and soon returned carrying Reva on her hip as Shashi herself carried her. The baby was sucking her thumb, but her eyes were wide open with anticipation.

"Where'll we put her?" Shashi asked, assaying Shiva's narrow bed.

"You lie down right next to Shiv," Tara said, seeing he had already plumped up Gopu's pillow next to his. "We'll all share the pillows, and I'll lay down with the baby on the other side of you. If we squeeze in, we should be able to all fit."

In a moment, they were all cozy, and Shashi began,

Once when I was six years old, I saw a magnificent picture in a book, called <u>True Stories from Nature</u> about the primeval forest. It was a picture of a boa constrictor in the act of swallowing an animal. Here is a copy of the drawing.

In the book, it said "Boa constrictors swallow their prey whole, without chewing it. After that, they are not able to move, and they must sleep through the six months that they need for digestion."

I pondered deeply, then, the adventures of the jungle. And after some work with a colored pencil I succeeded in making my first drawing. My Drawing Number One. It looked like this:

She pointed out the accompanying picture to the children.

I showed my masterpiece to the grown-ups, and asked them whether the drawing frightened them.

But they answered: "Frighten? Why should anyone be frightened by a hat?"

My drawing was not a picture of a hat. It was a picture of a boa constrictor digesting an elephant. But since the grown-ups were not able to understand it, I made another drawing. I drew the inside of the boa constrictor.

"So you see," she told her kids, "don't automatically doubt yourself when challenged by grownups. You have more imagination than them and may see the reality of things more clearly than them."

"But, Mom," Shiva said. "How could anyone tell from the first drawing that it was anything but a hat?"

"Shiv," Tara said, "you have to look inside to see what it really is."

"That's right, honey. Just like the snake had to digest the elephant before it could move again," Shashi said, "sometimes we have to take the time to digest what we see before we really know what there is in the inside of things."

She paused. "Like this war with China our Prime Minister is talking about all the time. If he is so concerned with whose land it is in the north of Kashmir, shouldn't he be more concerned with whose land Srinagar Valley should really be under the Partition Agreement he signed?"

And they went on to read and discuss two more chapters before the kids got sleepy. It was so cozy, and for perhaps the first time in Shashi's life, she was teaching her children what she had learned from life.

More than anything she now wanted her children to know what they can learn from reading and how it could give them the strength to make their own conclusions about what they encountered in life. Yet she did not want them to use a book in the way that its story became their reality as it had happened with her.

She did not think that disconnect, that escape from reality, would lead to finding happiness. As much as she have tried, it has not made her happy. Now she did not know who she was – the one reading the book or a character in it – so she never really knew whether she should be happy or not. In fact, she still did not know whether she was happy or not. She just pretended to be happy or sad or feel whatever she thought others wanted her to feel.

THE RAINS

Chapter Five

Mohan got off the bus at the entrance to Patna Market on Ashok Raj Path and walked briskly the minutes it took to reach its deepest recess, above which was the office of Verma Realty. Together with the ten-minute amble he took each day from his home to Prem Chand Circle to catch his bus, he got his blood circulating by the time he skipped up the stairs to the second glass door on the first landing, on which was perfectly printed the same thing he had on his business card ---

VERMA PROPERTIES

Specializing in family burial sites

Prop. Mohan Verma
B.A. Patna College 1943

--and usually made good decisions while he was there. This morning his assistant Arju Kumar had reached the office before him and was already on the phone when he heard the tea in the pan on the hotplate begin to bubble.

Mohan walked directly to the table on which the hotplate was set up, looked out the window to see the white winter smoke from the wood stoves below drift up into the blue sky above, and then quickly leaned over to watch the bubbles reach the outside of the pool of milk which told him it was time to remove the mixture for the tea from the heat. He did so and set the pan on a tin plate to stir the chai *masala*. When he had scraped the residue of tea leaves and masala powder off the bottom of the pan, he replaced it back on the burner and waited for the mixture to come to a final boil. As he waited, Arju came to the end of his business on the phone.

"*Khoda hafez, Khajendar sahub. Jaldi milengee,*" he said, putting the receiver back in its cradle and turning to his boss. *"Kya hota hai, Mohan?* Everything okay?"

"Couldn't be better, *bhai,*" Mohan said. "As they say in Hindi movies, 'I feel like a million dollars' after my quarter hour of power walking."

"So you left the Mrs. the car again, I take it?" Arju said. "Is she getting a better feel for the Maruti, *sahub?*"

"I haven't noticed any dents yet," he said, grinning. "She's probably grinding a gear here and there, but at least she's not hitting anything." Mohan removed the tea from the burner to stir one last time. "Umm, it smells good, Arju," he said. "Where'd you get the *masala?* From Chandan on the Raj Path?"

"*Bilkul nahii,*" Arju said, pumping out his chest as he walked over to unplug the hotplate. "We still have all the spices in the cupboard, so I got in early and mixed them up myself."

"Well, then, can I pour you a spot, *babu?*" Mohan asked. "You deserve the first taste."

Arju sipped from the glass his boss offered him and licked his lips. "Not bad if I do say so myself."

"*Chini chaate hai?*"

"Maybe one," Arju said, taking the proffered sugar jar and picking the *cammac* off the table cloth to add one table spoon.

"So what's on the agenda for today?" Mohan asked, returning to his desk with his own glass of tea. "God, this stuff is good," he said, taking a sip and waving his head after he sat down.

"I think I'd better go out to Fatepur and see if I can close the Miyan deal," Arju said picking up a document from his desk. "Old man Singhji says he wants a half *lakh* for the family plot the Miyans want, but I think he'll take forty thousand if I go out and buy him a cup of good *chai*."

"Sounds like a plan." Mohan smiled. "I think I'm going to go out to Gulzarbagh and talk to Nagarsir *babu* about that old bus of his. He says he's tired of making the same run to Hazaribagh and Ranchi every day, but no one wants to take the route off his hands." He looked out the window again and then turned back to his office manager.

"You're doing such a great job running this shop, there's not much for me to do here anymore. I think I need to try something new," he added. "If I've learned anything from Nehru's death, it's that a person should step aside when he's starting to get stale. Panditji hadn't done a good job running India since before the Sino-Indian War. If he'd have turned the country over to someone else back then, we'd all be better off, and he'd probably still be alive."

"What do you mean, Mohan?" Arju said, leaning forward. "You want to sell out?"

"Not exactly, *bhai*. But I think it's time you and I came to a different arrangement." He paused and focused on his assistant's face. "Like maybe I put in less time here and just help you when you want me to. If it works out well, maybe you can run the business after a while, and we can call it Wazir & Verma Ltd. or something like that."

"I don't know if I know enough about this business to run it without you, Mohan. It hasn't even been two years yet since I started working in properties."

"You're plenty quick, Arju. You'll be surprised at how much you've learned," Mohan said. "Besides I'll always be available to help you anytime you need me." He paused. "You're good enough to be making a lot more money, son, and you're reaching the age where you should be thinking about starting a family."

Arju nodded slowly.

"If you want to explore the idea, I can go to that solicitor Gupta we've used down on Station Road," Mohan went on. "He can probably give me some ideas about how to formally bring you into the business."

Arju was silent for a minute. "Have you talked to your wife about this? You've got two sons, you know," he finally said.

"I know," Mohan said. "But I want them to become whatever they want to. If one of them wants to get into the gravesite properties business, I'll still be a part owner here. Hopefully we could figure out a way for him to take my place if that situation arises."

"Sounds good to me."

"It only makes sense, *bhai*. The Muslims are by far our biggest customers. Being raised one yourself, you know their ways better than me, so you're more likely to make our little enterprise reach its fullest potential ...."

*   *   *

When Mohan got home that night, he alerted me that he had something to tell me as soon as he had kissed me hello.

"I talked with Arju today, Shash," he began. "I told him I wanted to give him a stake in the business."

"You *what*?"

"You know, like what we had talked about," he said. "I told him I wanted him to take more responsibility in Verma Properties, and I knew I had to pay him more to do it."

"I suppose you volunteered to give him more money just like that. Just because he's a Muslim," I said. "You're always feeling sorry for the Muslims, Mohan."

"It's not that, dear. But Arju's Muslim, and ninety percent of our deals involve Muslims," he said. "It only makes sense that we'd do more business if he was the front man and that the company name reflected that he owned part of the business."

"But, like I said before, Mohan, we can't afford to pay him anymore and still provide for the kids the things that they need."

"That's exactly the problem, Shash. They're only going to need more and more as they grow up," he said. "If we're going to have any chance of getting them the things they'll need to have a decent chance in life, Verma Properties is going to have to sell more burial plots." He paused for a moment but before I had a chance to say anything, continued, "Changing the company name to Wazir and Verma is a sure way to selling more gravesites, I reckon."

"What about the boys?" I said. "And has it ever occurred to you that one or both of the girls' husbands might just want to go into your business?"

"C'mon, Shash. I'd hope we'd bring up the girls well enough that neither one of the men they choose to marry would want to go into business with me."

"Who can guarantee that, Mohan? Who's smart enough to be sure they know what someone else is thinking?" I asked. "Anyway, the boys certainly might want to take after their father."

"I hope so, but in ways that count, darling," he said. "I hope both of them become men who'll have no more desire to go into business with me than I did with my own father."

"You're such a dreamer, Mohan. You remember that foolish ruckus the Kashmiris were making a few years ago about that Hazratbal shrine in Srinagar, about stealing the hair of Mohammed that was supposed to be inside it?" I said. "This country could have broken apart over that." I paused to let that sink in. "It still could break apart over something so ridiculous…. Then where would we be? There wouldn't be any jobs for anyone, much less the boys."

"Nehru handled that Hazratbal thing, didn't he, babe?" he said. "And he got the Supreme Court to limit the reservation of jobs in the government to fifty percent, didn't he? If the boys study hard and are willing to do any honest work, they'll always do alright."

"What if they want an easier life than we've got, honey?" I said.

"Life's never easy for decent people, Shashi. If they turn out to want a life of comfort, we wouldn't have raised them properly."

I didn't say any more. Mohan was never as good a student as I was, but he was every bit as smart. He got out every day and had learned something new every time he came home.

"Besides, sweetheart," he said. "I need a new challenge too." He paused. "Nagasir's got this bus route he wants to get rid of, and I think—"

"What do you know about buses?" I demanded. "That's as crazy as that idea you had about growing lychees."

"Give me a chance, Shashi," he said. "You didn't like the idea of selling gravesites either."

"That was different," I said, but I realized I was never going to be able to make Mohan just like my father. He was an original and definitely his own person.

"You have to have some consideration for my needs too, Shash."

"I do," I delayed. "Don't I try to make your favorite dishes all the time?"

"Which I can't always get home to eat, because you're always saying I'm not making enough money," he said. "You can't have it both ways, Shashi."

I knew that, but I believe that anything is possible if you want it bad enough. Look how far I've come from Maniarwa. And suddenly I realized how I could get what I wanted. "Okay, Mohan, have it your way," I said. "I'll see if Dr. Chandra can fit me with one of those loops, so we don't have any more children. Then you'll be able to slow down a little."

You should have seen the smile that came over his face then. But Mohan would never know for sure if I inserted it. If I worked it right, I could have it both ways yet....

*   *   *

"Hey, Mohan," Nagarsir said, grinning broadly at his friend as he entered the tea shop across the street from the stand at the intersection where the first bus was due from Gaya, Ranchi, and Jamshedpur in another quarter hour. "What's up with the old jalopy that you want my advice about?"

Mohan had added the three new buses to the operation he had bought from Nagasir several years before, so he was now running two fully-sold buses in either direction to and from Jamshedpur every day. Everywhere in the drought that had enveloped most of Bihar, people were leaving the fields in which nothing would grow without rain and flooding to the cities to look for work or food. But the 1952 Tata bus Mohan had bought along with the route now strained to make the full trip in eight hours. "I wanted to pick your brain about the repair history on old Ganesh," he said, referring to the surname he had given to the vehicle he had inherited from Nagasir along with the authority to make the run he had purchased. "I can't get the old fellow to cover the whole route in the time I advertise any longer."

"What do you mean?" Nagasir asked, his dark brow furrowing. "Ganesh has done okay for you until now, hasn't he?"

"It ran fine when it was the only bus I was operating," Mohan said. "It took closer to 9 hours to make the trip than 8, but now that the demand for seats has increased so much and I had to keep adding buses to meet it, the new Tata following Ganesh each day sometimes even passes the old fellow before it reaches the end of the route. I want to add two more buses now, but I'm wondering whether I should take Ganesh off the road and hold it in reserve or just trade it and try to finance three new vehicles at once."

"Have you been keeping up regular servicing on Ganesh like I told you?"

"Of course. If I hadn't, the old codger wouldn't have kept up this well," Mohan said. "I've put on nearly a half million kilometers on it since I got it from you."

"I can't remember what its odometer read when I sold it to you," Nagasir said. "It wasn't a half million yet, was it?"

"No, it's still below nine hundred thousand," Mohan said, then paused a beat. "But is that a true reading?"

"I don't know for sure," Nagasir said, shifting in his seat. "I bought Ganesh used too."

"Well, did you have any major trouble with it the five years you ran it to Jamshedpur?" Mohan asked.

"I told you I had a valve job done in 1964, I think."

"And that's it?" Mohan followed up, looking deeply into his friend's eyes. "Never had a full engine overhaul?"

Nagasir didn't say anything right away.

"Look, *baraa bhai*, I just want the truth," Mohan said. "Buying your business has already been a plus for me. I just need to know what's best to do with my fleet now."

Nagasir blew on the tea the *baira* brought him to cool it. "Now that I think about it," he said slowly, "I did do an overhaul on the old fellow back a year or so after I got it. Back in 1959, maybe."

"So that's when the odometer was probably reset," Mohan said while doing some further calculations in his head. "I guess you're saying I ought to trade Ganesh in? Tata says you can't expect to get more than a million kms out of that model."

Nagasir nodded, then lifted his eyes to look behind Mohan. "Looks like the old codger's still doing fine, though," he said pointing his head across the road in back of his friend.

Mohan turned around to see Ganesh come easing into the bus stand. Its exhaust was hardly darker than that of the newer model he'd seen coming in from Bhagalpur when he'd arrived. "I guess you're right," he said, grinning and lifting his tea glass to Nagasir. "*Dhanyavad, dost.*"

Mohan shifted his seat to watch the sixty or so passengers getting down. His driver Mahmud opened the luggage bin underneath the bus and stood back while those who had checked items retrieved them. The last piece was a big overloaded cardboard box of an *adivasi* woman. Mahmud picked it up by the rope tied around it and carried it across the road to our tea stall, setting it down outside. As she passed us on her way to the table behind, she smiled brightly at Mohan.

Mahmud followed her inside but sat at our table. Mohan turned his eyes from the woman and looked across the table at him to ask, "How'd old Ganesh do on the trip, Mood?"

"Just fine." He lifted his forearm to glance at his wristwatch. "Only about 18 minutes late," he said. "I had to stop a lot to pick up passengers along the road around Hazaribagh." He pointed his chin toward the tribal lady behind me, grinning and saying quietly, "That beauty got on there after Ramgarh. She's coming to Patna to sell embroidered *kurtas* up here."

Mohan shifted his seat again so he could include her in the conversation.

"What time did you tell your brother, Lily?" Mahmud asked her.

"She must be one of those new Christian converts down south," Nagasir leaned over to Mohan and whispered. "They're not so hard to talk to as the Hindu and Muslim ladies, they say."

"I said I'd be in by six," Lily answered Mahmud. "Did you see any *adavasi* men waiting here, *sahib*?" she asked Mohan.

"Nobody's come in since I got here about a half hour ago," he answered.

"I think she likes you," Nagasir again whispered in his ear.

"What time is it now, mister?" she asked Mohan.

He looked at his watch. "Almost six-thirty."

"I hope Babu didn't decide to get drunk today," Lily said to no one in particular. "Mata thinks that's why he moved over here," she added more quietly to Mohan. "If he did have too much to drink, he'll forget all about picking me up."

Mahmud and Nagasir smiled at him as if they knew something he didn't. They ordered more tea, and Mohan asked Mahmud more about the trip and the Jamshedpur terminal Mohan used when he had to work done on one of his buses down there. Then he asked Nagasir more about Ganesh's repair history.

"What time is it now, mister?" Lily called over to Mohan. "What'd you say your name was anyway?"

"Mohan." He looked at my watch. "It's five after seven."

"You have a car here, Mohan?"

"I do," he answered, then continued talking to Nagasir about Ganesh.

"Any chance you can give me a ride into Patna City, Mohan?" she called over to him again after a few more minutes. "I've got to find where my brother lives," she paused a beat now then continued, "or find somewhere else to stay."

Mohan looked hard at Mahmud and hunched his shoulders, then responded again, glancing back without turning around, "I don't think so, miss. My wife's waiting supper for me at home."

"What about you then, Mood?" she asked quickly. "Can you help me find a place for the night?"

When Mahmud got up to lift her carton again and she followed him out onto the street with her wooden suitcase, Nagasir looked long at Mohan and finally said, "You know, Mo, women like you. They find you very handsome."

"What are you talking about, Nagu?" he could feel his face warming.

"I mean that Lily wanted you," Nagasir said. "My daughter even told me she thinks you could be in the movies. Every time I've been out somewhere with you, women are turning around to look at you." He looked up at him. "You mean you haven't noticed?"

"You're just saying that because now we have a female Prime Minister," Mohan hurriedly said. "Besides I'm married, Nagasir. I love my wife, and I don't want to risk my marriage.'

"And I love my wife too, Mo," he said, clearly struggling how to put what he wanted to say next just right. "But after being married awhile, a man needs a little variety."

Mohan didn't agree, but he didn't say anything. He'd never thought about it before, to tell the truth. Nothing Nagasir was saying had ever occurred to him. "Nagasir, do you mind if we finish up about Ganesh?" he said. "It's the reason we got together today after all."

He looked at Mohan incredulously. Then he laughed and said, "Sure. What more do you want to know about that old jalopy."

"I think it'd be wiser to trade in Ganesh now," he said slowly. "Do you think you can give me a complete record of its repair and maintenance so I can pass it on to Tata or when I buy my new buses?"

*   *   *

The monsoon having at last returned to Bihar, life got a bit easier, and the kids being older, Mohan began taking Shashi out alone again occasionally. This night they had finally gone to see the film *Teesri Kasam*, which had been filmed in North Bihar several years earlier.

When the showing was over, Mohan at last was able to flag down a rickshaw on the other side of the street and instructed Shashi to stay where she was in front of the cinema hall as he dashed through the traffic to the edge of the Maidan, and jumped in. In short order, the rickshaw-waalah did a U, and soon they cruised to a stop in front of Shashi under the marquee above and headed toward Station Road.

"That was quick," Shashi said, chuckling in approbation. "You still run like you were playing football in college."

"I still play," Mohan said, lifting himself up to take the seat next to her. "Remember, just last Sunday, Naj and I whomped Arju and Bhagat in the park behind the college." Then to the rickshaw-waalah he said, "*Sidhee jaiiyee, bhai.* Then take Bari Path till Arya Kumar Road."

"I thought Bugs was supposed to be so good," Shashi said. "How'd you ever win with Najib on your side?"

"Bugs still smokes like a chimney," Mohan said. "I'm so glad I quit. But remember, Babe, I'm younger than you." He smiled. "I still got a ways to go till I'm forty."

"Well, if you don't start on the cigarettes again, your lungs will probably clear up again eventually." She paused as the rickshaw neared the junction with Bari Path. "I haven't smoked since after Reva was born. Mine probably are clear now."

"You want to stop at the Kit Kat and have a nightcap?" he asked, seeing the streetlights leading off to the left from the Maidan down their street. "We've haven't been out, just the two of us, for months."

"Naah, sweetheart," she said. "Let's just go home and be together there."

The rickshaw-waalah, overhearing the name of the bar, slowed and turned around as they approached the turnoff. "*Kidhur jaana manta hai, sahib?*"

"*Baya haath par, bhai,*" Mohan said, pointing down Bari Path, and the rickshaw followed the sweep of his hand.

They rode in silence for several minutes.

"That was some film, wasn't it, darling?" Mohan finally said.

"Almost better than Renu's story," she answered. "That *nautanki* play about village women in North Bihar was perfect."

"I know," he said. "I'm not surprised that the powers that be made it difficult to be shown in Bihar until now. It's almost like Hindi movies are making the point that actresses aren't necessarily prostitutes."

"The story's pretty radical for here, I agree." I don't know why Mohan's always thinking about loose women, Shashi wondered. "That Raj Kapoor is a dream, though. He even spoke with a pretty good Maithili accent."

"It was all filmed in northern Purnea, you know. Renu's homeland. The scenery there almost looked beautiful."

"Shankar and Jaikashan could make anyplace seem beautiful," she said.

The three-story Machhua Hotel emerged out of the darkness in the light of the streetlamps up ahead.

"What'd you think about the ending, Mohan? Do you think it was convincing?"

"What do you mean by *convincing*?"

"Realistic, I guess," she said. "Would a *nautanki* girl be that decent to let a nice, handsome guy like Hiraman escape her clutches?"

"I think so," he said, then laughed. "Remember dancing girls can be human beings too."

"Actresses," Shashi said, recalling her own impossible dreams of being in the movies when she was a girl. "Dancing girls are another thing."

Mohan nodded and didn't say anything as the Moin-ul-Haq Stadium appeared in the distance while they approached the junction with Arya Kumar Road. "Do you want me to get down here to go around the circle, *bhai*?" he asked.

"*Ji nahii,*" the rickshaw-waalah said, lifting his left hand from the handlebar as he slowed to pat the air. "*Sub thik hai.*"

On the other side of the circle, Shashi said to her husband, "You know, honey, Hiraman sort of reminded me of you."

"Why? Because I'm a hick from Bhagalpur," he said, smiling. "Remember you're from North Bihar, babe. In the shadow of Nepal," he added.

"In Darbhanga," she said. "I may be a village girl, but I always was a lot more sophisticated than you, Mo." She thought a moment. "Where I come from used to be one of the most important Aryan kingdoms back in the days of the *Mahabharata.*"

When they got home and tipped the rickshaw-waalah, they found Gopal and Shiva bent over a chess board at the kitchen table. "Are the girls asleep?" Mohan called quietly in their direction as they looked in on them before going on down to their bedroom.

"No. I think at least Tara is still awake," Gopal said. "She's got the winner if we ever get to seven games."

"*Seven* games," Shashi said. "That's not fair. She'll never get to play."

"Tell Shiva," Gopal said. "He's the one who insists he can beat me at chess now."

"So what's the score?" Mohan asked.

"Three-and-a-half to two-and-a-half, my favor," Shiva said.

"She never will get to play," Mohan agreed.

"I'll go up and tell her," Shashi said, turning and starting back toward the stairs. "You boys better wrap it up too. It's a school day tomorrow."

"C'mon, Mom," Gopal called after her.

"Don't talk back to your mother," Mohan warned his oldest son, while Shiva looked up and grinned at his brother.

"Can't we at least finish this game, Dad" he said.

"No way," Gopal said, starting to fold the board and spilling the pieces off it. "We'll pick up at 3 ½ to 2 ½ tomorrow."

"Yeah, because you're behind in this game. You knew you've got a test in calculus *aaj kal*," Shiva cried. "You're such a bad sport, Gopal. That's why you want to be an engineer"

"That's enough, you two!" Mohan said. "Now go up and get ready for bed too. *Abhii*. And fast!"

When Shashi got her daughters settled in for the night and came back down, the kitchen light was off, and Mohan was stretched out on their bed in his pajamas reading. She quickly changed into her *nuteez*, then brushed her teeth and let down her hair. Then she climbed under the covers and snuggled up to her husband.

"Wha'cha readin', honey?" she asked, hooking her top foot around his near knee.

"Nothing very elevating," he said, showing her the cover of *And then there were none*. "You know how mysteries are guaranteed to put me to sleep."

"I've got something," she said, rubbing her pubis against his hip, "that's guaranteed to give you better dreams. And more quickly too."

"Sweetheart," he said, starting to turn away.

"You promised, Mohan," she said, following him and reaching her hand over. "Besides," she continued, laughing, "now that I can see what happened to even an innocent *tonga-waalah* like Hiraman, I've got to defend my property."

"You don't have t—"

"Oh yes I do," she said, beginning to rub his penis until he put aside his book.

"Okay, if you insist." He turned his body to face her. "Have you put in your loop?"

"Don't you worry about that," she said, knowing he would be reassured....

*   *   *

By the time the freedom fighter Jay Prakash Narayan called for revolution against Indira's Congress in Patna's Gandhi Maidan, Wazir and Verma Ltd. was among the biggest property dealers in Bihar, and Mohan was running seven buses daily to and from Jamshedpur and had ventured into his first lychee orchard of nine or so hectares in Khajauli near Maniarwa. It was a good thing too, as Gopal was well into what was now Patna University and Shiva, who had received early admission, was right on his heels. The girls Tara and Reva were not far behind, showing that they could do anything their brothers could, and Mohan had had his last child, a third boy Ramesh, who Shashi believed the brightest in all the family and the one who would make her the proudest.

Then one Sunday morning during the rains, one of Mohan's buses coming back to Patna slid off the highway between Ramgarh and Hazaribagh in South Bihar, and early the next morning Nagasir in his tow truck was driving Mohan down the road through Nawada to retrieve the disabled vehicle, which though it had supposedly rolled once to end up on its side and damaged the engine, was otherwise unharmed. Since the accident had caused only minor injuries to the passengers and occurred on the very day of Nag Pachami, a holiday that was celebrated by most communities for at least two days, Najib decided to ride along for a diversion.

The skies were clear that Monday, so Nagasir reached Hazaribagh in time for a late lunch there. At the tea stall where they stopped on the south edge of town, they learned that the bus was only a few miles on down the road in the midst of forested hills frequented by the Hill Karia people. While Naj ordered *puri* and *alu* curry at the café, Nagasir carried Mohan to the police station with the intention of having the sergeant there lead them directly down to where the accident occurred. At the accident site, medics were still apparently attending to the most serious abrasions and sprains of the last two or three passengers.

When they reached the accident site, the bus was resting on its right side down the incline pretty much parallel to the road, and Vishnu the driver, who had been resting on his seat while the medics attended to the remaining casualties in the aisle, jumped down from the door and passed through the several score of tribal people milling around in front of the bus to greet the men who had arrived from Hazaribagh when they came down the incline.

"Ai, sahib, am I glad to see you," Vishnu said to Mohan. "The last two passengers are saying they must be taken by the ambulance back to the hospital in Ranchi, and these *adivasis* around here are making me nervous. They say a storm is building up over there," he said, pointing to the dark clouds gathering around the peaks to the east, "and the sky is going to open up with a downpour any minute now."

"Well we better get this Number 14 back up on the highway then and quickly," Mohan said, nodding to Nagasir who raced back up the incline to get his tow truck. "Turn it around and back down in front of the bus," he shouted after his friend. "We'll get the bus righted and some chains around its front axle, and we should be able to get it back up the hill to flat ground before it gets too wet."

Some of the tribals standing around seemed to understand what was said, and most of the men stepped closer to Mohan as he spoke clearly in Hindi, "I've got five rupees for everyone who helps us get this bus back on its wheels without tipping it over, *dost.*"

They turned inward toward each with confusion on their faces, and a pretty, dark, young woman worked her way through them to the front while wrapping a thin, white shawl around her head to cover her hair. "I'd say about half of you should go around to the uphill side of the bus," she said in Hindi, "and the other half should stay here."

The woman then shouted out a translation in the tribal tongue, while Vishnu and Sgt. Govindra and finally Nagasir gathered around Mohan, who told them, ""We'll stay over here on the downhill side to make sure the bus doesn't flip over. Vishnu, you jump in to make sure that emergency brake is on so it doesn't roll, and I'll go help the medics get the last of those passengers out of the vehicle."

Before he climbed through the door to follow Vishnu inside, though, he turned back to the woman, who had stayed with the tribals on the downhill side, and said, "*Aapka nam kya hai, srimati*?"

"My name is Kira, sahib," she answered, coming forward.

"Can you be the leader for the people who'll lift the bus on the other side, Kira?" he asked. "If you translate and get them to do everything I tell you to when we're ready to have them lift the bus, I'll give you ten rupees as soon as the bus is standing."

"*Bahut achaa,*" Kira said. "With you being the boss here on this side, we'll keep the bus from coming over too far when we lift it. I'll keep the men quiet over there, and you just let me know what you want us on the other side to do."

"*Bilkul thik hai,*" Mohan said as he started to climb up into the bus.

Inside he proceeded carefully down the aisle, placing his hands on the tops of the interior aisle seats to balance himself as he went. "How are things, Doctor *sahib*?" he said to the nearest medic ministering to an elderly woman, who was propped up against the uphill side of the bus in the fifth row of seats. "This is my bus. How's your patient coming along?"

"She's better," said the middle-aged female medic dressed in gray scrubs. "She suffered an awful fright, though, with the bus falling on its side, slow as it was, while it came down this hill." She pointed her head outside beyond her patient, and the sound of Kira's voice talking to her compatriots on that side could be heard through the open door. "It doesn't appear she has any broken bones, however, thank Lord Shiva for that," she added quietly.

"So can you get her ready to be moved?" he asked. "We've got to clear the bus completely so we can get it back standing on all four wheels to pull it back up to the highway."

"I don't know," the medic said. "She keeps dozing off on me. Maybe you can convince her she has to be moved now."

"Srimatiji," Mohan said, taking hold of the patient's wrist and shaking it gently. "We have to get you out of the bus so you can lie down properly."

The frightened passenger opened her eyes and nodded her head listlessly.

"Do you think you can do it if we give you plenty of help?" Mohan said.

The woman nodded again and started to lift herself. Mohan cautiously assisted her by her left arm, while one of the medic's peons took a hold of her other arm. Slowly they slid her across the seats so she could place her feet down on the floor of the aisle.

Mohan beckoned another peon from the group of people standing above the second passenger, who was laid out on the aisle floor further back. Carefully then the two peons stood the old lady up and helped her toward the front of the bus.

"Can a couple more of you men help get her through the door?" Mohan said to the rest of the group behind. "They've got some stretchers outside, and you can help her onto one of them and carry her up to the police wagon on the highway."

After two more men slid by him, Mohan moved on back to the last injured passenger. He was being attended by a younger male medic also dressed in loose gray scrubs.

"What's this man's condition?" Mohan asked the second medic.

"He doesn't want to be moved except by an ambulance crew."

"What are his injuries?" Mohan asked.

"He's probably got a hairline fracture of his right elbow," the second medic said. "I've set it and got it into an immobilizer, so he should be alright."

"Did you hear that?" Mohan asked the last passenger, whose eyes were open wide and following every word.

"*Ji ha*," the middle-aged man said. "But I want to be taken to the hospital in Ranchi in a fully-staffed ambulance. I'm a clerk for the Divisional Development Department there, and I can't take any chances with my arm. It is part of my position to take minutes of our meetings, you understand?"

"You'll be fine," Mohan said. "We'll get a stretcher in here and carry you up to the police wagon on the road. The medics will be able to take care of you there until we can get you safely to the hospital. You understand, of course, that there's still a food shortage here in Bihar, so all official vehicles are being heavily used."

"How long is it going to take to get to the hospital?" the injured man said.

"I don't know," Mohan said, looking at the second medic. "But this fine doctor here will stay with you all the way. He'll do everything he can to get you to the hospital as quickly as possible."

"I don't know," the injured clerk said as he saw the stretcher being carried down the aisle toward him from the front. "Alright," he said, raising his arms so they could lift him onto it. "But make sure they're careful getting me out of the bus."

"You heard him!" Mohan said, looking hard at the remaining peons. "This man is in pain, and I want you to be especially careful."

As the stretcher with the clerk lying upon it was gingerly moved down the aisle to the door, Mohan followed it patiently and made sure that the injured man was kept level as it was passed through the door to the bearers outside. Then he turned back to check one last time that the emergency brake was fully engaged. Before he emerged from the bus, he turned back to make sure that everyone else had been evacuated from the rear of the vehicle. Just below the open door, he came upon Kira still peering through the outside front window, taking in everything that went on inside.

He nodded at her, and she smiled backed. "Alright," he said to her, stretching his feet to the ground and pulling the door shut behind him, "let's get this bus back on its feet."

It was not an easy task. Kira had to send for more villagers from the forest to lift the long vehicle's uphill side and keep the bus fully balanced as Najib and Arash joined the downhill side to make sure it held an upright position as its weight was passed to them. When the bus at last was righted, Kira came around to watch Mohan direct the preparations for its tow back up to the road. "We're probably going to have to put our muscle behind the bus while it's being towed up to the level ground on the highway," he said to the people standing down below and Kira in particular.

"Don't worry," she assured him before she began her translation to her tribesmen. "Nobody will ask for more than five rupees for the whole operation till we get it back to the highway."

Up on the highway, when he got the bus ready for the over-the-road tow to Patna and paid off everyone who had helped, Mohan came over to Kira to pay her the foreman's wages. Notwithstanding their agreement, he handed her the last six five-rupee notes in his hand.

"Oh, no, sahib," she said, counting out and taking only the top two bills and closing his hand over the others. "I can't take all that. An agreement's an agreement."

""Kira, I insist," he said. "We never would have got the bus back up to the road in one piece without you."

"Well, you can buy me supper in Hazaribagh, then," she said, smiling.

"I'll do that too," he said, then pressed the other four bills into her other hand and closed her fist over them. "I insist."

Okay, she nodded and climbed into the tow truck with Nagasir while Najib and Mohan rode back with Sgt. Govindra back into Hazaribagh....

That evening Mohan treated everyone – Govindra, the female medic as well as Vishnu, Naj, Nagasir, and Kira – to the best meal in town. When they finished and Vishnu was dispatched with Nagasir in the tow truck back to Patna, Mohan announced to his friend that he intended to stay the night in Hazaribagh's Kabul Hotel rather than joining them on his next bus coming through going north. "I want to check with all the passengers here and in Ranchi to make sure they've gotten the treatment they need," he said. "Not only is it the right thing to do, but it will minimize the chance of any lawsuits."

"You're absolutely right about that," Najib said, moving his eyes over toward Kira, who was watching the goodbyes from the front of the bus stand across from the hotel. "I think I'll stay the night here too rather than go back to Patna."

"No, you're not," Mohan said, pushing him toward the steps into the bus. "I don't want to get in trouble with your wife, and besides I've a lot to get done down here tomorrow. I don't want any distractions."

"How's she going to get home?" Naj asked, pointing his head toward Kira.

"Don't worry about it," Mohan said. "I'll take care of it after I call Shashi…."

Chapter Six

The changing conditions of Shashi's internal parts was not improved by Mohan's absence the entire night to attend to the loose ends of the accident between Hazaribagh and Ramgarh. After he called her to let her know he would not be able to get back that night, she went down to the corner tobacco shop and bought her first pack of Rothman's Gold Leaf since her teaching days in Bhagalpur. Like all good mothers, she had given up cigarettes for her family, and now that Mohan had insisted that they have no more children after Ramesh, there was really no good reason she could not smoke again. Then too she was determined to regain her youth even if she was approaching fifty.

But after she came back home that night and went down into the storage room so the kids wouldn't see her smoke, she sensed she would have difficulty staying away from that secret hiding place. Things were in chaos above ground. J.P. Narayan had held a mass rally in Delhi in which he proclaimed that Indian citizens no longer had to follow immoral laws passed by their national government, and Indira promptly imprisoned him without a trial.

And from the time she drew on her first cigarette again, everything began to seem negative – she was sure Mohan had met another woman and knew that their financial house of cards was certain to collapse – and then all of a sudden she was euphoric. I know I can keep him, she thought. I am confident that I can accomplish anything if I just put my mind to it.

But I'm not beautiful anymore, she began to sob silently to herself. It's so sad that Mo and I have lost that wonderful thing we had together. I know we'll never recapture it. I know

Mohan now realizes that I've always been a fallen woman, that I'm no good..., and now I have nothing more to live for.

And I'm a bad mother too. None of the kids are close to me. And I don't really love them either. I just wanted to have Ramesh so I could win Mohan back, but now I know I never will. At least with the other kids, I connected when I suckled them. With Ramesh, I can't stand it when he wants my milk. And I haven't even told Mohan that I've been buying breast milk from Srimati Yama down the street.

But the kids are so beautiful, and they love him so much. And despite the fact that he's away so much now, I have to admit he's a perfect husband and father, hard-working, honest, and still handsome as a movie star.

But why don't I want to make love with him anymore. It's more than the fact that it hurts me so. Because I'm so dry down there. I was sore for a while after the other kids, but it was never like this. After the older kids' births, we were back into our lovely intimacy in no time – but I have a feeling it won't happen so easily this time. But I also know I'll never find the wonderful sex Mohan and I have had with another man.

Worst of all I can't concentrate on anything else but my misery. I can't sleep, and I have no interest in sex. I'm tired all the time, and I get no joy in anything I eat, yet I'm never hungry. My mouth is so dry from smoking all these cigarettes, but I don't feel thirsty. And I can't even concentrate to read. There's nothing in life for me anymore. I want to die. How can I do it so it doesn't look like suicide?

Yet still I have to pee, Shashi thought as she put the current Rothman out half-smoked and carefully balanced it on the edge of her now-filthy saucer she used as an ashtray. I have to pee all the time now.

As she climbed the stairs from her hiding place to go to the bathroom, she thought of her children for the first time. What kind of a mother have I become? Ramesh is still a newborn, and how long is it since I've thought of him?

After going to the toilet, she opened the refrigerator to warm some of Mrs. Yama's milk for him. But to be honest with myself at least I can't stand it when that little boy – he a beautiful little thing, the most perfect of all my kids – puts his tiny mouth on my nipple and begins to suck so greedily.

Suddenly Shashi started sobbing again. God, I've failed in everything I've ever tried in my life … even in being a mother. Everyone says motherhood's the most natural thing in the world for a woman, yet I honestly don't feel anything at this moment for those creatures I've brought into this world.

Then the craving for the taste of a Gold Leaf again came upon her. I have just enough time to pee once more and finish that one I started and left downstairs before this milk is warm enough, she thought as she poured it from the bottle into a pan on the stove and turned the burner on low. Then, just before she closed the door to the basement behind her, she heard Ramesh upstairs begin to wail again for the milk she was supposed to have given him a half hour ago….

*   *   *

India by 1977 was falling apart. Indira's son Sanjay Gandhi was bulldozing the homes of squatters in Delhi and Bombay, and rumors abounded that Congress party workers were sterilizing villagers by force all over the country. Mohan was never at home now with the demands of his far-flung business interests. He added buses on the run to Jamshedpur and opened one to Dhanbad and on to Calcutta and back, so he had to set up a terminal there for servicing them and often had to stay a night or two to straighten out the wrinkles in his operation in the south. Then, with the bridge from Patna across the Ganges finally completed, he also began in earnest to develop his lychee orchard up in the Khajauli Block.

At first, inasmuch as Mohan got my father to help him with the orchard, he would take the children and me up there with him on the weekends, and he, Pitaji, Gopal, and Shiva would go out to Khajauli to work with him while the girls, Ramesh, and I visited with my mother and Lakshmi in Maniarwa. When he would come home in the evenings up there, I could tell he was exhausted, but he always insisted that the cooling breeze blowing off the mountains refreshed him like nothing else could.

Those trips were happy times, and Mohan grew close to my father, who became fascinated with growing lychees and eventually even helped in marketing them. During these visits, Aunt Gauri often came over from Darbhanga, and she schooled me in the style of Madhubani painting in which she had become interested as a way for rural women to carry their families through lean years in the fields. My mother had already grown proficient in the Kayastha style of that art used for decorating bridal chambers in red and black, but I and especially Reva, under my tutelage, became decent in colorfully depicting outside walls with Hindu mythological figures in what is called the Brahmin school of Madhubani painting. Tara, who showed great imagination in working in the Kayastha style with my mother, could have earned money in the art, but she was approaching that age where she wanted as little as possible to do with her family.

Hence, these halcyon weekends soon came to an end for me. Gopal especially and Shiva to a lesser degree quickly developed an aversion to working in the orchard, claiming that their work at college did not permit them such extended time away from their studies, and Tara began to be difficult about even coming across the river for the weekend. Several times I left her to stay and study at the family home of a her friend Varsha, but when I discovered from Gopal that the two of them were sometimes chasing around Bankipur with boys already in college, I had to stay home and watch over her and let Mohan travel out to his orchard for a while with Reva only but later by himself. If Tara was going to be admitted to the university as we hoped, I had to make certain she kept up with her schoolwork and didn't misbehave.

By early 1977 Indira Gandhi finally ordered elections to be held, and Congress was resoundingly defeated by the Janata coalition. By then, Tara had as little to do with me as possible, and I grew bored with reading, cooking, and supervising the activities of the younger children. Mohan reverted to spending at least one weekend a month in Jamshedpur, and when I started to smell another woman on him when he returned, I was convinced he was seeing someone else down in South Bihar.

Thus, though I did a little volunteering at the Museum near the Serpentine, I began to pour all my attention and energy onto the baby Ramesh, who would be my salvation. I felt guilty about not offering him my breast, so I saw Dr. Ray at Kurji, who helped me build up my capacity to produce *dudh* and allowed me to start breastfeeding him once more even though he was over a year old.

Mohan was furious about it. One Saturday night he unexpectedly came home from Khajauli and demanded we resume the relations we hadn't had since Ramesh was born. He came upon me as I was preparing to give our youngest his last nourishment for the night and insisted that I put him down immediately in the crib upstairs and that we "have this out."

I had no more interest in him than he apparently had in me, but I knew our marriage was doomed if we abandoned our intimacy. So when I returned from putting Ramesh down upstairs, I resolved that I would try and resurrect our passion in the marital bed.

It was a disaster. It had been months since Mohan had had his vasectomy, but I could not even begin to get him hard.

Finally he turned away from me after we were both sweating profusely. "Shash," he whispered. "I just can't."

"Maybe it's the vasectomy."

"Maybe, but I don't think so," he said after a long silence. "Since you pulled the quick one on me and had Ramesh, you just don't appeal to me anymore."

After giving in and trying even when I didn't want to, this was devastating.

"You have another woman," I finally said. "Someone in South Bihar. I know it."

"No, Shash, it's not that." He began crying softly. "It's just that I can't forgive you for what you did by tricking me into having Ramesh."

"Don't you love Ramesh?" I said, laying on my back looking at the ceiling for several minutes. "Well, at least I've got to feed him," I said when I realized he wasn't going to answer, getting up at last. "He hasn't had anything since midday."

Ramesh was whimpering too when I got to him. When I gave him my nipple, he took it eagerly.

He sucked and sucked and sucked, and the milk did not stop flowing. I unpinned his diaper and took his little penis and began to stroke it gently. It grew harder than Mohan's had, and he began to hum as he continued sucking.

Yes, he was my little man. Yes.

And, all at once, I sighed happily and came. Then I kissed his little head with a love I'd never felt before....

*   *   *

Tara got married the month after she graduated from Patna University in fine arts. She and her husband Deepak moved into a flat in the Pataliputra Colony. When Tara promptly got pregnant, Shashi spent more and more time over there. Initially she provided advice about the hardships of the female body during the gestation period, but after Tina was born, she became a doting grandmother and the go-to babysitter for the young couple.

One evening when the Patna premier of the film *Muqaddar Ka Sikandar* was on the agenda for Tara and Deepak, Shashi arrived less than an hour before its 7:10 show time at the Majestic Cinema on the Maidan, and she immediately rushed to attend to Tina, whom Tara had just fed.

"And how's my little sweetie tonight," she baby-talked while caressing the infant's cheek and clamoring to take her into her arms. "I swear every time I see her she's more beautiful than the time before."

"Oh, Mother, that's a little much," Tara said, rolling her eyes to her husband who was reading the *Hindustan Times* in the easy chair. "You don't want to get her all excited just after her feeding. If you do, you'd better be ready to face the consequences," she added, putting her arms in the jacket Deepak picked up and offered to slip on her.

"Don't you worry, Tara," Shashi said. "Tina and I love to be together. We'll have a great time."

"Okay, then," Tara said. "We've got to rush or they won't hold our tickets."

Shashi carried the baby to the front window of the flat to watch Deepak flag down a cab for her daughter and him down below. "See, Tina," she cooed to her granddaughter, "there go your parents off to the movies."

"My little darling, what do you think of this world you've come into?" She rocked her gently as she strolled back across the sitting room. *"Achaa laagta hai?"*

The baby looked up, wrinkled her nose, and whimpered.

"Now don't you start crying," Shashi admonished her. "I'm your grandmother, and I've come over especially to be with you. So you better treat me nicely.'

I know women are supposed to love their grandchildren, she thought, especially the first one, especially a girl. So I have to say I love you. Your mother was a handful for years, but that doesn't mean you have to be that way.

And you are adorable – but suddenly she smelled gas – and felt the little body she was holding convulse and deposit something in her diapers and that carried an even stinkier odor into the closed apartment.

"You would have started this already," she scolded the baby. "Tara won't be back for hours, so there's no way I won't have to change you." She laid the little girl on the pull-out sofa and stepped out of range of the putrid smell.

Sometimes this grandparents' thing isn't all it's cracked up to be, she laughed to herself and held her nose as she returned to Tina and began to undo her diaper....

*   *   *

In the revived economy that Janata brought, Mohan began to spend more and more of his time in the south or on the other side of the bridge working on his lychee orchards. I could not stop loving Ramesh when we were alone. He was the only one who loved me anymore.

One night Mohan came back from the south and quietly barged in on us just as I came.

"I suspected something like this was happening," he yelled and grabbed Ramesh from me even though the baby wailed in fear. "Do you know what you could be doing to him?"

"I'm just loving him."

He carefully set the baby down in the crib which was in our room. "You're crazy, Shashi," he said. "You need help!"

I just continued sobbing while he stood above glaring at me. "And I think I know where to get it," he said at last. "I know just the place...."

FALL

Chapter Seven

The first step, though, in dealing with this emergency, Mohan learned, was medication to stabilize Shashi and help her sleep. Najib and Arash pulled some strings, and Dr. Kurthan in Pataliputra saw her on short notice and prescribed a moderate dose of Desyrel, an obsolescent anti-depressant that still had a remarkable capacity as a muscle-relaxant and thus could facilitate sleep. So after a good night's sleep or two, Mohan was able to convince the normally obdurate Shashi that she should check herself into the Central Institute of Psychiatry in Kanke just outside Ranchi.

Mohan determined to have them take his own express bus down to Ranchi, with only twenty-minute stops in Nawada, Koderma, and Hazaribagh before reaching the headquarters of Chotanagpur. He would lose little time by not driving and gain much opportunity for important communication in the bus with his wife, who was clearly at an important turning point in her life. And whether or not she got ahold of herself and faced her inner problems would, of course, be supremely critical to his own life and those of his children.

The first hour or so out of Patna took the couple across the Gangetic Plain into the heart of the old Magadha Empire and was similar to the beautiful countryside they had picnicked in around Islampur a little to the east. Shashi was reminded of their lovely daytrip along the Mohana River there not so long ago, and the memory gave her hope that Mohan and she could find joy in each other's company again.

But it was so many years back, she thought, and I am so much older now. And I did some despicably selfish things to little Ramesh. How will Mohan, not to mention Ramesh himself, ever forgive me for that?

Coming into the Nawada stop, I leaned over to my husband and said, "Do we have time to get something to drink and walk a bit here, Mohan? I want to ask you something."

"We'll have 20 minutes here," he said. "Let's do it."

After we got some sodas from a vendor near the bus stand, Mohan suggested we could probably get a glimpse of the nearby Handiya Sun Temple. "The pond alongside of it is where the Magadha King Jarasandha's daughter Dhaniya was cured of leprosy," he told me. "It is a place of healing, and a short *tirthyatra* there will be a good way to begin this journey."

"Do you think you can ever forgive me, darling, for what I did?" I asked him after we got directions and set off walking at a brisk pace. "This Central Institute of Psychiatry has got to cost a lot of money."

"That's the least of it, Shashi," he said. "If the people there can help you to get well, it's worth everything we have."

"But even if I can be made well again, Mo, will you ever be able to forgive me?" I didn't even want to explicitly say for what. "And will I ever be able to forgive myself for what I did to little Ramesh?"

He looked long and hard at me as we turned the corner onto the street at the end of which the *mandir* stood. "To be honest, I don't know, sweetheart," he finally said as we continued walking briskly toward it. "Who knows what damage you might have done to him? Hopefully he is so small he won't remember it."

I shuddered to imagine what would happen to me in my next life if Ramesh did remember. "Please, Mohan," I cried as acid arose in my stomach. "I don't want to think about that now."

He walked on in silence then looked at his watch. Decisively he stopped and turned around at last, saying, "We'll have to start back now. But if you get well, Shashi, I'll never mention what you did again."

We got back on the bus just as it was ready to pull out of Nawada, and soon we passed the turnoff to Kakolat Falls, where Lord Krishna was said to have bathed during his time in Bihar. "Remember, Mohan, how happy we were the day we rode out of Islampur to the Mohana," I said. "Wasn't Krishna supposed to have visited the spot where we had our picnic?"

"I think so," he said and a tear slid down his cheek. But he wiped it off as he turned away to look out the window in the direction of the falls. "I think it was Vishnu actually."

"Do you think we can ever be that happy again, Mo?"

He took a long time to answer. "I hope so, Shashi," he said at last. "We can't go back to the past, but if we open ourselves to the future, we'll have a chance. But each of us is going to have to work hard to break some bad habits we've fallen into."

Soon we passed into the rolling green hills of Hazaribagh District. Near the town of Kodarma, there were some trucks running back and forth on a side road leading to a bare scar on the side of one of those hills.

"See over there, Shashi," Mohan said, pointing to the red scar. "The Janata must have got the mines working again. They say this area has the largest deposits of mica in the world."

"What is mica used for?" I asked because I knew he would want me to.

"Mostly to aid in conducting electricity, I think. It's very heat-resistant and a good insulator," he said. "In a powder form, it's very useful as a lubricant when drilling wells, so it is one part of the economy here in Bihar that has benefited from the drought." When he saw that I didn't understand, he went on to explain, "This endless supply of mica around Koderma facilitated drilling the water wells has made us less dependent on the monsoons."

"How can you possibly know so much about this?" I asked, genuinely impressed, as we pulled into the stop in Koderma town.

"One of the reasons I was coming down here so much is that I thought about trying to get into mica," he answered. "People say it even has a potential application in nuclear research."

"So why didn't you get into mica, as you say, then?" I'm embarrassed that I was so certain he was always coming to South Bihar because he'd found a woman down here.

"I didn't really have the money to get into it in a potentially profitable way," he said. "Also the Santhals coming to and from the mines around here made expanding Bihar Bus a better investment in the short run."

The bus pulled out again but within minutes stopped on the side of the road to pick up a group of tribal men. "See what I mean," he said, smiling.

Within the hour, we got out to stretch at the stop in Hazaribagh city.

"You want some lunch, Shash?" Mohan asked me. "I'm famished."

"You go ahead," I said. "I'll just have a cup of tea."

We found a tea stall by the bus stand and ordered. While we waited, many *adivasis* on foot passed by.

"Aren't those tribal people too?" I asked.

"It looks like most of them are Santhals," he said. "They've been coming over here to mine for years."

"I thought tribals mostly lived in the forests," I said. "Moving around gathering nuts and roots and hunting animals."

"They used to. But the Santhals have been farming in the Gangetic Plain for generations. Now there are just too many of them there for the available land like everywhere else."

"So how did this city come up?" I asked. "Because of the coal in the area?" I had noticed trucks filled with black rocks all over Hazaribagh.

"I don't think so. Akbar conquered the tribals in the area long ago, and the Mughals established an outpost here," he said. "Later it became part of the Raja of Ramgarh's kingdom and under the British a base for the great white hunters of the tigers around here."

"They still have tigers here?" I asked absently.

"Not today, I don't think. Most of them that still exist in Bihar are in the Palamau National Reserve further south near Ranchi," Mohan said. "Hazaribagh itself is way too industrialized now for any animals to survive other than domesticated ones like cows and dogs."

The next stop was Ranchi, the capital of the Chotanagpur Division and my home for the immediate future. As we crossed a plateau and then the hills that surrounded that second city of

Bihar, I noticed the air was fresh, and when the sun neared the western horizon, there was less haze on the ground to diffuse its colors as it did along the Ganges.

Mohan continued to tell me about the area, but as we got nearer to the Central Institute of Psychiatry where he had arranged my admittance, I became more distracted.

"Ranchi's on a plateau with only a few peaks and ridges jutting out," he said. It was getting dark enough now that these rock formations were taking on an ominous character. "The town itself grew up around an old Oraon village near a bamboo grove," he went on. "In Oraon, they called bamboo *archi*. According to legend, long ago a spirit in the grove is supposed to have become angry with a farmer from the village. So the farmer beat him, and the serpent fled crying *archi, archi, archi*. Thus, the village was named *Archi*, which the Aryan farmers misnamed as Ranchi when they came into the area."

That's all I need to hear, I thought. That this town was named for all the spirits which haunted the bamboo groves here. Coming from the shadows of the Himalayas, I have enough of my own personal demons astir within me already.

Ranchi when we got there did not seem like the Wild West town Mohan had described to me. It was spread out, with open fields between the clusters of buildings that began to appear on both sides of the road. Only in the very center of town did the congestion even approach the cities of the north, and only the area around the bus stand about a block from the end of Hazaribagh highway was as crowded as most Bihari centers.

"I don't see how Ranchi reminds you of those towns in North America we've seen in those Westerns like *High Noon*," I said as we stood in the aisle waiting to get off the bus. "As we were coming in, it looked more like an old British cantonment, and here in the center, the buildings are unmistakably Indian."

"I really meant the feel of the people here reminds me of the Wild West," he said. "One time when I was trying to get official permission to add another daily bus run from Patna, the District Transport Officer took me to eat at the Ranchi club just up the way. The people in there were drinking and playing cards during lunch just like Gary Cooper and those other Hollywood stars who used to be in the old movies."

"So where's the Sanitarium from here?" I asked to change the subject. "Is it is near the center here too?"

"Not at all," he said, helping me down the steps out of the bus. "It's on the outskirts of the town, but on another highway that goes by a reservoir. We'll have to take a cab to get out there."

"Will there be anyone to see us at this time in the evening?" I hesitated a second and then posed another question. "Won't we have to find a place to stay down here for the night?"

"We've got an appointment set with the hospital's deputy administrator at 7 tonight," he said, moving forward to get my bags from the luggage chamber under the bus which the driver was unloading, while he looked at his watch. "If we hurry, we should easily get there in time."

In the back seat of the taxi, I explained my anxiety to Mohan. "Is this hospital absolutely necessary, Mohan? Other than for bearing the children, I've never been in one in my life."

"We've discussed this, Shashi. You agreed you had a nervous breakdown, and at a minimum, you need rest, which you're not going to get at home."

"But can we afford this, Mohan? A psychiatrist has to cost a pretty penny," I said.

"We don't have any choice, honey. We can't go on like we were," he said. "You're going to have to come to grips with what had you holed up in the laundry room chain-smoking cigarettes."

"I already know why," I argued. "You weren't there, Mohan, and I could feel you slipping away forever."

"How can you think that, Shash? I love you!"

"But you're never home."

"I am when I can be," he said. "But someone has to feed us." He paused before continuing. "That's what a husband does when the kids are young like Ramesh. Besides it's good for us that I have to go out into the world to do it. It makes me keep getting better, so you'll keep loving me."

"What do you mean by that, darling? I'll always love you no matter what," I insisted. "I promised you that when we got married."

"That's something else," Mohan said. "It's not what I'm talking about. Maybe you'll understand better after the rest you will get here...."

*   *   *

Consistently with the conditions of my admittance to the Central Institute of Psychiatry in Kanke, Mohan checked me in that night, and we agreed not to see each other again until Dr. Virchand Seth, a friend of Arash Narriman with whom he had discussed my history over the phone, had arrived at a diagnosis for me. The first step in that process toward a treatment was my initial consultation with Dr. Seth the first morning in the hospital.

I was awakened about the time Mo caught the earliest of his express buses back to Patna. I was fed a lovely breakfast – grapefruit juice, bran grain and nut cereal with reduced-fat milk and a banana and blueberries on top – and was sitting in wait of Dr. Seth in front of his office door at 8:27. At eight-thirty sharp, a slim, light-skinned man in shirt sleeves and a tie opened the door and called me in.

As soon as I entered the dark, medium-sized room, its malodorous mustiness made me sneeze. It did not appear the old, brown, leather chairs had been dusted for several months.

The doctor had nothing on his walls but a triptych of framed diplomas – his M.D. in Psychiatry from the University of Chicago a little above his B.S. and M.Sc. in Psychology from the University of Allahabad – behind his desk. The desk faced the only window in the office, and looking out on the Institute's only parking lot and thus the only paved portion on its grounds, the view provided little relief from the interior's somber décor. The sole bookshelf in the office, situated behind the desk below the diplomas, was mostly lined with brown, expandable files, and the hard covers of the few actual books there were uniformly of a darker hue with their gold, embossed titles on their spines giving the room its only brightness.

"How are you, Mrs. Verma?" Dr. Seth asked as he led me into his office to a chair situated in front of his desk. There he shook my hand and moved back around his desk to take his seat there. "My name is Virchand Seth. I trust you slept well?"

"Very well, thank you," I said. "I'm Shashi Verma, as you undoubtedly know, Dr. Seth."

"I surely do, Mrs. Verma," he said. "I spoke with your husband at length when he was arranging your stay here at the Institute."

"Which I'm not entirely certain is necessary." I wanted him to know from the beginning that I wanted results from him quickly. "I still have two children at home, Dr. Seth. I am needed there, so I am not able to stay here indefinitely."

"Of course not, Mrs. Verma – do you mind if I call you Shashi – we are going to have to become friends, and being on a first-name basis might help with that," he said then returned to the issue at hand. "I can assure you, Shashi, that we at the Institute understand that there are a number of good reasons why we should not keep anyone here any longer than necessary."

"Of course you can call me Shashi, Doctor. But I don't believe I am psychologically ill," I said. "I was worn out and not sleeping, but my husband got me to a physician in Patna who prescribed Desyrel for me. As a result, I am sleeping fine now, so I think my difficulties are already mostly over."

"That's rarely true with only a prescription," the doctor said, looking at me intently. "Medication is the first step when someone has a nervous breakdown, and it opens the patient up to the possibility of getting at the root cause of the disability, however temporary that disability may be." He paused a moment to formulate how to word what he next wanted to say to me. "But," he continued, "I personally can assure you that I will not keep you here at the Institute any longer than is necessary to resolve your psychiatric problems."

I looked hard at Dr. Seth and decided to trust him. "Then we understand each other and are in agreement as to my treatment," I tried to say with confidence. "So what else would you like to know about what landed me in this place."

"What do you think did get you in here, Shashi?"

"I was overtired because I was not able to sleep," I had rehearsed this answer. "A lot of things were bothering me."

"What sort of things?"

"Well, for one thing, doctor, my husband doesn't spend as much time at home as he used to," I said nervously. "I'm wondering if he's seeing another woman."

"Assuming he is, Shashi – and, mind you, he did not tell me he was seeing anyone else – do you think you have any part in him seeking the company of another?" he asked me.

"Absolutely not," I replied with certainty. "I've been a good wife to him and a good mother for his children. I've never even thought of seeing another man, and I've always been completely devoted to my children."

The doctor again looked intently at me and didn't say anything for a while. Then he picked up a pen and wrote something down in a notebook that lay open on his desk, saying slowly, "Okay" and looked back up at me. "We'll come back to this later."

"I can't see why we have to," I said. I did not want to even think about anything I had done that might have driven Mohan away. "But for now, I'm not going to take issue with you about anything."

"So if I understand you correctly, Shashi," he began, "you don't think that anything you have done," he emphasized this phrase and paused after enunciating it clearly, "was out of the ordinary, shall we say?"

I thought carefully about what he was asking and finally responded. "No, I can't recall anything *out of the ordinary*, as you say, which I have done that might have driven Mohan away."

"There's nothing you've done that you now regret?"

"No," I said slowly, struggling to remember everything that had kept me sleepless during the nights before my breakdown. "Nothing that I can remember...."

*   *   *

I began to see Dr. Seth twice a week, every Monday and Thursday at 8:30 sharp. I cannot say we were making progress toward my release, though, as he seemed determined to make me acknowledge that which I could not.

I could not, of course, admit to myself that I had been inappropriate with my baby boy, for then I would never get out of the hospital. What I had done to him I had done because I was having a nervous breakdown, and now that I was getting enough sleep I would not do it again.

End of story! There was nothing more to be discussed. There was nothing more behind my breakdown than Mohan seeming to be drawing away from me and my resulting exhaustion. Now that he seemed to be dedicated to me getting well, all that remained to be accomplished at the hospital was that I would become stabilized enough so that I would not have another breakdown in the future, which would cause me to lose him.

The solution to that problem seemed to reduce itself to Dr. Seth finding the right medication for me to continue taking. Desyrel got me to sleep but didn't do much else. While taking it, I felt unable to accomplish the most rudimentary of tasks to keep my family together, and I had no interest in intimacy with Mohan. My participation in both of these activities was essential for me to get what I wanted, which was to keep my family together, so, I reasoned, my medication had to be changed.

One Monday morning after I had been at the sanitarium about a month and a half, Dr. Seth suggested we might get further if we took a walk on the grounds during the beautiful autumn day. Of course, I was thrilled at some change in what seemed to be becoming a tiresome routine.

The sal trees were still green, and some of the late perennials like phlox and nasturium that were bedded all over the gentle slopes on the CIT's grounds still displayed their mauve or red. "My goodness, Dr. Seth, we should have done this some time ago," I said, inhaling the lingering fragrance of the season. "Everything still seems so much more possible out here today. I feel like I can tell you anything about myself."

"In that case, let's walk all the way down to the reservoir," he suggested, heading toward the water I could see behind a dense growth of rosewood trees and willow boughs that drooped over the well-maintained lawn. "Maybe it'll put us in the frame of mind to discover what's really bothering you."

We set out on a long, curving lightly tarred path that followed the contours of the land across the grounds. "I think I should first know the solution we are searching for, Doctor," I said once we were on our way at an even pace. "The problem, I think, is the Desyrel I have been taking."

"How so?"

"Well, I think both of us have to admit I'm much better," I said confidently. "I am no longer so fatigued, and my outlook is much brighter. The future no longer seems so bleak."

"That, of course, is important, Shashi, but—"

"The only thing I'm still fearful of is that the medication saps me of the will to do what I have to do," I continued as we followed the path between converging beds of orange geraniums. "To discharge my responsibilities as a wife and mother, if you know what I mean. There has to be some other kind of medicine that will keep me relaxed yet not so relaxed that I find it difficult to do anything else but read and loll around in this beautiful place all day long."

"Of course, there are new anti-depressants becoming available that are much improved over Desyrel, but," he said, choosing his words carefully as he spoke, "they are much more expensive also. Like everything else, you pay for what you get in medications too."

"I'm well aware of that," I said, my arm catching on the rough bough of a low-hanging oak. "But it can't be cheap to stay on at this place either, and my husband is paying for a housekeeper back in Patna too. Surely another course of medication couldn't cost as much as all that."

"Probably not," Dr. Seth agreed, nodding as we continued walking. "But I'm not sure we've gotten at the reason you had to come here in the first place. So I can't guarantee that even with a prescription for Haidol, for example, you won't be back here again pretty soon anyway."

"I can," I said affirmatively. "I'm never again going let myself deteriorate to the same state I was in when I came here. If I feel I'm headed in that direction in the future, I promise you I'll call you."

We were just nearing the lakeshore, and he walked silently up to it, seeming to digest what I had just said. It was a lovely day, warm and clear, and the lapping water ahead pushed magic rays of light upon us. "Okay, Shashi," he finally said. "I'll talk to your husband…."

*   *   *

Mohan drove down to collect me two Mondays hence. Dr. Seth had discontinued the Desyrel immediately and already started me on Haidol by the Friday following our talk. By the end of the next week, he was certain I could tolerate it. I was much less drained of energy on it, and my sleep and optimism seemed just as good.

When Mohan arrived the following Monday, he came into the cafeteria while I was eating breakfast before our appointment with Dr. Seth. He leaned over and kissed my cheek before I realized he was there. "I missed you, sweetheart," he said, straightening up. "All of us have."

I stood up and kissed him on the lips for a long time, while tears of joys poured from my eyes. "And you'll never begin to know how I've missed you all," I whispered to him when we drew back at last to look at each other.

Both of us met Dr. Seth in his office briefly before we all took a last gambol around the grounds. I don't much remember what we said, but the fall morning was as perfect as two weeks before. I know I did say as we wound our way through the trees and last flowers, "I'll never forget this beautiful place and what it's done for me."

I hugged Dr. Seth when we parted. "Thank you so much, Virchand," I said. "I hope it's alright if I use your first name this last time."

Mohan and I started on the Hazaribagh road in his silver Maruti. I sat close to him as he drove, and it reminded me of how it was when we were young.

"Why did you decide to drive down this time, Mohan?" I asked when we were clear of Ranchi. "When you took me here to the sanitarium on the bus, you said you wanted us to be able to pay attention to what we were saying." I laughed and grasped his arm. "Don't you think it's necessary this time, honey?"

"No, it's not that," he said. "I just want—"

"I hope you didn't come down here early to spend time with your girlfriend," I teased him.

"Shashi," he said, turning his eyes on mine. "Don't star—"

"I'm just kidding, Mohu," I said, laughing and looking ahead. "I'm just kidding."

*   *   *

It was not too long before Shashi started sneaking down to the storage room for an occasional cigarette again. She said it helped her to remember where she did not want to go, but Mohan was still concerned. When Arash called him early in 1979 from Benares to tell that he was coming over to Patna again for a family visit and further research on his book about Bihar, it was Mohan this time who arranged an evening for him to spend with Arash and Najib.

This time it was at the Bankipur Club, which he had joined earlier in the year, and Shashi, who had supped there with Mohan several times already, didn't utter a word of protest to his going there with his two old college friends. And this time it was Mohan who was waiting there when Najib and then Arash just minutes later came in to join him.

"So how's Shashi?" Najib asked almost as soon as they hugged each other. "I'm not sure whether Arash knows about what happened to her, so I didn't want to say anything in front of him."

"It's okay, Naj," Mohan said. "Aru's father gave me Dr. Kurthan's name when she needed medication right after she broke down, so I'm sure Aru knows by now at least that much."

"So how's she doing now?"

"So far so good," he said, choosing not to mention the situation with Ramesh or her renewed smoking of cigarettes in the cellar. "But I'm not sure she's seen the last of the Central Institute of Psychiatry in Ranchi."

"Why's that?"

"It's just my intuition, Naj," Mohan said. "Her doctor warned me that she refused to delve into any issues that arose in her childhood which may be at the root of her problem."

"What exactly is her problem anyway, Mo?"

"She had a nervous breakdown, *bhai*," he responded quickly. "What exactly caused it I have no idea."

"And the doctor down in Ranchi doesn't know either?"

"That's what he says." Mohan saw Arash enter the room and was glad to change the subject. "*Kaisa hai, Aru*" he said, getting up to hug him. "*Sub thik hai*?"

"Fine with me," Aru said. "You don't look so great, though."

Mohan looked at Najib, certain now that he had spoken to Arash about Shashi, but Naj turned his palms up to disclaim it. "Why do you say that?" Mohan asked Arash.

"I don't know," he said. "You just looked worried, Mo"

"I do?" he said, trying to examine myself. "Well, our children are getting older, and Shashi and I are looking at just being married again. It's a frightening prospect in a way."

"I understand you had another child since I saw you last," Arash said.

"Yeah," Mohan admitted, shaking his head. "Ramesh is his name, and he just turned two. He's our *last*," he said meaningfully. "How about you, Aru?" Mo asked. "You have any kids yet?"

"None yet," he replied. "We're not sure we want to bring any children into this vale of tears."

"Are you kidding?" Naj demanded. "I'm not certain I'd still be married if it wasn't for my children."

"It's that bad, Naj?" Mohan asked him in surprise. "I had no idea you and Mira were having a hard time."

"It's not that we have problems," he said. "It's just that I don't see the point of getting married if you're not going to have kids."

"Oh, I don't know about that, Naj," Aru said. "Having a helpmate in life is reason enough for marriage."

"Maybe," Najib said, thinking a moment. "But I'm still not sure I see the point of staying married if it isn't for children," he added. "There's plenty of pretty women in the world." He laughed and turned to me.

"What are you looking at me for?" Mohan asked Naj and felt the blood rush to his face.

"Oh, I was just thinking of that tribal woman you stayed in Hazaribagh to take to dinner after she helped us get the bus back on the highway," Naju said, laughing.

"What's this all about?" Aru said, joining him in laughter. "Is there something I should know, Mo?"

"Not really," he lied. "This *adivasi* lady I met when one of our buses went off the road wouldn't take more than thirty rupees for helping to get it back on its feet. I couldn't have managed the tribal labor I hired there without her, so I wanted to thank her.'

"That's it?" Naj looked at Mohan knowingly with a smirk on his face.

"That's it," he said, turning to Arash. "So what about you, Aru? Without kids, you must have the pick of the girls at Benares Hindu University."

"Hardly," he said. "I'm not interested in that even if I could." He halted a second then looked up at me. "I love my Hitosa. She's not the most beautiful woman around, but I married her for other reasons," he went on. "She's a fine Sanskrit scholar, and we want the same things in life."

"Like what?" Mohan followed up, wondering if Shashi and he still did.

"Like the arts, for one thing," Aru said. "We get to at least one performance a week. A play or some music at the university, or maybe a movie if there's nothing else exciting going on."

"I guess you'll never move out of the city then," Najib said.

"Oh, I don't know about that," Arash said. "We're both so sick of the noise and pollution we can hardly stand Benares. If it weren't for the money we're making teaching, we'd leave in a second."

"Benares Hindu University pays well?"

"For a Parsi it does," he said, smiling. "Come to think about it, maybe that's why my birth mother likes Benares so much too."

"Have you heard more from her?"

"At least once a week," Aru said. "Would you believe I even send her money?"

"What?"

"That's right," Arash said. "At least once a month. She likes to play the horses." He paused. "Besides my salary, she thinks because my adoptive parents are doctors, I have plenty of extra money lying around. She's always threatening to visit us," he went on, chuckling ruefully. "It's another kind of pollution we've encountered where we are."

"Well, you sure picked the wrong place to settle down," Mohan said, realizing how uncomfortable Aru was talking about his birth mother and that he wanted to change the subject. "Other than Bombay, there's probably not a worse place in the country for noise and pollution than Benares."

"There has to be more you and Hitosa have in common than the arts then," Najib observed.

"Oh, there is," Aru said. "Oddly enough, Benares is just about the center of the Buddhist revival in India, you know. Both Hitosa and I are interested in it and spend a lot of time in the temple at Sarnath."

"Why?" Mohan asked "Except for its meditation practices, isn't Buddhism about the same as Hinduism?

"I don't know about that," Aru said. "Sure, some Hindus have made a god out of Lord Buddha now, but He still doesn't believe in the caste system, no matter how much they worship him. Buddhism has a fundamentally different view of life."

"How so?" Mohan was interested in learning more about this. He had never been very comfortable about compartmentalizing people by the circumstances of their birth or telling people they had to wait for their next life to be rewarded for their good deeds in this one. "How does Buddhism have such a fundamentally different view of life than Hinduism?"

Arash thought for a while before answering. "In Gautama's original conception, his whole purpose was to find a way out of the cycle of reincarnation," he said. "He realized there is only so far man can go in life on this earth."

"What do you mean by that?" Najib demanded.

Again Aru thought for a moment before speaking. "Modern science has shown us that we use at most about a tenth of our brain. What other worlds will we come to know if we can learn to use all of our capacity?" he said.

"Oh, c'mon, Aru," Najib said, gesticulating. "You're talking about that *nirvana* hogwash again. Isn't that just another way to escape your responsibilities as a human to other people?"

"Call it what you want to, Naj," Mohan intervened. "Aru's raised an interesting point. Maybe this vale of tears is not the end all of what we can know…in this life…."

Chapter Eight

Who would ever believe that her own bodyguards would kill her, Shashi thought as she got up from her favorite chair in the front room on Seventh Road to turn off the news. Indira was a Gandhi and a Nehru, in the direct line of our country's founding fathers. Who can you trust these days now that even the loyal old Sikhs want their own Khalistan completely separate from India.

She went into the kitchen to get another cup of coffee and turned on the radio to hear some relaxing evening ragas. I don't know why I've taken to drinking coffee these hours before Mohan gets home – he always gets home late now that all the kids are out of the house except Ramesh – I don't even want to think about what he's doing out there, so I guess it's good I have my Hadiol. It keeps me mellow, and I haven't smoked for months now.

She walked back to the house's front window and pulled aside the corner of the curtain to see if there was any sign of Mohan yet. Ramesh was upstairs in his room, reading or doing homework. He was an excellent student and the best reader in the family – better than I ever was, she thought, especially now when I can't seem to concentrate long enough to finish anything but newspaper and magazine articles. Twice Ramu's learned things so easily the school has pushed him ahead a semester to the next class above so that now he's going to begin intermediate-school classes when he should be starting his last year of primary school.

She went to her chair near the sofa and picked up an *India Today*, glanced through a few pages, but then threw it back on the coffee table. I've got to quit following the news so closely. It's usually all bad anyway, and it'll drive me crazy. Every time I go to the market or when I'm volunteering at the museum or the University Ladies now, I just freeze when I see a bearded man with a turban. I can't stop myself from thinking my time has come, he's going to take us all down now.

I got up and went back to the window. It was completely dark at last, but I still pulled the whole curtain back just a crack. Otherwise that Srimati Hasan across the street will be able to tell I'm waiting for Mohan again – at least he doesn't drink much anymore, though I'm pretty sure he'll take *bhang* anytime he gets a chance. He got that habit from working his damn orchards up in Khajauli – a lot of people up there do it to make the slowness and monotony of life tolerable. Mohan certainly doesn't do it for that – he's got more than enough to do with his buses and properties and now those blasted lychees Dad's helping him with. I guess Mohan's one of those people who take *ganja* to relax. I can't say that I blame him with all the stress he's got – I couldn't live without a little pick-me-up too if I had half the worries he's got.

But why does the damn Shyla Hasan have to be out on her porch every time he comes home. It's like she's got a sixth sense when he'll be late, and I'm sure she can tell he's high even when he doesn't stumble or smell. And I'm sure she tells all her friends like Mrs. Jalal down the street and Mrs. Ali over on Mahadeo Road who seems to come over and rock back and forth with Shyla every morning on her porch swing.

I can see them talking and looking over here almost every day. I'm sure the whole neighborhood knows my marriage is falling apart.

I went back into the kitchen for last cup in the pot. I poured it and took a first sip, and it was as stale as I expected. But somehow it was a comfort to me, like an old, trusted friend.

I carried it back into the front room and wondered if I'd have to make another pot before Mohan got home. I picked up the *India Today* once more, but this time didn't even look inside of it before I set it back on top of the *Hindustan Times* again. I didn't want to go back to the window just yet because I was sure I had seen Shyla peeking out the last time I looked.

Yes, I'm sure she talks about Mohan and me. She probably says I should never have had Ramesh when I was so old, that it wasn't fair to him. But he's doing fine, he's skipped a grade and still at the top of his class.

That old Mrs. Singh next door, she's not Muslim, so Shyla doesn't talk to her about Mohan and me, but she's such a liar. Her son Vijay is still a year ahead of Ramesh, but the way she brags about him, you'd think he's the smartest kid in this whole school district. She says Vijay always gets straight A's, but I've never seen a single report card to prove it. When Ramesh got those A's in Science and Hindi in the upper class he moved into last year, you can be sure I showed his card to her.

What's that engine noise approaching from down the street? It sounds like Mohan's old Maruti – when's he going to get a new car anyway? – but I'd better make sure it's him before I go upstairs.

I cracked the curtain one more time, and it was him. I rushed to the light switch and darkened the front room before taking my cup to the sink. I got the kitchen light off before he turned in the driveway and headed for the stairs. I don't want him to know that I'm still waiting up for him.....

*   *   *

As the years went by, Shashi continued to smoke in secret and brood about what Mohan did when he was not at home. Clearly it was time-consuming for him to monitor his growing transportation empire which he had expanded with routes to Gopalganj, Motihari, Madhubani, and Kishanganj north of the river and a fleet of thirty-five Tata buses never more than five years old. And he still got succor from tending to his lychee orchards that now brought in half again as much money. And, of course, he still had to attend to particular problems that arose in the gravesite business like the aftermath of the '89 Bhagalpur riots, which had led to a greater emphasis in sales to Christianized tribals in South Bihar even as they agitated for their own separate state there.

Of course, the education of the children cost a lot of money – Gopal had gone on to a doctorate in Computer Engineering in the U.S. and finally settled into a good job with Apple in Silicon Valley – but no sooner was Mohan largely free of supporting his eldest son than Reva was deep into Management Studies in New Delhi. While Shiva went on for graduate degrees in English in Calcutta and eventually got a university position there to support his writing habit, Tara continued growing the family she started after graduating with honors from Patna U in Biology. But when it came time for Ramesh to enter college, he indicated he really wanted to go into the bus business where he had been working weekends and vacations since he was a teenager, though Mohan joined Shashi in insisting that he enroll in Patna College and at least get a B.A. first.

Mohan was immensely proud of his children and would have kept on working full-time to further their education alone if that was necessary, so it was a weekend of great pride when his youngest child graduated from Patna University. Neither Mohan nor Shashi really had any Brahmin background, yet all five of their offspring had secured an education that would prepare them to survive in the 21st century. And as they gathered in the Bihar capital for Ramesh's commencement ceremony, it became apparent that all were doing well as each marched to the beat of his or her own *tabla*.

Gopal, who had come from the furthest away, was the first to arrive, and not surprisingly, his wife and children found it easier to relate to his father than his shy and often anxious mother Shashi. So Gopal helped Mohan arrange the party for Ramesh while Shashi supervised her sister Lakshmi and her mother Neela in the cooking of the celebratory dinner.

"Okay, then, Dad," Gopal asked as they pulled a trailer of stacked plastic chairs and tables home from a rental store on Boring Road during the Saturday afternoon of the graduation, "Is mother over her menopause problems at last? It seemed like it had been going on for a while already even before I first went to the States, and I've been there a good dozen years now."

"Let's hope so," Mohan said as his Ford SUV rounded the familiar corner onto Seventh Road. "Pull into the alley in back, Gopu, so we don't have to carry all this stuff through the house." His son complied and pulled the trailer up just past the gate into the Verma backyard. "Perfect," Mohan said as he climbed out. "I'll fill you in on the details of what's going on while we set up the tables."

"Good," Gopal said. "I've been wondering when Mother and you were going to come over and see our new house in San Jose. Everyone finally has their own room at last, and our backyard ends right at the beginning of the national forest. We'll hike up to the ridge overlooking the Bay when you come, Dad."

"It may be some time before I can get away for that long," Mohan said as he lifted out the first stack of chairs. "Your Nana Aravind does a fine job with the orchards, and Wazir doesn't need me much with the properties anymore. But I've got nobody who can really handle Bihar Bus when I'm gone."

"C'mon, Dad, is that really the reason you haven't visited us yet?" Gopal asked, taking the second stack.

"Your mother is still pretty fragile," Mohan said, opening the gate. "I think we'll have to wait till Ramesh gets settled before we can come all the way over there."

They each carried three stacks of chairs into the backyard and leaned the stacks against the side fence. Then they went back to the trailer for the first of the folding tables.

"Is she ever going to be alright, Dad?" Gopal asked as he backed his way through the gate.

"I don't know, son," Mohan said, pointing his head toward the left back corner of the yard as he followed him through carrying the other end of the table. "But how about you? Are you happy working at Apple?"

"I am. Steve Jobs is brilliant," Gopal said and paused momentarily. "He's a little bit strange, but every time I work with him on something, I learn something new."

"You think you'll ever move back to India, Gopu?" Mohan said, setting down his end of the table while his son squared it up with the fence line.

"I doubt it," Gopal said, heading back to the trailer after they had stood it up. "Marianne loves it over here, but she doesn't want to raise the kids in India. And right now they don't want to live here either."

"But things are much better here now," Mohan said. "Lalu Yadav is running the state government, and he's built his base on the backward castes, the *harijans* and Muslims and even tribal people. For a while, I thought he was making it harder on us businessmen," he went on, 'but now I think he's creating the kind of climate that's perfect for the Indian entrepreneurial spirit."

"Lalu's part of the problem for me," Gopal said, backing through the gate with the second table. "He's more socialistic than Nehru and the Gandhis. I work hard, and I want to be rewarded for it like I am in America," he continued. "I'm in on the ground floor with Apple, and there's no limit to what I can make if I stay there."

"How much money do you need, Gopu?" his younger brother Shiva said, striding from the back door across the yard. "A man should have only one house until everyone has one."

"Shiva," Gopal said, setting down the table and running over to hug him. "I'm not sure I agree with you, but you're still my brother," he said joyfully.

"That's what I mean," Shiva said, embracing him. "We're all brothers, and we should treat everyone like it. America doesn't allow that possibility. India does." Mohan came over to hug his second son, and Shiva winked at Gopal. "I've just about got Dad convinced of this."

"Since Shiva's got tenure at the University of Calcutta, he's started to remind me of myself when I was in college," Mohan said, joining in the teasing. "When did you get in Shiv?"

"Just this minute," he said. "There was a cancelled reservation on the Punjab Express, and it was on time for once."

"You still don't have a car?" Gopal demanded.

"No. why should I?" he said. "It's expensive and – how is it you Americans say it? – a car is more of a pain in the ass than not in Calcutta."

"You're still not blithering that Naxalite rubbish, are you, Shiv?" his little brother Ramesh, the guest of honor said, coming out of the screen door from the house. "I thought you got over that after they started beheading landlords without trials in West Ben-- ."

"I suppose you picked him up at the station, Ramu," Gopal interrupted. "Even Naxalites like a little curb service once in a while, I guess."

"Not at all," Ramesh said. "I had to go home to get changed after the ceremony, and just as I got to our street here, I saw him getting his bags down from the auto-rickshaw outside."

"Where in the world is your new place, Ramu?" Gopal asked. "The ceremony was over hours ago."

"Way out in Gulzarbagh. I found a nice little flat way down by the river," he said. "I have to work at the Bihar Bus garage in Patna City on the weekends, so it's convenient."

"You're still working for Dad?" Shiva said. "Here you're graduating university in three years with all kinds of awards, and you're still servicing buses?"

"When I have to, sure," Ramesh said. "What's wrong with that?"

"He helps me with a lot of things," Mohan offered. "I'm getting older, you know."

"Of course, you are, Pitaji" Gopal said, turning back to his youngest brother. "What Shiv means is that Ramesh is probably the smartest one in the fam—"

"C'mon, Gopal," Ramesh said. "Reva got just as good grades as I did at Patna University.'

"You bet she did," Tara cried, bursting out of the screen door now carrying a box of plastic silverware and plates and napkins. "And I got better grades than she did."

"And look what you did with them," Shiva said.

"What do you mean by that crack?" Tara demanded.

"Yeah, what *do* you mean by it? Reva said, following her sister out of the kitchen. "That because she's a woman it doesn't count."

"Not at all," Shiva said, backing up. "Only that Tara got married right out of college. She never even tried to do anything with her education."

"And I suppose you think I didn't either," Shashi called out from inside. "Well, if you *prima donnas* don't quit arguing and get those tables set up, all my slaving here in the kitchen these last two days will be for naught."

"Amen," Tara said, starting to lay out a setting. "And that goes for everyone, not just Reva and me."

"Yeah," agreed the diminutive Reva. "I can't believe you think Tara hasn't used her education to raise her kids," she said to her older brothers. "I may be a career woman at this point, but I have enough sense to know that bringing up your own children from the cradle to classroom is the most important job in the world." Then she laughed. "Anyway I probably supervise more people at Info-Tech than any of you," she said, beginning to set the plastic glasses she was carrying on the one table already standing, "so let's get this show on the road. And that means everybody!"

Mohan saluted and popped out the legs to the second table he and Gopal had left leaning against the fence. "Yes, sir…er…I mean, madam…Madam Vice-President."

Shiva and Ramesh headed out to the trailer to bring in the third table, but not before Shiva turned to his sisters and said, "I'm sorry, Tara and Reva. You're absolutely right about what you said about motherhood. I didn't mean to minimize what you've done or hope someday to do with your lives."

"Oh, that's alright, Shiva," Tara said. "It's probably because you're still a crotchety old bachelor and now a full Professor of English to boot."

Out in the alley, Shiva apologized to his younger brother too. "And I didn't mean to diminish you either, Ramu," he said as they lifted off another table. "If you want to work for Dad, it's your choice. At his age, he should be slowing down."

"And his business is a challenge to me," Ramesh said. "I like to see concrete results in what I do. After I don't know how many years of school, I'm kind of sick of just talking."

"We're all different, brother," Shiva said as they were setting up the table in the yard. "Me. I love literature. I know it's talking, often on and on, but I fancy I'll change society through the students I teach."

"And you might, Shiv," Ramu said. "Maybe I'll try it someday, but right now I want to get my hands dirty." They lifted out the next to last of the six tables the Vermas had rented. "You must understand that I respect you too, *baraa bhai*, all the changes you've been through.

"Yeah, I guess," Shiva said. "It broke my heart when I found out the Naxalites were starting to indiscriminately kill people out in the villages they had liberated."

"I can imagine how you felt, Shiv."

"But now, Ramu," he said. "I think this Lalu's the genuine thing. I think he's going to prove to the world that democracy works in India...."

*   *   *

Shashi's recurring outbreaks of depression and eventual breakdowns, however, kept Mohan's nose somewhat to the grindstone into his seventies even with Ramesh's enthusiastic assistance. Lalu Prasad Yadav's reign in Bihar seemed to particularly rankle Shashi, who despised the personality cult Lalu established, and later Shiva, who as a Marxist felt betrayed when Lalu was implicated in the fodder scam that derailed the Janata Dal Party in Patna just before the end of the century.

Shashi, in fact, had been down at Ranchi in the Institute for a little "rest" when Mohan received the news that Shiva had been found dead in his apartment near the University in Kolkata. He immediately phoned Dr. Seth and asked him to shield his wife from the news until he had a chance to break it to her. He also asked the doctor to start getting her prepared pharmaceutically for the trip to the West Bengal capital where they would have to arrange for their son's last rites.

Ramesh, who had become Bihar Bus's General Manager following his graduation in General Humanities from Patna University several years earlier, drove his father down to the Institute in his new Ford SUV, and then they would all proceed to Kolkata by road. Tara and her family, who also still lived in Patna, would come down by train and meet them there for Shiva's cremation. Reva would fly in from Delhi and Gopal from San Francisco for the actual rites once arrangements for them had been made at Nimtala Ghat on the Hoogly.

Mohan and Ramesh arrived in Ranchi mid-afternoon on the Tuesday Shiva's body had been discovered. Their names had been left at the Institute gate by Dr. Seth, and they parked between several vehicles as he had instructed them in front of his office. They proceeded inside to his waiting room, and the doctor came in to get them within five minutes.

"I'm so sorry," he said, shaking their hands before seating himself behind his desk. "He couldn't have been very old, I am thinking. It must have been a terrible shock."

"It seems like he just turned forty," Mohan said, shaking his head. "He had no health issues I know of, so it was completely unexpected."

"And you, Ramesh," Dr. Seth said, turning to him. "I imagine he had a big influence on you."

"He did," Ramesh said. "We were very different, but he was always protective and a very good friend to me."

"How much did he know of the reasons your wife was originally admitted here?" the doctor asked Mohan. "Did you talk to him about it?"

"No more than I did with the other children," Mohan said. "But Shiva was very intuitive. He seemed to know things he was never told."

The doctor thought about that for a moment, then moved on. "So, I've told her you were coming," he said. "And I have a prescription of Xanax filled for her," he added, removing a small bottle from the drawer. "She should take one capsule now and another before she goes to bed. Thereafter one with breakfast, one at bedtime each day until it's gone or refilled."

Mohan nodded.

"This bottle should get her through the last rites," Dr. Seth said. "If you cremate him in Calcutta, you should probably bring her back here on your way home."

"How's Mother doing anyway?" Ramesh asked. "Hopefully she's in better shape now than when she came down here this time."

"I'd say so," Dr. Seth said. "She probably was about ready to go home before this tragedy happened, but I'm sure this news is going to set her back."

"Have you made any progress in finding out what's behind her illness?" Mohan asked then quickly followed with another question. "You're still quite certain her diagnosis is schizophrenia, are you not?"

"No and yes," Dr. Seth said. "Ever since she began to resist looking into her family of origin, there haven't been any breakthroughs." He stopped and looked down at the notes on his desk for a moment. "But yes. I am quite certain she has a mild case of schizophrenia."

"Well, at least we know what we're dealing with, Doctor," Mohan said after thinking about it. "Where exactly on the Institute grounds is she right now?"

"I saw her on the porch when I was making my rounds just earlier," the doctor said. "I suggest you go pick her up there and take her out for a walk. If you need help after you tell her about your son, bring her back to her room and call me."

"Thanks, Dr. Seth."

Father and son found her on the porch, and she happily agreed to the idea of taking a walk. When the three of them were alone outside, it was Ramesh who told her about Shiva.

"Mom," he said, stopping her and taking a hold of her hand, "this morning they found Shiva's body in his apartment in Calcutta."

"What....?" She started to moan. "What do you mean?"

"The police said he's been dead for two days," Mohan said.

"Oh, nooooo...." My tears wouldn't come, so I shook loose my hand and started walking on the path again. They soon caught up with me. "What happened?" I asked. Somehow I felt nothing, numb like Emily Dickinson. "Do they know?"

"I don't know, honey" Mohan said. "We're going down there. We'll find out."

I stopped and stood there a minute, cold and trembling. "Well, I'd better go pack a suitcase," I finally said and turned around to start back toward the buildings.

Ramesh said it would be better if Mohan and I went on to Calcutta alone, so we dropped him off at the Bihar Bus terminal in Jamshedpur, where he had some things to do. He will come along later for the cremation....

*   *   *

We finally reached Shiva's apartment building at about eleven that night. The building superintendent Guha had told Mohan that he would be available to us to let us in whenever we got there, so we knocked on the door of the super's apartment next to the lobby on the first floor.

"He always had a short day teaching on Fridays," Guha said in his front room, "and this Friday he got home about midday as usual.

"Normally he came in and talked with me as he came by on the way to the stairs, but this time he waved and that was all."

"Did he look out of sorts?" Mohan asked. "Like something was bothering him?"

"Not really," Guha said. "We had made a date to play chess down here Sunday at dusk. I figured with mid-terms coming up at the University he had a lot of grading to do. His classes were very popular, you know."

"Shiva was especially proud of his *Literature of the American West* class he had developed," I said. "The last time he was in Patna he was just unveiling it, and he told us over a hundred students had already signed up for it. And it was an upper level course too," I added proudly. "Not just anyone could sign up for it."

"He used to talk about it when we played chess," Guha said. "I must have known more about novels in English written by American Indians than any building superintendent in Kolkata."

"Was there anything that was troubling him?" Mohan asked. "Had he seen his old girlfriend Bharati lately?"

"I don't think so," the superintendent said, shaking his head.

"He was shocked like everyone else when Lalu in Bihar got implicated in the fodder scandal, of course," Superintendent Guha added. "But he had read everything he could lay his hands on about it, and in the end I think he had accepted the fact that there was a reasonable chance Lalu had been taking money."

"And?"

"It disappointed him for sure," Guha replied. "But he didn't seem to be brooding about it. As a matter of fact, he told me had an idea for a new novel he wanted to write."

"Shiva was always a sensitive boy," I said. "As his mother, I could tell when things bothered him, but he was very good at hiding his feelings when he wanted to."

"Did you ever see him go back out of the building after he came in Friday noon?" Mohan asked. "I realize you weren't in your office over the weekend, but you probably live in the unit right next door, don't you?"

"I didn't," Guha said. "Shiva liked to write outside of his apartment or office at the university, in the library or a café, so he was always coming or going." He thought a moment. "But I never saw him again after he waved at me Friday around noon."

Mohan digested this. "So can we go up to his apartment?" he said at last, and we went out and started up. "How did you discover the body?" he asked as we began to follow Guha up the stairs.

He waited for us at the first landing. "Like I told you, we were supposed to play chess at 5 or so on Sunday," he said, facing us and catching his breath between phrases. "He was a punctual man, so when he didn't turn up, I started to wonder." He turned and began to climb the second flight of steps, and his voice trailed back as he continued, "Then when the Rahmans from 312 told me there was a smell coming from his apartment, I knew something was wrong."

'Why?"

"Shiva never shut his windows," he explained as he stopped at the top of the second floor. "One morning when he was teaching a class during the monsoon a couple of years ago, he called me from work during a downpour and asked me to go in and close them."

"So you went in again on Sunday night?" Mohan led him.

"What'd you find?" I asked before Guha could answer I didn't want to know, but I had to.

"He was sitting in his chair," Guha said, starting down the hall. "The cushioned one by the window. But all the blinds were pulled, and it was dark as a tomb—dark as *midnight* in there," he went on. "And the smell was awful." He opened the door to 310 and snapped on the light. The blinds in the front room were still down, and I thought I caught a whiff of death in the room. "His head was slumped over in the chair," he said. "Otherwise everything's the same as when I found him unless the police moved something."

"Did they take anything?" Mohan asked.

"They didn't tell me if they did," Guha answered. "When they left, I told them I had called you, and they said you could take any of his personal affects you wanted."

There was a long silence as we started to look around. I went into the bedroom, but I could hear Mohan eventually say, "What was the cause of death?"

"Heart failure," Guha said. "The medical examiner said his heart just stopped."

I didn't want to hear more, but I could hear Mohan persist as I headed back into the front room, "What caused it to stop?"

"I don't know," Guha said. "When they took the body, they said they'd have an autopsy report in a day or two. Here," he said, taking a card from his shirt pocket and handing it to Mohan. "I wrote the number on the back where the doctor said you could reach him."

Then he gave Mohan the key and left. I looked around the front room a bit, but Mohan just sat down on the old couch. On Shiva's desk, I found the novel he had been writing in a notebook. I didn't tell Mohan and slipped it into my handbag.

Then we undressed and went to bed in his room. I took my Xanax, but still I lay there all night without sleeping....

The next morning Mohan went down to Nimtala Ghat to make arrangements for the cremation. On the way back, he said he would stop at the coroner's office to see about the autopsy report. I stayed in the apartment and read through the pages of Shiva's notebook. I didn't want to say it, but I knew he wanted to die.

Then I began to collect mementos of his life from the flat.

When Mohan got back, I asked him about the medical report. He said something about a prescription called Oxycodone. Then he began to call the family about the last rites, which were set for Saturday.

That night we went to the Temple of the Twelve Shivas on the Hoogly. Both of us sobbed like babies.

The next morning we picked up Tara and her family at Howrah Junction. Reva flew in from Delhi that night.

Ramesh came in from Jamshedpur the following morning, and Gopal and Marianne were scheduled to reach Dum Dum that night. Those days passed like a blur.

We went by the University of Kolkata and cleared out Shiva's office. We prepared some cartons and shipped them back to Patna, and I remember we visited the Black Hole of Calcutta, where the Nawab of Bengal held a number of British soldiers until they suffocated, and Kalighat where they say this terrible city began.

Saturday morning we went to the end of Nimtala Ghat road where Shiva's body was laid on a pyre at the riverbank. My husband lit the perfumed wood at the bottom, and when the flames began to burn my boy's corpse, he started to sit up, as they say the body does at all cremations when the soul ascends to heaven.

My beautiful son was dead and had departed....

WINTER

Chapter Nine

After the cremation, the family scattered to the winds again. Ramu took my father Aravind back to Maniarwa on the train, and Mohan's father having died several years previously, Tara's family caught the Punjab Express for Patna and escorted the rest of the Vermas back as far as Bhagalpur. Reva went back to her job in Delhi, and Gopal and his wife flew back across the Pacific to California. That left Mohan and I to drive back to the Institute in Ranchi.

Dr. Seth met us in his office and since it was a beautiful cool day outside, quickly suggested that the three of us stroll alongside the reservoir. Purposefully, I think, he took the position between the two of us as we walked and began asking each of us questions about our son.

"So what do you think happened to him, Mohan?"

"I don't know," he said darkly. "All they told us was that for some reason his heart stopped almost exactly a week ago to this hour."

"Had he a history of heart problems?" Dr. Seth probed.

"Not that I know of," Mohan answered, looking at me.

"What do you think happened, Shashi?" the doctor asked me.

I thought for a minute as we walked. I didn't want to hurt Mohan, but it was time we started to speak the truth. "I'm not certain, of course, but I think Shiva killed himself," I said evenly.

"What makes you say that?" Mohan cried. "I know he was depressed about Lalu being indicted, but Guha said he had worked through that and accepted it."

"Accepted that Lalu was stealing," I said. "But I suspect it hurt him very badly. Shiva was a very sensitive man," I went on. "Kind of like you, Mohan dear. He was so passionate about politics, and he'd already made a big mistake about the Naxalites. This news about Lalu must have been the last straw."

"Enough to commit suicide?" Dr. Seth asked.

"Yes," I said, nodding as we approached the shimmering water, "enough to commit suicide." We kept on walking a moment in silence. "You know, Shiva was a lot like me. He never said what he was feeling, but things like this disappointed him far more than other people."

"You mean this cattle fodder scandal?" Mohan asked.

"I mean it hurt him deeply to learn that Lalu was corrupt," I said. "I know it hurt me too, but," I slowed my cadence, "justice for the little people of the world wasn't as important to me as it was for Shiva. I'm much more selfish than he was."

"You're not selfish, Shashi," Mohan said. "When you're well, you're one of the most giving mothers imaginable."

"That's what you believe, darling," I said, "and that's the way I'd like to be." I stopped. "But I'm not. It's all fake..., play-acting. Something's fundamentally wrong with me."

"What's fundamentally wrong with you, Shashi?" Dr. Seth demanded.

"The only one I really care about is myself," I said quietly. "It's been like that since I can remember. The only thing that's important is what happens to me. It's always been that way."

"Has it?" Dr. Seth asked. "Has it always been that way?"

"I think so," I said, thinking back to my childhood in Maniarwa as we walked slowly. Then I remembered about what I'd been too ashamed to tell anyone. "At least since...."

"At least since what?" Dr. Seth said softly. "Tell us." He paused and came to a halt as we reached the path that diverged and went in either direction along the shore. "This is important."

I remembered those nights in Ranibala's house. Those nights when Chacha Lal came into my room. I burst into tears, and Mohan put his arm around me and laid my head on his warm chest. "I'm so ashamed." I wept.

"So ashamed for what?" Mohan said gently.

"For what he did to me?" I finally cried.

"For what who did to you?"

I could taste the acid in my mouth now and spit it out on the ground. "My Uncle Lal," I said, building up my courage. "He touched me.... Down there," I said, dropping my eyes.

"How old were you?" Mohan demanded.

"Eight...almost nin—"

"You didn't know any better, darli—"

"Yes, I did," I cried. "I knew it was wrong ... but I liked it.... After he first did it, there were times when I stayed over there again, and I wanted him to come into my room...."

*   *   *

"There are reasons for the law proscribing statutory rape," Dr. Seth explained in my exit interview about six months later. "There is no way a girl of eight or nine was mature enough to understand this."

"Of course not," Mohan said putting his arm around me as my tears began to fall once more. "But the doctor here tells me that you've pretty much worked through this trauma in your life."

"I'd blocked it out, darling," I said calmly. It had been months since I'd seen Mohan, and I had a lot of things to explain to him.

"I hope you've forgiven yourself for whatever happened, Shashi," Mohan said, squeezing my shoulder reassuringly. "No one can place any blame on you for it."

"I know, Mohan," I said, kissing his cheek. I had no idea what he had been doing these months when I had been away, but Dr. Seth had convinced me I had to forget about him for a change and concentrate only on getting myself well during this time. "But at last, I think, I've gotten better." I turned to the doctor. "Dr. Seth thinks I'm ready to go home now."

"Yes," Dr. Seth said, "when your wife finally admitted to herself what her uncle did to her, it opened up the possibility for her to get well. Only when she realized that survivors of childhood abuse were likely to repeat it, could she accept what had happened to your son without blaming herself for it."

"I understand, Doctor," Mohan said, looking hard at him. "I can't tell you how grateful I am for what you've done for us."

"Your wife has had a number of shocks to her system," the doctor continued. "Perhaps, the most severe she hasn't revealed to you yet," he said, looking at me meaningfully.

"Yes, Mohan," I began after nodding to Dr. Seth. "Probably the hardest thing was to finally realize that my mother really didn't want me to be born. And I came to understand that she didn't want to believe that Lal had abused me, because she didn't want to disturb her relationship with him as her older brother, She didn't hear what was I was saying and made me doubt my own experience, so I internalized a feeling that my existence and well-being was worth nothing to anyone except myself. So above all I had to protect myself." It still hurt me to say this, but I had learned to accept it. "But I'm over it now. I've forgiven my mother, and I'm ready to go on."

"Sweetheart, I'm so happy," Mohan said, facing me with tears in his eyes. "Welcome home. I've missed you so much."

"And," Dr. Seth said, "I should add that now that I know what's behind Shashi's problems, we've found the medication regimen that should keep her on the right track in the future." He paused, looking hard at Mohan. "Hadiol was not addressing her alternating feelings of depression and anxiety. Among other things, it was stripping her of her vitality, her energy. For her particular condition," he went on, pronouncing each word slowly and clearly, "we've arrived at a course of Chloropromazine. It's a relatively new compound available here in India, and she's been trying it out for the last few months." He paused before concluding. "I am recommending that she continue taking it daily after she goes home."

I could tell from Mohan's face that it was difficult for him to hear that I would have to continue to take medication. But it had been difficult for me to accept my need to do so too.

"Many people in the world today just need their chemistry to be tweaked to be able to tolerate the challenges of modern life," Dr. Seth continued, looking from Mohan to me and back again to Mohan. "We've settled on a moderate daily dose of this medication and have learned that it alleviates her symptoms without undermining the unique and beautiful person Shashi is."

"How long wil—"

"For the best result, she should continue taking 100 mg at bedtime for the rest of her life," Dr. Seth said quickly, picking up a slip of paper from his desktop and handing it to Mohan. "Here's a prescription that will keep you in business for a year." He smiled at us. "I've sent a letter to your physician Dr. Kurthan in Patna, and he will refill it when the year is over. God willing, Shashi will never have to see me again...."

* * *

Back at home on Seventh Road in Rajendra Nagar, Mohan and I got used to each other again, all alone for the first time in the old house. While we no longer had the ardent attraction for each other that had brought us together in the first place, there was still sporadic intimacy between us, and we became more accustomed to and comfortable with one another than we had ever been.

We saw a lot of Tara and her family, and Ramesh did an excellent job of directing the businesses with less and less input from Mohan. While I didn't particularly like his girlfriend Priya, who more or less lived with him now in his Gulzarbagh flat on the river, we were the same type of women and got along tolerably well, and with Mohan and Ramesh the four of us often went out to dinner, a film, or even some performances at the university.

The biggest development in our family was that Reva finally met a man in Delhi. The only problem was that Sunil was Muslim.

His parents from Ahmedabad liked their relationship no better than we did. To be fair, Mohan never said a word about it, but as much as I had been forced to grow in the years since Shiva's death, I still could not abide the way Islam treated women.

In time, Sunil, who worked for Challenge Systems, was transferred to America in a move that I hoped would solve the problem, but in Reva's case, more than absence made her heart grow fonder. At age 39, she became pregnant – a result I suppose from periodic rendezvous they arranged in Europe or the Middle East – and before I could decide to give grandmothering a second chance, she was moving to join Sunil in the Washington DC area.

Prior to her leaving, though, Mohan insisted upon putting on a wedding for his "little girl" in Patna. Three of our four parents were still alive and not far away, and he convinced me that since Sunil and Reva were willing to marry on short notice, a ceremony on the riverbank behind our *alma mater* could be put on without major embarrassment or incident. Since it was the exact spot where I had first met Mohan and fell in love with him, it would be a good springboard for our youngest daughter's marriage and a likely rejuvenation of ours. So I could no longer resist his argument that with what was left of our family now spread around the world, this wedding might be the last chance for its four generations still living in India to meet and forge relationships with their blood relatives overseas.

I gave Mohan the green light, and just before the new millennium took hold, dozens of Vermas and Chaudrys and in-laws and friends began assembling in Patna one last time. To assure that things started out smoothly, Mohan and I picked up Sunil's parents at the Jayprakash

Narayan Airport and took them to our home in Rajendra Nagar for a small reception several days before the ceremony. Tara greeted us at the front door at our old house on 7th Road with a broad and gracious smile, and Mrs. Abdullah set the tone for what would be a wonderful celebration when she greeted her by saying, "I know who you are! You must be Tara, and you must be her sister," she then added, looking at me and chuckling in advance at her own joke. "Until this minute, I thought we were going to have the most beautiful daughter-in-law in the world, but now I see why your husband's parents can claim the same thing."

I was not normally fond of such over-the-top flattery, but for Mohan and my youngest daughter who was getting married at last I made an exception for once. "You're very kind, Mrs. Abdullah," I said. "You've made a conquest of Reva's best friend and closest advisor. It bodes well for a happy marriage between our children," I concluded, laughing myself.

Reva and Sunil did not arrive from Delhi until the evening before the ceremony. Tired, especially because of Sunil's long journey that had begun in America, they called to indicate they would stay in their hotel room on the Maidan for the rest of the evening, and the bridal shower that Tara had arranged at her home had to proceed that night without an appearance of the guest of honor.

The ceremony was set for 11 AM the following morning in the Park that was now called Chandripore behind the University. It was the same spot where I was introduced to Mohan nearly six decades earlier, but the small *maidan* running down to the Ganges there had been much beautified in the intervening years. The vows before the Magistrate proceeded exactly when scheduled, as Mohan led Reva through the rows of folding chairs up to him right on the stroke of eleven while more than one family of guests straggled into their seats as the short and simple civil ceremony was being performed.

Afterwards the reception and lunch was held at the venerable Bankipur Club, which was in walking distance for most of the guests. Shashi remembered her rickshaw ride with Sangeeta down to the college that fated day in 1943, and ironically she found herself walking over to the reception between Mohan and her father, probably the oldest guest in attendance.

"So, *beti*, now you've got everyone married off but Ramesh," Aravind said, then corrected himself. "Except for Shiva, of course. Maybe, he'd still be here if he had married that pretty little Bengali girlfriend he used to talk about."

"Maybe so, Dad," Shashi said as they followed the bridal party toward the Club. "Marriage isn't the easiest thing, but it's pretty hard to go all the way through life without it."

"How about you, Aravind?" Mohan said. "Are you getting along alright without Neela? You must miss her terribly after all the years you were together."

"Of course I miss my sweet, little Neela," his father-in-law said. "But Lakshmi and Hari keep a pretty close eye on me. They're still no more than ten minutes walk from the old house." The mist in his eyes cleared quickly. "Sometimes I actually wish they'd give me a little more space, but to be honest," he added, shaking his head and laughing, "But I don't know what I'd do with the free time if they did.'

"That's what happens to us, Pita," Mohan said, clapping him gently on the back as they entered the narrow lane leading from the park to the Club.

Before they sat down in the banquet hall which they had rented, they discovered many of the guests had gathered on the patio for something to drink from the bar. While Mohan went inside to get drinks for himself and Ramesh who with his girlfriend Priya had joined Shashi and her father at a patio table outside, Najib came up to him at the bar as he waited for his drinks after the bartender had taken his order.

"So you're still drinking beer, Mo?" Najib said as they hugged.

"You, my friend, more than anyone should know that alcohol was never my problem," Mohan said, smiling.

"You're right about that," Najib said, showing him the drinks he held for Mira and himself in his hands as the bartender returned with his order and Mohan paid.

"But if you've got any *bhang* nearby, Naj," Mohan whispered, "I'd go out in the alley with you for a glass of it in a heartbeat."

"I know you would," Naj said with a laugh while they walked toward the patio. "If I'd have known you would become such a pothead, I never would have introduced you to it back in the Emergency, which, I might add, we might never have gotten through without."

"Oh, I've gotten it under control now," Mohan said quietly. "I think."

"Sure you do," Naj said looking hard at his old friend.

After everyone finished their refreshments outside, they joined the rest of the party in the banquet room. Shashi and Mohan were seated at the head table with the bride and groom, Mr. and Mrs. Abdullah, and Tara and Sunil's childhood friend, Salim from Gujarat, who had stood up for the newly married couple at the ceremony.

Mira, who was sitting with Najib and some of the rest of the old gang at the next table, leaned over to greet Shashi. "You're so lucky your husband only likes to drink *bhang*," she said, looking disdainfully at the whiskey Najib was savoring. "Mine's forbidden to drink alcohol by his doctor as well as his religion, yet he still overdoes it anytime the opportunity presents itself."

When Shashi turned back to her husband, she pulled him away from the table and quietly asked him, ""You're not still doing so much *ganja*, are you, honey?"

"Not really," he answered. "I got used to it when I was working so hard with Bihar Bus, and I still like the way it relaxes me. But I'm sure I can stop anytime I wanted."

"You didn't have any of it with almonds and *garam masala* this morning, did you?"

Mohan didn't answer for a moment, looking at her "Just a little before everyone had breakfast," he admitted at last.

"Mom," Reva called to her from the other side, "are you ever going to come and visit us in Washington? I want my children to be as close to you as Tara's are."

"Not only that," Sunil added, leaning forward from the seat next to her. "Reva's going to go back to work as soon as he can after we have our chil—"

"Not right away," Reva corrected him.

"But she does want to continue her career in management," Sunil went on, "outside the house. So we could use as much grandmotherly help as we can get. My parents have promised to visit, but getting them out of Gujarat is like pulling teeth."

Shashi looked at Mohan then turned back to her new son-in-law. ""Does everyone in the U.S. smoke *ganja* as much as the Americans who come over here do?" she asked him out of the blue. "If they do, I'm not sure I want to come so much either. I'm really not that fond of most of the Americans I've met the way they act here with their loud music and all."

"Americans can't legally use drugs in the United States, Mrs. Verma," Sunil said. "That's why they always seem to be high here. Even marijuana is against the law there." He paused a second. "It's probably the reason a lot of them are so crazy to come to India."

Shashi digested this a minute. I wonder if we'd like it in America, she asked herself. I never even thought of moving out of India before, but at least Mohan wouldn't be drinking *bhang* in the morning there. "Is it hard for an Indian to get a visa to visit America?" she asked Sunil.

"Not with two children there and grandchildren who are citizens like you have," he said. "With your resources," he added, looking at Mohan, "you two could probably even retire there if you wanted to."

"Actually I've always dreamed of seeing America," she said. It could be a fresh start for us, she thought. "I've always heard that every kind of people live there, so it would probably be fascinating. I bet I'd like it…"

*   *   *

This would perhaps be our last journey on the Ashok Raj Path, Shashi mused as Mohan and she maneuvered their SUV to get on the bypass to go out to Ramesh's flat in Gulzarbagh. At this time of day, they would meet little traffic before reaching the junction with the feeder to the Gandhi Bridge across the Ganges, which gave out onto the Raj Path just a few blocks from the flat, but the substantial congestion at this intersection during this time of day was mostly caused by roadside vendors of produce and every other imaginable household need there.

But even the newly widened Raj Path, which was usually jammed with *lakhs* of humans and every other kind of animal for the full ten miles from the Maidan to Patna City, seemed clear for the half mile or so they had to travel upon it before the turn to the river where Ramesh and his family lived. It was a good sign for their journey back home that they would take on this ancient artery of commerce along the sacred Ganga after dinner. Their son Ramesh was taking them to the airport in the morning for their flight to America and would then drive the SUV to their old house in Rajendra Nagar that he would inherit when they left India tomorrow.

Shashi imagined that Mohan could well be more sentimental than she about this final journey. He had, after all, labored so hard along this Path for the better part of a half-century while she had ventured upon it only when activities of their children had absolutely demanded it or for a special occasion when she and her husband had managed to sneak out for a night on the town alone. More recently, after all the children were out of the home, however, her volunteer duties at the museum or the College Women's Association, or even the auxiliary to the Rotary Club which she was much more faithful to than her husband whose businesses were the reason for her membership, had required her to battle this familiar street on an almost daily basis, a task she could well do without now that they were moving to America.

It had been hard to coax Ramesh out of his humble workingman's flat on the river, but when it had become certain that Mohan and she were leaving and not coming back to the house he had been born into and grown up in and that they would sell unless he took up residence there, he finally assented to make the move. His longtime fiancée Priya, with whom he had created two of their grandchildren, would remain on the river, tending to their children's education in the Gulzarbagh School District they did not want to depart. They would join Ramesh at Rajendra Nagar only on the weekends, if even then. Ramesh was a strange boy – no a man of almost thirty now – and Shashi did not even want to speculate why he was so different from the norm.

As soon as they turned north on the highway that would cross the Setu into her homeland of North Bihar, the portable roadside commerce began to thin, but there was still the ubiquitous smoke curling off into the reddening sky. "How peaceful India becomes in the evening," Mohan said as he edged the SUV past the few shoppers who seemed to wander aimlessly looking at the array of goods still displayed on the blacktop. "I have to admit I'm going to miss this hour when we're in America."

"Are you anxious about what we're going to do there?" I asked him, knowing full well that all the signs from Reva's relocation to the Washington area to her plea for help with her soon-to-be three year old twins Sam and Leila were that we should make this move now. Especially my sense that Mohan would not live long if he was not soon taken away from his new and too-intimate friend *bhang*. "I must admit I'm a little frightened too."

"Of course, I'm uncertain about it," he finally said. "It'll be completely different from the life we've known, and we're getting old. We won't know anything there, and it won't be so easy to adjust," he added as he took the right turn off the highway to go north on the Path.

"But what a challenge, dear," I said. "It'll be just the thing to give us a new zest for living."

"Of course, Shash," he said, now taking the left turn off Ashok Raj Path to head down toward the river. "I don't have anything to do here now that Ramesh and Wazir's son are running everything. I don't know anything about these new computers they have, so I'm more of a hindrance than a help when they do ask me to come in to help them with something," he continued wistfully. "I have plenty of weaknesses, but I've always been one to accept the reality of things."

"Aap ke pas bahut daya hai, Mohan," I agreed. "You've always been much more selfless and insightful than me. You were the one who saw Reva needed us more in America now than anyone does here."

The road down to the Ganga was only surfaced for about a block off the Path. It had originally been paved all the way to the water, but after years of patching the cement with blacktop closer to the river after the monsoons, the municipal authorities had given up and let most of the lane return to dirt. Ramesh, Priya, and their neighbors now were more than happy to have this touch of the village in their colony.

At the door to the flat on the street facing the river, Shashi looked out to the receding shoreline as she got out of the vehicle. The last time I was here the water was no more than fifty meters from this lane, she remembered. Now it's almost twice that far.

In the softening light, she heard her name called by the shrill voices of her grandchildren, who had disengaged from their friends with whom they had been playing on the beach and were running toward them.

"Dada, Dadi, you're here," they cried happily. "It's been so long since we've seen you."

They all embraced each other before starting to climb the stoop to the door, when it opened from the inside and Priya stood there beaming. *"Svagat,* Mohan and Shashi," she said, sweeping her hand back into the flat. *"Svagat hamara ghar par."*

Ramesh emerged from the kitchen smiling with an apron tied around his waist and a big spoon in his hand. "At last you got here," he said. "Good thing you're a little late, because we're a little behind on dinner. Priya's got the chapattis ready, but we haven't cooked them yet, and I'm just finishing putting in the last spices for our *murgi masala.*"

"Since when did you start cooking, *beta*?" Mohan asked, laughing. "You've always made fun of me when I made something at home."

"That was because Shiva and the girls always did," Ramesh said.

"The times are changing, Mr. Verma," Priya added. "At least once a week some emergency arises at the hostel, and I have to stay late. So Ramesh has to feed the kids, and he's gotten in the habit of cooking for everyone."

"I never made Mohan do that," I interjected. "The only time he cooked is because he wanted to cook."

"But you never worked out of the house, *Mata*," Ramesh said.

"I did too," I said. "I worked at the museum and for the College Women's Association at Pat—"

"But those were volunteer jobs, Ma," Ramesh argued. "You were able to schedule your own hours so you would never get home too late to cook dinner."

I looked at Mohan for support. "He's right, sweetheart," he said.

"Priya's helping to support the household," our son offered.

"And I didn't in our household?" I asked. "It would have cost us more to hire help with the children than I could have made teaching."

"Maybe so, Shash," Mohan said, "but that's not the point. Priya can't always get home before Ram and Richa do, so Ramesh had to learn to cook."

"Usually I would prepare our dinner the day before and leave it in the fridge," I said. "Then I'd warm it up. If she did that," I went on, pointing my head toward Priya," Ramesh would never have to do more than put what she prepared on the stove."

"Okay, dear," Mohan said, then turned to Priya. "Now that we're leaving, you'll be able to quit your job," he said to her. "Ramu and I have made an agreement to have him buy me out of Bihar Bus and the orchards for an amount he should be able to pay off in several years."

"Why should she quit her job?" I demanded. "They're not even married."

"I don't want to quit my job anyway," Priya said. "I'm really helping the girls in the hostel who've just started college make the adjustment to living on their own. I hope to continue doing it till the twins are out of school. Then if I'm able to," she added, "I'd like to go back to school myself and get an advanced degree in psychology or some kind of counseling and maybe open my own business."

I didn't say anything even though it seemed she would say anything to show me up in my son's eyes. After dinner as Ramesh was driving us home and learning the finer points of operating Mohan's SUV, it became clear to me she had been successful in her endeavor.

As we were leaving their flat, the last vestiges of the day lingered beautifully over Bhadra Ghat, and Priya followed us outside and kissed Ramesh goodbye passionately before he got behind the wheel. Then he started the car and drove it up to the Raj Path in silence without asking Mohan any questions about operating it, and by the time we were passing the Polytechnic College on the main street, he took up the issue of the orchards back near Maniarwa in a way that seemed designed to preclude my participation in the discussion from the back seat. "Do you think Nana's getting too old to handle all the marketing of the fruit, Dad?" he asked.

"Not as far as I'm concerned," Mohan answered. "Aravind's mind is amazing for someone who's a hundred. But he is fragile physically, so you'll have—"

"He's just as sharp as you are, Ramesh," I contributed. "You should be so lucky to be that—"

"What about his taking care of the irrigation system, Dad?" Ramesh asked.

"He still loves going out to the fields, son," Mohan said, "but…."

My mind drifted away from the conversation. Passing under the bridge, I remembered when Mohan bought that land up in Khajauli and the whole family started crossing the river this way to go up for the weekends. Mohan and my father got so close then that he could have been Pita's son, and I must admit I got a little jealous. Mother never allowed even me to get that close with Dad.

Soon after we reached the Vilayatan Mosque, I wondered if Mohan liked my father so much because he found out at our wedding feast that Pita probably had some Muslim blood. It seemed too like Mo got even closer with Najib after we were married.

Going through the Alamganj Cowk and seeing all the *musalman* in *lungis* there, I admitted to myself that I had a harder time with Dad's Muslim blood than Mohan did. I remembered how he had quarreled with his own father about the Muslims working in the family silk shop the last time we were in Bhagalpur before we moved to the Patna area.

At the Sher Shah intersection, I recalled the tension around Ramu's birth in the hospital there. At first, I thought Mohan was so upset with having a fifth child that he would stint on the costs of the delivery, but instead he picked the best maternity ward in Patna. Now that Shiva's gone, it's a good thing that he insisted upon Tripolia Hospital, as Ramesh has always been very healthy.

Not much further down the Path as we passed the Janta bus stand, I remembered how Lalu was just beginning to gain popularity when Ramesh was born. How could I have predicted that Shiva's disillusionment with that political clown would have contributed to my son probably taking his own life. How important of a cause it was I will never know....

While we continued on down toward the University from which all of our children graduated, I noticed the fine retirement housing they had put up off to the right. Are we doing the right thing by moving to America? The signs seem to point toward doing it, and I've always wanted to see the place. But I'm going to miss this old burg too. For the most part, we've had a wonderful life here.

There on the other side, well before we would turn south for Rajendra Nagar is the hostel where Sangeeta and I roomed together our last year at Patna College. It was so nice to see Sukhmay and her at Reva's wedding, but I wished I'd seen more of her these last years. It's hard to believe that it's almost sixty years ago that we took that fatal rickshaw ride from the hostel down to the College where I heard Mohan speak. I think I fell in love with him the minute he opened his mouth that day....

It's not too far on down the Raj Path where we got off the rickshaw for the auditorium where they held the senior class meeting. Just behind it down toward where Reva got married is where Mohan and I first talked with each other after we were introduced by our friends.

Now things are really coming back. On beyond the College on the other side of the Path is where Mohan found his first office in Patna Market for his realty business, and just beyond that back on the other side is where St. Xavier's used to be, where Mo met Naj and Aru and the rest of their old gang. And not much further on, the Path runs into Gandhi Maidan, where I think Mohan and I have heard just about every important Indian politician speak since Independence.

I got a last glance down the rest of Ashok Raj Path as Ramesh turned left on Makhania Kuan Road to continue on home. Yeah, for all its faults, I love Patna. And I'm going to miss Mata Bharat....

Chapter Ten

Mr. and Mrs, Mohan Verma settled in Vienna, Virginia, hardly venturing into the frenzied pace of Washington DC that was no more than thirty minutes away. The Virginia suburb where the main production facility of Challenge Systems that employed Sunil was located was a big enough shock to their systems. Reva worked part-time as a management consultant for the company out of an office in nearby Fairfax, but Challenge so appreciated her contributions that she was working literally every day. Though it was Shashi's grandparenting skills that were mainly called upon by the Abdullahs and the commute between the two homes in Vienna was relatively easy by American standards, Mohan was much more overwhelmed by the U.S. than his wife.

Driving, which continued to be primarily his responsibility, on the right-hand side of the road was the initial and one of the biggest hurdles for him. He survived a series of fender benders although at some cost. Marijuana was, as it turned out, readily available in the greater DC area, and as a result his *ganja* habit became worse rather than better. Being high calmed his anxiety on the roads enough to make him marginally safe when he drove.

Since at least at the outset of his time in America, the ingredients to prepare a *bhang* drink – fresh marijuana leaves and flowers, blanched and chopped almonds, and the cloves, cardamom, and cinnamon to make *garam masala* – were unavailable to him, he had to take to smoking again after so many years with the result that his general health deteriorated, and he needed to smoke all the time to kill the discomfort. In just a few months, Shashi could see he was more dependent on marijuana than he had ever been in India.

So she confided in Reva about the problem, and her daughter through her friends at work searched out a substance-abuse counselor for Mohan, who would never have imagined that he needed such help. Shashi broached the subject with him when she returned to their apartment one evening after she had cooked dinner for the kids before Reva and Sunil got home. She had come back to the apartment to find Mohan on the couch watching Donald Duck cartoons on TV.

"I had no idea you found these silly stories entertaining, Mohan," she said after changing into a housecoat and returning into the tiny living room. "Have you eaten anything since lunch?"

"Funny thing is I haven't been hungry," he said, continuing to stare at the television. "Actually these cartoons are hysterical."

"For Leila and Sam maybe," she said. "For you … I think you're a little too old for them."

"I don't know, Shashi. Arash told me the Buddha used to say 'let us be like little children."

"When did you become so fascinated with the Buddha?" she demanded. "There are other avatars of Lord Vishnu just as impressive as he is."

"In your opinion," he said, hitting the *Off* button on the remote to kill the screen and turning to acknowledge me as I sat on the chair facing the sofa. "To me, Buddha is more than just an avatat of Vishnu."

"You never could have told it by me," I snapped back at him. "You're stoned so much now you might as well be a Hindu *sadhu* in Varanasi."

"Aha," he said, holding up his forefinger. "I knew that was what this was all about. You can't stand to have me relax, can you, Shashi?"

"Of course I can," I said. "You've worked hard all your life." Then I noticed the can of air freshener and empty bag of Cheetos on the end table next to him and said, "But you're not going to last long if you keep smoking so much and don't eat decently."

"Maybe I never had time to be young," he said. "Besides the only reason I'm still smoking is because you won't let me try to mix up some *bhang*."

"I don't care what you say, it's not legal here, Mohan. If they catch us with marijuana in any form here, we'll be in big trouble," I said. "Especially after what happened at the World Trade Center. To people here in America, Indians are as suspect as the Arabs are now. In fact, most people here don't even know the difference."

"That's overstating it," he said. "Why are you becoming such a goody-two shoes anyway? You can hardly stand anyone you meet in this country."

"That's not true," I said, though he had a point. "I'm doing my best to adjust to a very unfamiliar place."

"So am I. Why do you think I smoke *ganja* all the time. I'm becoming an American," he said, laughing. "I can't relax without it. Anyway, it's the only way I can drive without starting out on the left-hand side of the road or hitting someone in all this traffic."

"That's an excuse, Mohan. The biggest reason I wanted to move here was because I wanted to get you off *bhang*!" I started to cry. "I thought you'd stop because it's illegal here."

"Why does that not surprise me, Shashi. You're as crazy as your mother was."

"Don't you start on that," I shouted then tried to compose myself again. "Why can't you admit that what you're doing isn't good for you. Or good for anyone else."

He didn't say anything for a long time. "You're probably right, Shash," he finally said in a measured tone. "But I don't know what else to do with myself here. I don't know anyone, and I don't know how to entertain little kids like you do."

"That's about the only thing I can do better than you," I said. "I got plenty of practice at it when you were off to work outside our home all the time." Before he could protest, I quickly added, "Look, I know you had to work hard with five children to put through college. I just couldn't ever find anything I wanted to do in Bihar."

"You were a great teacher, Shashi. You could have gone back to it."

"Well, I didn't, Mohan." I glared at him. "And the past's the past. We can't do anything about it. Anyway, if I didn't want to return to teaching, it was probably what the gods wanted to happen."

"Don't start this Hindu bullshi—"

"You're a Hindu too, Mo—"

"You were just accusing me of trying to be a Buddhist."

"Well – what is it Leila says all the time – *whatever*. So what. Buddhist or Hindu, you're smoking too much pot, and I don't think you can stop unless you get help."

"And I suppose you know where I can get that help," he said evenly.

"I don't. But, as a matter of fact, Reva has learned about a place…."

*   *   *

Who'd have ever thought he'd end up in Wickenburg, Arizona, Mohan thought as he was beeped out of the cafeteria at the Patio Treatment Center into the first morning session of the day. He had been in the facility for two weeks and was now accepting of such intrusions into his personal space. Once he had been convinced to try the Patio by its impressive record of success in overcoming addiction, acceptance of its methods and rules had been no great leap of faith for him.

Today was a special one in that Shashi, having spent last night at the Best Western in nearby Sun City after her flight from DC yesterday, was scheduled to begin her family visit. Through the lectures, groups, and individual therapy in which he had already participated, Mohan had learned that while his wife was not responsible for his marijuana addiction, she was certainly a necessary partner in his cure, so her presence at this juncture of the process was indispensable to his success.

Mohan had in the restful confines of the Patio had little difficulty with not smoking marijuana in his fortnight's residence there. Despite his celebrity in the facility as the Hindu who wanted to kick his pot habit, there had been almost none of the heightened stress or pressures that had pushed him into daily smoking in the first place.

So Mohan was halfway home. He had learned that his resort to *cannabis* had been situational caused by his geographical and social displacement. Not only was he adrift in a new culture he did not understand or appreciate in many of its aspects, but he had been stripped of his identity as a doer by the displacement. All of his life he had gained self-esteem from his labor, and his ingenuity in achieving his financial goals in the complex and difficult milieu of Bihar had given him a confidence that previously had never been invaded by self-doubt.

When all of that was gone and he had less to do than even his wife who was functioning as nothing more than a baby sitter to their grandchildren Sam and Leila, he was completely lost. Lost and without mooring in a self-important metropolis that saw itself as the center of the world and was more extensive and faster and louder than anyplace he had ever experienced before.

Understanding this (which he had intuited prior to his arrival in Wickenburg) had stabilized Mohan temporarily, though he had no idea how he would cope when he had to go back to DC. But his counselor, the lovely and accomplished Mia Farreti, had assured him that all would be well if he remained open to the Patio process the rest of the way through his course of treatment there. So, although he was nervous and ashamed and a bit frightened about seeing Shashi again after two weeks apart, he walked down the hall to Small Group Room B with a certainty that he was where he had to be.

"Good morning, Mohan," Mia greeted him as she pointed him to the open chair among the seats in the circle opposite from her. "I trust your yoga lesson before breakfast has energized you this morning for the meeting."

Shashi, dressed in a pink blouse and dark slacks, was seated on Mia's other side. And Michael, the actor from California, and Muriel, the Seattle software saleswoman, occupied the two chairs on the other side of the circle between the counselor and him. The Chicana lawyer from Scottsdale named Beatriz followed him into the room and took the chair between Shashi and him.

"It's got all my pores opened up as Marge likes to say," Mohan responded. "I'm ready for a beautiful day."

"Terrific," Mia said, turning toward Shashi. "As you can see, your wife made it too."

"Hi, Shashi," he said, smiling and waving to her. "How was your trip?"

"No problems," she answered. "Reva got me to the flight in plenty of time, and I had a good night's sleep in the hotel here last night."

"What about the rest of you?" Mia asked. "You ready to help these two get reacquainted?" Everyone nodded, and she looked across to Beatriz. "How was your night's rest, Beatriz?"

"Couldn't be better," she said.

"And what about you, Michael?" Mia said.

"Excellent," he said, leaning forward and rubbing his hands together. "I'm ready to do what I can."

"Me too," Muriel offered. "My acupuncture session's got me beautifully relaxed."

"Perfect then," Mia said, looking up at me "So, Mohan, do you have anything you want to tell Shashi about what you've been doing here the last two weeks?"

"Well, for starters, I haven't smoked any *ganja*," said. "After the first few days, I haven't even thought about it." He smiled. "They keep us pretty busy here."

"With what?" Shashi asked.

"Meetings mostly," he said. "Every day I start the morning with a yoga lesson and after breakfast come to this group. Before lunch, then, there's usually a speaker about a specialized subject relating to addiction for the whole center."

"What kinds of things do they discuss?" Shashi said.

"A whole range of issues from relationships to family-of-origin issues," Mia interjected, "to the psych-physiological aspects of addiction ...."

"After lunch, we try to take a hike," Mohan continued, "and then I generally have a one-on-one session with Mia for about an hour. Afterwards, most days I finish out the afternoon in a discussion with a group of about a dozen other patients—"

"You know we don't call you patients, Mohan," Mia said.

"I'm sorry. Students, other *students*," he said. "Then, after supper, we read for an hour or two before we go to sleep, mostly from self-help books we get from the library here."

"That sounds like a pretty full day," Shashi observed.

"It is," he said. "I've learned a lot."

"You've listened to Mohan every day, Muriel," Mia said. "What in particular do you think he's learned?"

"Well, for one thing, he's – we've – talked a lot about how different the U.S. is from India," Muriel said. "And the different ways people use marijuana in each culture."

"And he's talked a lot about your family," Beatriz said, looking at Shashi. "You and your kids are really important to him, you know."

"What about you, Michael?" Mia asked. "What do you think Mohan's learned?"

"It seems to me he's been doing a lot of thinking about what he wants to do with the rest of his life," Michael said slowly. "He told us how traditionally Hindu men are supposed to end their lives as an itinerant beggar or a *sunyassi* but how that's not going to work so well for him," he went on, smiling, "because he wants to become a Buddhist, as I understand it."

Mohan nodded in agreement and looked at Shashi. "He's right, honey. I think you know I've wanted to do this for some time."

"I have," Shashi said then cleared her throat before she spoke again. "I have no objection."

Tears came to his eyes.

After a minute, Mia asked him, "And what do you think is the most important thing you've learned here, Mohan?"

"I've learned that I can break down too," he said at last. "Because that's what happened to me when I started to go into la-la land every day. I thought it was the only way I could cope," I continued. "I've still got a lot of work to do on myself, Shash. But I've definitely made a start on it here."

"Why do you think you've taken so long to realize these things, Mohan?" Mia finally asked me.

"To be honest, I think people get sick when they can," he replied. "Until now I had to take care of other people. Now that you seem to have found yourself, sweetheart," he said, fixing Shashi with his eyes, "I can focus on myself for a while." He paused a moment. "I'm not mad at you, Shash. You had to go through what you did. Hopefully now I can grow into the person you deserve."

Shashi started to cry.

He went over and put his arms around her and started to cry too....

       *   *   *

When Mohan got back to DC in another month or so – he had stayed on a bit longer than the normal course for intensive individual therapy with Mia and the Patio's psychiatrist Dr. Feldstein – Reva had gone fulltime with Challenge at its Alexandria headquarters, Sunil had left the company to open his own consulting business, and they had moved into a house in Arlington. So Shashi had found a new apartment nearby in Alexandria about equidistant between the Abdullahs' home and the Buddhist Center for Meditation in the area.

Mohan began his Buddhist studies, drawn to the Theravada school not only because of its Indian lineage but also because his college friend Arash had come to be a Tibetan monk and a Theravada scholar. Arash and his wife had earlier become significant patrons of the Dalai Lama after the death of Aru's parents in the late Nineties. When Hitosa herself passed away in 2002, he became a Bhikktu and then one of the principal representatives of the aged Lama who could no longer make the necessary journeys abroad to harvest the fertile field of Western devotees, which was growing exponentially.

Meanwhile Mohan and Arash, because of these monumental changes in their lives, had lost touch. By the time Arash made his first trip to the Meditation Center in Alexandria at the beginning of 2005, Mohan was far along into the Noble Eightfold Path to Awakening there to learn that his old friend was coming to town. On the other hand, Ramesh had told Arash of his parents' relocation to Washington.

So when the two old friends found themselves in close proximity just after the Indian Supreme Court had delivered a directive permitting the videotaping of Bihar polling places to protect the sanctity of the vote, they were expecting to find each other in the crowd which was gathering at the Meditation Center to hear Arash speak there. Shashi, though, could not come, having taken the occasion to go by train up to New York to hear Guru P. Rishi read his new article on 'Principles for a Worldwide Sanatan' to an equally large audience of Hindu reformers in downtown Manhattan.

At the center that night, Arash spoke on the doctrine of Right Resolve and its relationship to preparing to transcend this world. While the American electorate had just failed in the effort to oust an increasingly unpopular President, Mohan competed with hundreds of well-wishers who came up to meet the speaker after his words. When Mohan reached Arash in the line, more than just Arash's right hand was fatigued, but the sight of his *purana dost* brought a broad grin to his face.

"*Kaisa hai, bhai?*" he said as he embraced him. "I knew you would come."

"Even more because I am now following your faith, Arash," Mohan said. "I hope you will forgive me for not addressing you as Panchen Lama as I really should do."

"We are still old friends, Mo," Arash said quietly. "My officially becoming a Panchen Lama does not change that." Then he leaned forward to direct his next words only into Mohan's ear. "Can you wait for me somewhere nearby for a half hour or so till I'm through here?"

"How about the Howard Johnson coffee shop on the corner?" Mohan said. "I'll be at the counter."

Arash arrived there alone shortly before ten o'clock. "So what's been happening with you these last few years?" he said taking the stool next to Mohan. "Do you like living here in America?"

"It's better now since I've been on the path to Awakening," Mohan said. "When we first arrived here, I hated it, so I fell into smoking *ganja* every day. I couldn't face life without it."

"So that's why you decided to explore Buddhism further?"

"I wouldn't say that," Mohan said. "But I was in such bad shape I had to go into a rehabilitation program. They asked me there what I wanted to do with the rest of my life." He paused and looked into Arash's eyes. "You know I've been interested in Buddhism for some time."

"Are you following the Theravada way?" Arash asked. "I'm assuming that you are since you seem to know your way around The Meditation Center."

"I've been going to the Vaj Rayogini Center in the District," Mohan said. "It's Theravada too. I feel more comfortable with Indian Buddhism," he explained. "Its language and process are more familiar."

"And Shashi?"

Mohan didn't answer for a while. "She's fine about it now," he said at last. "She's finally come to terms with her problems and seems to find a purpose in helping raise Reva's kids here. She wants Reva to succeed as a mother as well as a manager."

"What does she think about the way of Buddhism?"

"She's not interested," Mohan said. "She says Hinduism will be her salvation one way or the other. In fact, she's up in New York right now looking into the 'radical universalism' of Dharma Acharya there."

"Does that bother you?' Arash asked. "The fact that Hitosa became a Buddhist before she died made it much easier for me to want to become Awakened."

"I don't think it's a problem, Aru," Mohan said. "Shashi and I are headed for a different kind of relationship – can you imagine that at our age? We've been preoccupied with preparing our children for years, so now we don't have to be involved in everything together anymore."

Arash looked at his friend for a long time. "If you can make it work that way, Mohan, that's great," he said. "Believe me, I know that to reach the end of the Eightfold Path, it's easier to go it alone … without any distractions…."

*   *   *

On the advice of Arash, Mohan went on a Bhavana Society retreat the following summer to learn the Forest Tradition in High View, West Virginia. When he would return to Alexandria, he would have to become more engaged in mentoring Leila and Sam at least for the moment, however, as Shashi had scheduled more than a week in Manhattan to study the Dharma Evolution with Rishiji as soon as Mohan got back.

The Bhavana Retreat Center was several hours west of DC in the mountains just across the state line from Virginia. So Friday evening after entering West Virginia on US 50, Mohan took the first highway south and wound his way a quarter hour up the still-green and lovely

Appalachian hills till he reached the Bhavana grounds. Perched on a hilltop overlooking the Shenandoah Valley to the east, the *stupa* was beautifully situated, and Mohan was greeted at the door by a monk who appeared to be South Indian.

"*Namaskaar, ji.* Are you here for the *Seeds of Dhamma Taking Root* retreat?"

"I am, Bhante," Mohan answered, bowing slightly. "Here is a copy of my accepted application."

The old Indian looked through a list on the lectern next to the door. "Ah, yes, I see you are from the Meditation Center in Washington."

"Yes, that is where I have taken refuge in Lord Buddha, his Dhamma, and the Sangha of Panchen Lama Nariman," Mohan said.

"Wonderful," said the monk, smiling. "I am Bhante Gunapola, the Preceptor of this Forest Monastery. I think I remember seeing you when the Panchen Lama spoke there in January." He paused. "Can you tell me why you are taking the ceremony, Mohan?"

"I am more than eighty years old, Bhante, and I have been in this country for less than two years," Mohan said. "As you can see from my name, I am from India."

"And I am from Sri Lanka."

"Then you must have a sense of how difficult it was for me to adjust to the States," Mohan continued. "After six months in the suburbs of Washington, I found myself wanting to smoke *ganja* all the time."

"Washington is not America, Mohan," the Bhante said. "You will find it very different here."

"I expect so," Mohan said. "Don't misunderstand me, Bhante. I no longer smoke *ganja*, and my hard work at The Meditation Center is a major reason for my stopping. But long before I came to the U.S., I was interested in Buddhism, and I am thinking this retreat is my next step on the way to Awakening," he went on. "I'm getting older, and as everyone my age, I have suffered much in this life. I would like to pass over to a better place."

"And you shall, Mohan," Bhante said as the door was opened from the outside again. "Your room is the last in the building to the left out front. Tomorrow morning at 7 you will get a bite to eat at the canteen in here, and then we will gather in the conference room where I will give a little presentation on Theravada morality. Then after lunch we will practice Noble Silence and meditate until bedtime."

"Will we follow you in Vipassana Meditation tomorrow, Bhante Gunapola?"

"I am hopeful we will have the time," Bhante said, smiling radiantly. "Then Sunday in the ceremony you will receive your Pali name to attest to your commitment to the Eight Precepts."

"Excellent. I am looking forward to it...."

The following morning after oatmeal and tea, Bhante Gunapola spoke to the approximately three dozen initiates, all barefooted and dressed completely in white, "Good morning. Welcome to the High View Forest Monastery's Pathway to Eight Precepts Retreat.

"I am Bhante Gunapola of the Bhavana Society Meditation and Retreat Center. As many of you know, I was born in Sri Lanka almost eighty years ago, and after Buddhist studies there and missionary work in Southeast Asia, I came to this country to work in the Vihara society in

Washington DC. Then after many more years of study culminating in my final degree at George Washington University about ten years ago, I came here.

"In 1998, we inducted here our first group of laypeople who committed themselves to the Eight Lifetime Precepts of the Bhavana Theravada Society. Those precepts are the basis of our morality, and the first several of them are fundamental to all peoples. They are, first, to abstain from killing, and second, to abstain from stealing.

"The third precept is to abstain from sexual misconduct. While I as a monk have taken a vow to abstain from all sexual relations, many of you are married. So while those of you who are will be permitted to continue normal sexual relations with your spouse, you must abstain from sex with anyone else while you are married.

"Fourth, you vow to abstain from false speech or lying.

"Fifth, you vow to abstain from malicious speech, which is any speech that can harm others. In this connection, Lord Buddha said in Sutta Nipata 452

> 'Speak kind words, words
> Rejoiced at and welcomed,
> Words that bear ill-will to none;
> Always speak kindly to others.'

"Sixth, you vow to abstain from harsh speech. In this connection, the Buddha said that 'The fool thinks he has won a battle when he bullies with harsh speech. But knowing how to be forbearing alone makes one victorious.

"Seventh, you will abstain from useless speech. In this precept, we exalt Noble Silence instead of the constant chatter people are often encouraged to partake of. Instead, when we observe silence, we can achieve the mindfulness necessary to still the insults and injuries of daily life.

"Lastly, you will abstain from engaging in a wrong livelihood or in partaking in drinks or drugs in such a way as will cause you to become heedless in your actions...."

From the meditation hall, Mohan and the others were led to the canteen, where they were fed a simple lunch of water, rice and cauliflower curry, and tea. After eating they sat for several hours, sharing with each other the circumstances of their lives that had brought them to commit to the Eight Lifetime Precepts in pursuit of the mindfulness practiced by the Bhavana Society and their experience in the Society which had prepared them for this ceremony.

Mohan spent most of this time until 2:30 telling an American novice named Roger from New Jersey of his life in India and the DC area, emphasizing particularly his differences with his father over business ethics, Shashi's long term difficulties that were finally resolved after Shiva's death, and his own descent into addiction in the U.S. and his struggle to overcome it. Roger reciprocated by relating the course of his life from selling life insurance near Cape May to the death of his wife from cancer when they were reconciling after a long separation and his now-distant relationship with his three children. Both men had found some peace through their adoption of the Theravada Buddhism and were determined to achieve serenity by continued commitment to the Lifetime Precepts.

At two on Saturday, the aspirants entered into a Noble Silence that would last until the 10 o'clock bedtime. Each could meditate in the big hall and/or on the several hundred acres of forest land surrounding the Monastery and Retreat Center. Mohan began out of doors, trying to meditate while walking and during some sitting on the forest floor. At sunset, he joined most of his classmates in the meditation hall where he attempted to still his mind for the last few hours before sleep by practicing the Vipassana Yoga he had been learning in the Mediatation Center.

By 7 AM Sunday they all gathered once more dressed in white in the meditation hall and seated themselves in rows before Bhante Gunapola and the other monks. There they chanted their desire to commit to the Eight Lifetime Precepts, and Bhante began to administer to the aspirants. Each hopeful initiate was called forward to kneel before him, and the Bhante presented them a medallion of the Bhavana Society with an embossed figure of the Buddha in the lotus position. Then each initiate had a knotted string tied around his or her right wrist which symbolized the lifelong commitment to the Eight Precepts.

Later each celebrant was called back by the Bhante to receive a Pali name representing a specific goal toward which the recipient would strive for the rest of his/her life. Roger was called the Solitary One to remind him of his need to always try hard to establish community with those with whom he came into contact. Mohan was named *Nicca* for the constancy he had maintained throughout his life but for one time, which would cause him always to remember that each person is imperfect.

After a communal meal following the ceremony which ended the fast, the celebrants gathered one last time in the meditation hall to share their memories of the retreat and their intentions for the future. Mohan told his classmates of a bluebird, who had adopted him during the Noble Silence the previous afternoon and led him around the entire mountain, and then he declared his intention to perfect the Vipassana yoga technique.

Before five, Mohan and the others prepared to return to their homes. Roger and he embraced and promised to remain in touch in the years that would follow. Then Mohan set out in his Chevy down the mountain into Virginia again on the road toward the eastern sky fading from pink to mauve to black on his way back to DC....

*   *   *

In Alexandria later that night, Mohan excitedly recounted his High View experience to Shashi. "I want to go on following the Way of the Buddha," he said to her as they awaited the arrival of Reva, who was taking her mother to the airport for her flight to New York. "When Arash told me about this Bhavana Society retreat, he also told me of a Metta Monastery in California where one can be initiated as a monk. If I'm successful in mastering Vipassana Yoga here in the next few years, I may well go on to become a monk there."

"Wonderful," Shashi said as she got up to look out the window. "While I prepare to revitalize my roots in our Hindu birthright, you're already planning to become the most-observant Buddhist. How do you expect we'll be able to continue to live together?"

"Why should it be a problem, Shash?" he said. "Lord Buddha respected the sanctity of all faiths. Doesn't your dharma group do the same?"

"It's called the Sanatan Society, Mohan." she said. "It means the 'eternal way' for Vedic civilization, the way of salvation for all true Hindus. It might do you some good too, since its basic purpose is to develop bonds between Hindus here in America."

"There's plenty of Indian Buddhists here too, Shashi," he said. "And Muslims too. Do we have to give up our faiths to be included in this Sanatan Society?"

"I doubt it." She saw Reva's car pull into the parking lot. "But I'll probably find out for sure soon," Shashi said, heading to the closet to get her coat. "Reva just got here."

"I'll carry your suitcase," Mohan said, getting up. "In fact, I might as well ride with you out to the airport."

"Oh, you don't really have to, darling," she said, waving him off. "You must be tired after your long drive."

"I want to, sweetheart," he said, pickup up his jacket off the back of his chair.where he had laid it. "I missed you and I want to tell you about the rest of the retreat."

"Well, if you want to," Shashi said, going past her suitcase by the door. "But I was hoping to tell Reva about the Sanatan conference on the way to the airport."

"We should have plenty of time for both," he said, following me out the door. "There'll probably be a lot of traffic…."

On the way back from the airport to Alexandria, Mohan turned to his daughter as they got stopped at a red light before getting on the freeway. "Your mother sure seems enthusiastic about this Sanatan Dharma business, doesn't she?" he said. "Has she been talking it up a lot to you, Rév?"

"Not so much," Reva answered, then paused a moment. "She's worried about you, Dad. She thinks socializing with other Indians would be good for you."

"Why's that?"

"She knows you don't like it here. She thinks you'd be less likely to take up *ganja* again if you had some friends."

"What makes her think that I don't have friends at The Meditation Center?" he asked as the light turned green and they proceeded ahead.. "I heard Arash speak there, didn't I?"

"Mom's thinking Hindus, Dad. You know that some part of Mom doesn't believe that anyone except Hindus are Indian."

"Maybe she used to think that, *beti*," he said, looking out his window. "But now that she's well, I don't know if she thinks that way anymore"

"Maybe you're right," Reva said. "But Sunil's convinced she doesn't really feel comfortable with him because he's a Muslim. That she just pretends to like him for me."

They rode on in silence for a while.

Finally Mohan said, "Do you think she feels the same way about me because I've become a Buddhist?"

"You're not actually a Buddhist yet, are you?"

"I certainly am. I'm a Bhavana Buddhist," he said, turning to face his daughter again. "Why? Does that make a difference to you?"

"Of course not," Reva said immediately. "But then I wasn't born in Maniarwa. Mother may think you're running away from your Indian heritage."

"That's ridiculous," Mohan said, dismissing the thought by swiping his hand over the dashboard. "The Buddha reached Awakening twenty-five hundred years ago in Bihar. What could be more Indian?"

Reva didn't say anything right away. At last she turned to her father and said quickly, "You notice I didn't convert to Islam, don't you?"

"What's that supposed to mean?"

"Mom's still insecure. She doesn't do change well."

"So I'm insecure too," he said, looking straight ahead. "I find peace in Buddhism. It's been easier for your mother to adjust to the culture here than for me," he added. "She's had a ready-made purpose here helping you with your kids."

"Well, Bap," Reva said, laughing, "you're certainly about to get a little more of that purpose this week, aren't you…?"

*   *   *

Over the next few years, Shashi became more deeply involved with the Sanatan Society on the East Coast, while Mohan put more and more of his energy into becoming adept at Vipassana yoga. Then, in late 2005, Arash made another trip to Washington and offered his friend a private tutorial in the practice.

Seated in a small salon in The Meditation Center, he started Mohan in his first session, "First, we will assume the lotus position. Sit on the floor and cross your legs as you have seen the Buddha depicted so often, and keep your back straight. For now you may simply lay your hands in your lap, because there is no need for your arms to be in any particular position. Just let them rest on the insides of your thighs with your fingers hanging down to touch the floor."

Mohan did as directed, and Arash began to speak again. "May I also suggest that you approach the mindfulness necessary for Vipassana meditation by seeing yourself as you are situated in the universe. Imagine that the top of your head is pointing into the infinite sky above, and then that your spine is pressing into the Earth and on through it into the infinite sky on the other side. Then visualize your chest reaching out toward the horizon in front of you, and your back connected to the horizon behind," the Panchen Lama said. "Finally, visualize the right side of your body touching the horizon to your right, and your left side stretching out to the horizon on your left.

"Now you can feel your body in the center of a vast matrix, like a great top that is absolutely motionless as only the planet slowly spins and even more slowly rotates in infinite space, and your body is held perfectly still in this matrix connected to the infinity in all six directions. Feel the Earth slowly circulate in its orbit and turn on its axis. Now you are at once at rest and moving almost imperceptibly through the cosmos.

"Next you must wish goods things for all living things in this universe," Arash continued. "Send only positive thoughts to everyone you know and every creature you have encountered. Direct goodness to all of them and those you don't know and even those you don't like. To do this, you must fill yourself with generosity, kindness, and compassion. Link these feelings with wishes of joy and peace for everything. Purge yourself of any resentment, jealousy, or fear, and send only love to all living things."

Mohan felt a lightness take over his body as he followed these gentle commands.

"Once you have achieved this state of bliss, focus all your attention on your breath," Arash went on. "Feel the natural intake and outlet of air from your nostrils and out of the opening between your lips. Don't take deeper breaths than normal and don't try to hold your breath any longer than feels natural. Just let the process of breathing occur. Just let it be, and you will achieve the proper mindfulness of your body taking in the oxygen it needs to live, and letting out the carbon dioxide your blood cells have stripped of the oxygen you have taken in, which your body must expel to continue life."

Mohan was there in the intersection of breath that softly came into his nose and then out of it.

"When you have achieved this undivided focus on the natural cycle of your respiration, you are ready for the last step, without which you will not be able to free yourself from suffering. This essential final step is to become fully aware of your own nature, your own characteristics of attachment to things and dependence on them that cause you suffering," Arash said. "This focus on what you really are provides the window out of your suffering, which is everywhere in this life. The way to release yourself from these negativities that imprison you here is to focus upon their impermanence.

"Nothing in this life remains the same for more than an instant," he said, "nothing, not your breath or your resentment or your anger or any object of your negative emotions. Everything will be different an instant from now. Everything changes and is constantly in change.

"This realization of universal impermanence and change will liberate you from suffering," he began to close. "The understanding that all is change and the humility that comes with knowing that nothing you feel about anything will remain exactly the same from one moment to the next allows you to enter into a deep community with everything else in the universe. You will be in relationship with everything on an equal basis and dependent upon nothing anymore.

"You will be free. You will suffer no more...."

By this point in time, Mohan felt Arash's resonant tones to be literally inside himself, coming from and coursing through the very essence of what he was. He was one with Arash and everything else….

Sometime later he opened his eyes and saw Arash in front of him again. They smiled at each other, and Aru said, "It seems you have followed the process, my friend. You have gained a sense of what it can do for you."

"If you continue, you will be released," Aru went on. "But you must not expect perfection immediately. You must practice the process to achieve it."

"Perhaps, tomorrow Vipassana will not go so smoothly for you. But if you do it each day, you will get better, and eventually you will be at peace."

"This is the nearest I have come to it," he said to his old friend. He could hardly remember why he had harbored any resentment toward Shashi, or toward anyone else for that matter. He knew that his attachment to them would come back to some extent, but he had seen at last a way to rid myself of them, a way to be released from dependence and reach peace. "I have glimpsed the light at the end of the tunnel," he said to his friend and teacher, "and I will strive to reach it and disappear into it.

"*Dhanyavad, hamare dost….*"

COOL SEASON

Chapter Eleven

"When do you suppose Dadi is coming back?" Gopal's daughter Mina asked her grandmother on the seventh day of her visit at their Los Altos Hills home in January of 2006. "I've gotten to know you pretty well this last week, but Grandpa left before we could hardly exchange a word. Where did he rush off to anyway?"

"He was supposed to be back yesterday," Shashi said curtly. I'm the one who spends all my time with these grandkids, but it seems like every last one of them likes Mohan better. "And he didn't just rush off anywhere. He's up in a monastery a few hours north of here, which is in fact the very reason he came out here in the first place."

"What's a monastery?" Mina demanded.

"It's a place of meditation and spiri—"

"What's meditation?"

"That's where a person is silent and concentrates...," I said after some time, "on discovering the important truths," I added slowly. This one is smart as a whip. She reminds me of Reva, always having the next question out there before I've answered the first one. "We usually are in such a hurry that we can't take the necessary time to look at things and see what they really are."

"Why can't Grandpa do that here?"

"That's a good question," I answered, thinking quickly for a good answer. "Grandpa's become a Buddhist. And he's not just any Buddhist, he follows the very special Thai Forest

Tradition," I started again. "It believes that spiritual progress through meditation can be achieved only in the wilderness, which is where the Buddha himself gained his wisdom." I stopped to catch my breath.

"What's a Buddhist?" Mina persisted.

I ignored her and went on, "So Grandpa had to go to the Abhayogari Monastery up past Ukiah, I think it is. A friend of his from India told him about that place and was supposed to meet him there."

"So he didn't come back because he's playing with his friend in the woods?" Mina asked with, I think, a twinkle in her eye.

"That's probably about the truth of it," Shashi said, laughing, and then paused a moment. "But seriously, Grandpa doesn't feel he has any purpose to his life besides his meditation, but he doesn't feel he's ready to go on to the next world."

"What's the next world? India?"

"No, that was the previous one," Shashi answered immediately. "The next one is up there," she explained, pointing to the clear blue sky she had seen here every day.

"Heaven, you mean?"

"Hopefully," Shashi said. "That's if Grandpa doesn't play too much with his friend up in the woods in Ukiah."

Just then the back door of the house opened, and they could hear some male voices talking too loud for good Buddhists. Shashi turned and saw Gopal leading Mohan and Arash in full saffron robes out to join her and her granddaughter by the pool.

"Dad, you can't be serious you're going to join an order of Thai monks and go back to Bihar?" Gopal was saying as they approached. "You're going to leave Mother alone here?"

"If she wants to become a nun, she can certainly come along," Mohan said, taking the chair next to me. "It's up to her. But Bodh Gaya is where I can do the most good the next few years," he went on, shifting his eyes onto me. "That's what Aru says, and he ought to know."

"I thought Aru was a follower of the Dalai Lama," I said, smiling at Mohan's old friend whose robe was a much lighter shade of saffron while extending my hand to the chair on my other side. "Isn't he Tibetan?"

"Right on both counts," Arash said to me. "But His Holiness has long been interested in the Vipassana yoga practiced by the Thai Forest Tradition."

"Besides that, Aru has been telling me that Buddhism is making a bad name for itself these days in Bodh Gaya," Mohan said, "which is probably the single most important Buddhist site in the world. The Thai and Tibetan monasteries there are at such odds with each other over doctrinal differences that the Hindus have taken over the town council, which has control over the Mahabodhi Temple where Lord Buddha achieved Enlightenment."

"That's absolutely correct," Arash affirmed. "Not only is the Buddhist revival in India in jeopardy because of this rift, but the home country of all of us is being deprived of one of its richest spiritual traditions as a result."

"Is that so bad?" I asked mischievously. "India is a Hindu country, and Hinduism has absorbed the best of what Buddhism has to offer without absorbing its divisive baggage," I went on, turning from Arash to Mohan. "Buddha is the eighth avatar of Lord Vishnu, you know."

After taking a moment to cogitate this response, Mohan said, "Once again, let's not go there." Then he looked deeply into my eyes. "You have to accept that I've become a Buddhist, Shash. Hinduism is still completely wedded to the caste system, and most Indians are disadvantaged because of it."

I too decided that I shouldn't have gone there.

"Buddhism is an Indian tradition that is now as influential around the world as Christianity and Islam," Arash said at last. "And it is neither as volatile or bitterly divided as Islam nor as tied up with the Western power structure as Christianity. If you believe as I do that India has something critical to offer for the future of mankind, then Buddhism is the expression of India most likely to be accepted by other people today."

"I thought you just said Buddhism in Bodh Gaya is being riven between your sect and Dad's," Gopal said. "How's he going to be able to do anything about that?'

"Gopu's right," I jumped in. "Mohan became a Buddhist just a few years ago. What Tibetan Buddhist – or Thai Buddhist as far as that goes – is going to take anything he says about their doctrinal disputes seriously?"

"Don't underestimate my friend," Arash said, swinging his eyes from me to Gopal to his father. "He's a man of great persuasiveness, and he knows Bihar…and India like few people do."

"Who can argue with that?" I said. "Don't forget I met him the day he convinced Patna College's Class of '43 to support the British war effort against Subhas Chandra Bose when he was at the height of his popularity."

"And I've heard told he got a bunch of primitive tribals around Hazaribagh to help right a bus that crashed on their land in the Seventies," Arash said. "Mohan can be very compelling."

"But he's almost ninety years old now," I cried.

"So are you, Shash. And, to be honest, I don't think you've lost a step," Mohan said. "I feel very deeply about what the Vipassana meditation of the Thai tradition can do for the world, and Aru tells me the Dalai Lama himself wants to move his followers into its methodology."

"You might be right," I conjectured slowly. "So it's two against two among the old timers," I said, moving my eyes from Mohan to Arash to Gopal before settling them upon his Mina. "Let's hear what the younger generation has to say."

"I vote for Grandpa," Mina said without hesitation. "I'm going to miss him, but he should go back to India if he can help the people there."

       *   *   *

A year later Mohan did indeed heal the Thai-Tibetan division in Bodh Gaya. After that, he took to the forest and the road as a mendicant, preaching to his countrymen the Way of the Buddha, and we seldom heard from him over the next several years. During that time, my anxiety abated with a deepening involvement in the Sanatan Society, working toward a closer community among American and Indian Hindus. Then on February 17, 2009, Ramesh called to tell me Mohan had been hit by a police vehicle chasing Naxalite rebels near the Nepal border with Paschim Champaran and killed.

Ramesh indicated that the place Mohan died was not much more than fifty miles from both Lumbini, where the Buddha was born, and Kushinagar, where he left this world. No one seemed to know for sure to which place he was going.

Mohan had just turned eighty-seven years old. Immediately I prepared to return to India to cremate him at Varanasi.

In a day, Reva, Sunil, Leila, Sam, and I flew from Washington to Delhi. While they stopped for the night to check in with the Challenge Solutions headquarters in India there, I took a connecting flight right on to Patna, where Ramesh had brought Mohan's body. My son's family made room for me at our old home in Rajendra Nagar, and the next morning Ramesh and I dropped Priya and the children off at Patna Junction to catch a train to Varanasi, where they would meet up with the families of Reva, Tara, and Gopal at the Rashmi Guest House near Manikarnika Ghat in Varanasi where we would cremate Mohan.

We went on in the old SUV to collect the body from cold storage and carry it to Varanasi. By 10:30 we were out of the city, and well before noon we were crossing the bridge over the Son heading west toward Varanasi or Kashi, what we Indians like to say is the oldest city in the world.

While it was only the beginning of the cold season, the land on either side of Bhojpur District was already parched. Ramesh drove on toward Ara in silence, and my mind meandered over my sixty years of marriage while my Mohan was laid out in the back of his old vehicle.

"Did Bappa ever go to Varanasi since he came back to India, Ramu?" I asked, looking at our youngest through the misty film over my eyes. "Many Hindus, especially those who have garnered wealth like your father, come to the Holy City to get ready for their death." I thought about the kind of man my husband was and then added, "But I would guess Mohan never would have allowed himself that luxury, for which he had worked so hard."

"I don't know that he did or he didn't, Mom," Ramesh said, continuing to look ahead. "When Dad brought a form of peace between the Tibetans and Thais in Bodh Gaya, he went out as a mendicant like the Buddha to find his own way to escape the cycle of rebirth." He shook his head wistfully while he concluded, "So I doubt that would include a trip to Benares."

"Yes, for some reason your father found his peace as a Buddhist," I said, resigned at last to accepting his way. "And isn't it also ironic that he was killed because of the Naxalites while he was still in Bihar, skirting the Varanasi of us Hindus on the way to the beginning or the end of the Buddha's life."

"What do you mean *also*?" Ramesh quietly asked.

"I mean Shiva suffered also because of the Naxalites," I answered softly. "And like Mohan, he chose to minister to others, and even more than Lalu, the Naxalites were the big disappointment in his life."

"I never thought of it that way," Ramu said. "I always thought of Shiva and Dad together, though," he went on after a moment's pause, "and now they most surely are…I hope."

"Yes," I agreed. "Both of them did quite well in what they did. Yet still both of them were so helpless in a way. They were probably too sensitive for this world…."

Ramesh nodded in agreement and averted his head to gaze out his window for a minute.

Buxar, that last town in Bihar on the Ganges, was also already unseasonably dry and brown, as if it was in mourning. As we came near Ram Rekha Ghat on the river where Ram crossed it so many centuries ago on his way from Ayodha to meet Sita at Janakpur, I mused aloud to my son, "In these parts during 1765, the Mughal Emperor Shah Alam II was defeated by the British East India Company. This enabled the Company to bring Bihar fully under British control," I said sadly. "And here too Mohan leaves his beloved Bihar for the last time."

Ramesh said nothing for a time but then ventured, "And somehow it seems that we are bringing Shiva home to Kashi too." He looked over at me entreatingly. "Mata, I've always had a sense that you know more about his death than you have let on. Lalu's fodder cannot be the only reason he took his life."

I looked back at him at him and wondered whether he could bear to hear what I had read in Shiva's notebook so long ago. I hadn't wanted to tell Mohan…or anyone about it. It was too sad, too disturbing. Should Ramesh hear it now?

"Dad told me you had taken a notebook from Shiva's apartment before his cremation. But for some reason," he continued, "you had never showed it to him, never even talked to him about what was in it," Ramesh went on as we started across the bridge from Bihar. "Dad said you had to have had a good reason for that." We were well out over the river now. "Did you, Ma?"

"I thought so," I finally said as we crossed the midway point. "I don't think Mohan could have borne what Shiva said in his notebook."

"Do you still have the notebook, Ma?"

"It's in the storage room of the house, Ramesh. In one of those boxes in the basement. Its edges are charred, like Shiva tried to burn it before he died, but his words are still clear."

We listened to the hum of the tires on the bridge and looked at the sacred water down below for the longest time.

"What'd he say?" Ramesh asked. "Had you done to him what you'd done to me?"

My heart wrenched, and I wanted it to burst.

It didn't....

I couldn't answer till we were on land again, outside of Bihar. "No, of course not," I murmured at last. "I was unbalanced when I did that to you. Forgive me...."

When we were well into the last leg of our journey toward Kashi, I continued, "Shiva had begun a novel about a man, an intelligent, industrious man like your father. He was a good man, provided for his family ... and Shiva loved him," I went on. "But he didn't respect himself. He thought he had wasted his life, that he had hurt so many people by his pursuit of comfort, of riches ... people that he could have helped if he had lived as his dreams would have had him live."

Ramesh started to cry as Kashi came into sight across the river again from the highway.

"In the sketch of the novel – Ganesh was the protagonist's name – Ganesh loved only one person, told only one person that he hated himself ... a tribal woman from the south."

We hit a pothole in the road, and it seemed like there was a thump in the back of the vehicle which was too loud. It came from inside the coffin. It was as if the body was struggling to escape, to flee ... as if Mohan knew he should not be sent from this life from the banks of the sacred Ganga with this blasphemy on his soul....

*   *   *

We came into Varanasi on Mandan Mohan Malviya Road as the day began to wind down. Ramesh called Sunil at the Rashmi Guest House where we would all stay, and the three of us agreed to proceed directly to Manikarnika Ghat to meet the others.

Here it is said that in ancient times Lord Vishnu, with Lord Shiva watching over him from the heavens above, dug a pit before his jeweled earring or *manikarnika* fell into the pit. Shiva's consort Parvati, thinking her man would look forever for the earring somewhere on the banks of the Ganges here rather than run off with his disciples spreading the word of Lord Brahma, told Shiva that it was her earring, and Shiva whispered to Vishnu that if he found it for him he would go to Mt. Kailash rather than to Yama, the land of death. Still today it is said that Lord Shiva asks each soul that is released by cremation here if he or she has seen the earring.

We drove as close as we could get to Manikarnika, and after we parked, we hired coolies to carry the coffin to the burning *ghat.* The rest of the family was already there, and Gopal, Tara, and Reva helped us remove Mohan's body from the coffin and place it on the pyre.

Then Gopal lit the wood below Mohan. In moments, flames leapt from the boughs and lapped at his body.

Soon he sat up, and then – *whuuush* – his soul departed. Out of the unblemished sky of the dusk, there was a roar of thunder -- *grrrrraaam* – but I felt not a drop of rain. It was as if Lord Shiva was calling Mohan....

After the *brahmin* permitted us to collect a bit of his ashes in a jar I held, Ramesh filled a small pot with sacred Ganges water to take back to his home. Then all of us began to walk away from the river toward the Golden Temple of Vishwanath, probably the most famous Hindu *mandir* in the world. Dedicated to our destroyer god Lord Shiva, the original city of Kashi was built around it, so I guided our family there because I am certain Mohan would have wanted us to honor our Shiva at this time as much as he himself would have done.

As full darkness came along our way just before we reached the Vishwanath Gali quarter, a *sadhu* materialized from the horde of pedestrians around and offered his guide services. "You will need help tonight getting around Varanasi tonight, Srimati," he said, having apparently surmised I was the widow from the ceremony he had just witnessed at Manikarnika Kund. "Today is Mahashivaratri, the great night of Shiva, and it is the holy city's greatest festival. Parvati proclaimed it after she persuaded Lord Shiva to save the world he had intended to destroy. There will be thousands who have fasted all day here and will come to this area tonight to pay homage to Lord Shiva at the Kashi Vishwanath Mandir."

It was then I realized that Ramesh and I in the rush to get Mohan here to Kashi in time for his final passage had not taken the time to get even a morsel to eat all day. "Ramu," I called back and beckoned to him. "This man just told me that it is Shivaratri today here, and one is supposed to fast all day in honor of Lord Shiva." I waited a second for that information to light up his eyes. "Do you realize we've already performed that observance without knowing we were doing it," I said to him.

Ramesh caught up with the *sadhu* and me and walked several steps more into Gali before he said, "It is as though we were meant to celebrate this festival. What else does a devotee traditionally do today in Shiva's honor?" he asked, turning to the *sadhu* on my other side.

"For one thing, he performs a very precise ritual in the Kashi Vishwanath Mandir ahead," the holy man answered. "But it will be very difficult just now because of the rush of *bhagat* there who can break their fast after dusk. It would probably be better to first visit the Temple of Annapurna just beyond the Golden Temple."

"Maybe you should guide my family to the Vishwanath Temple now," I said indicating the crowd of relations following us as I saw how to kill two birds with one stone. "They probably did not know it is Shivaratri today either and would like to avoid the crowds inside. But they have already eaten breakfast and lunch and will not need the food my son Ramesh here and I must seek now," I added, taking Ramu by the arm and turning him back to face the family coming up the street.

Gopal leading the rest of the clan caught up to the three of us. "Gopu, this man told us it is Mahashivaratri today," I said, "and there will be hordes of devotees going into the Golden Temple right now. He is a native of Varanasi and has offered to guide you through it to celebrate Lord Shiva's Day."

"Exactly, *sahib*. Ganguly is my name," the *sadhu* said, extending his hand to Gopal. "I recommend you go to Annapurna Temple now and come back to Vishwanath when the crowd thins out."

Before Gopal could recommend that plan to the rest of the family, I said quickly, "Ramesh and I didn't have time to get anything to eat all day. We're going to find a tea stand in the *cowk*." I then proposed, "We'll meet you at the Rashmi after we finish paying our respects to Lord Shiva."

Before anyone could object, Ramesh and I darted off toward the Gali. We kept looking back, and when the rest of the family passed the golden spire and disappeared in the mass of people on the street beyond it, we turned back and hurried to get in the line to enter Vishwanath Mandir ahead of the masses approaching it from both directions.

"Look up Vishwanath Temple on the Internet, Ramu," I said, indicating the holster on his belt where he carried his cellular. "That way we as *bhagat* can know what to do on this night when we get inside here."

Ramesh read the "Shivaratri" sub-section of the "Kashi Vishwanath Temple" site as we proceeded slowly past a shrine to an aspect of Shiva called Dandapani inside the door. "At the time of creation," Ramu read, "the Creator god Brahma and the Preserver Vishnu were each claiming they were supreme in this new second world. To help resolve the dispute, Shiva threw down a bolt of light of infinite length from heaven. That bolt, which is the ultimate, indivisible reality out of which Shiva is often depicted as emerging, easily pierced the atmosphere and entered deeply into the earth. Shiva told the other two gods of the Trimurti that the first one of them to find the end of the bolt would be supreme."

We slowly moved ahead past another statue, this one called Kala Bhairava. "Brahma flew up looking for the higher end of the bolt, and Vishnu went down searching for its other end," Ramesh began again. "Soon Brahma claimed that he had found the end of the bolt in heaven, but Vishnu was furious because he knew Brahma was lying. So Shiva hurled down another bolt which he descended upon, and he condemned Brahma to be excluded from our Hindu ceremonies while decreeing that Vishnu would be worshipped by man forever."

As we edged past a shrine to Vishnu as promised by Shiva at the time of creation, Ramesh went on. "While Shiva is said to have dispatched many of these *jyotirlingas*, only the twelve of them that landed in India or its vicinity are considered auspicious and holy. This

Stambha Pillar or *lingam* that we will soon reach here in the Vishwanath Temple is the most sacred of these twelve bolts, which are scattered from Mt. Kailash in the Tibetan Himalayas down to Rameshwaram in eastern Tamil Nadu."

He now summarized from his screen as we finally went into the temple's inner chamber. "When we pass the altar of the *jyotirlinga* ahead, we are to bathe the Shiv Linga with the water from the Ganges that I have," he said. "If I had milk or food or *bhang*, I would offer it to assure the long and healthy life of Priya. Since you have already borne your children, our offering of the Ganga *pani* will provide us the best path to being liberated from the cycle of reincarnation."

"Ah," I said, accepting his offer of the pot holding the Ganges water, "I suppose it is okay for a woman nearing ninety like me to ceremonially douse the stone *lingam*." And when we actually reached the great bolt of Shiva, I splashed the hard black rock with the water and made as if to scrub it, while younger maidens still seeking marital bliss applied red clay and spread food and flowers around the huge *linga*.

Further on inside this inner chamber, we heard the chanting of *"Om Namah Sivaya…"* and the singing to bells of "Shanker ki Jai" made to Shiva's benevolent avatar of Rudram and the supplications of Chamakan and Dasa Shanthi for forgiveness of our sins….

When we at last passed on out of the *mandir*, Ramesh pointed to the martial Vishwanath manifestation of Shiva with his familiar trident atop the golden spire of the temple. "This place is properly called Kashi Vishwanath Temple for that particular destructive aspect of Lord Shiva," he said, bringing his eyes back down to me. "This Holy City of Kashi itself is said to have begun when Lord Brahma performed a fire sacrifice to please Lord Shiva. When the First Mother Goddess Shakti then separated herself from Shiva to help Brahma complete the creation, Brahma decided to return her to Shiva in celebration when it was done. But Brahma's son Daksha made several more fire sacrifices to transform Shakti into his own daughter Sati, who then had become the bride of Shiva.

"Yet, because Shiva had cursed Brahma for his lie about finding the first pillar's upper end, Daksha decided at the last minute to forbid the marriage," Ramesh continued as we reached the street again. "But Sati was already enamored with Shiva, so they married anyway, prompting Daksha to hold yet another *yajna* to which he did not invite the happy couple. However, when Sati attended the sacrifice anyway, she immolated herself in front of Daksha because of his repeated insults of her husband.

"This, of course, enraged Shiva, who beheaded Daksha and carrying Sati's corpse began his dance of destruction across all creation. When the other gods requested Vishnu to stop Shiva's rampage, Vishnu cut through Sati's corpse, and the pieces of her body fell throughout India at what are called Shakti Peethas," Ramesh explained. "At the places where the parts of her body came to rest, the goddess is worshipped today as an aspect of the Supreme being Adi Parashakti, the mother of the Trimurti of Lords Brahma, Shiva, and Vishnu.

"Manikarnika Ghat, where we hopefully dispatched Father this evening to Mount Kailash, is one of those Shakti Peethas," Ramesh said, starting back toward the Temple Annapurna Devi. "In fact, Kashi is said to have been founded at that very tank when Shiva came to earth up ahead there after the death of his bride Sati. Today we worship her at the Temple Vishalalshi or Annapurna just in front of us, where her likeness can be seen inside next to her companion Lord Shiva Bhairava."

"But the first Annapurna Temple itself was back in the early mists of history at nearby Vishwanath," Ramesh went on. "Sadly it was destroyed by the Turk Qutb Din Aibak in 1194 and rebuilt several times more at the site of that Gyanvapi Mosque over there before the Mughal Emperor Aurangzeb leveled it and finally built in 1669 the mosque we see today. It is said that the temple priest at that time saved the Shiva linga by jumping with it into the well there, so the original Vishwanath is thought to reside now at the bottom of the mosque's well."

We continued on down the crowded street. "The present Kashi Vishwanath Temple was built by the Maratha King Holkar about a century later. Around it are the other temples honoring the Kal Bhairava, Dandapani, and Dhudiraj manifestations of Shiva," he concluded as we turned off to enter the structure on our left. "But right now we're going to go into the Vishalakshi Temple here to pay homage to the Mother of Creation."

"I'm happy about that," I said jovially, following him. "I was tired of all these tridents and thunderbolts of destruction. It's time we did some celebrating the creation of life."

"Enjoy it while you can, Mata," Ramesh said as we proceeded toward the image of Sati. "The final rites of Shivaratri are a bath in the Ganges and a different fire ritual called the *aarti* or waving of the flame. As long as we're so near to Dasaswamedh Ghat down the river, we might as well go over to see it performed tonight. It's supposed to be beautiful."

When we left Annapurna Temple and got to that main square of Kashi, we momentarily stepped into the river and then got out to watch the *aarti* at the ghat. The sanctification of the fire and water elements was probably the same ceremony that Brahma performed to celebrate his creation of this world. Chants were intoned in the great amphitheatre here, and then about seven priests began waving aarti lamps around themselves to generate the air that would give them power in front of the sacred water of the river.

At the end of the ceremony, the priest cupped his hand over the lamp's flame, and the thousands of devotees laid flowers and incense and vermillion rice on the lip of the lamp to celebrate the fusion of these elements which had resulted in Creation. When I saw the countless humble village women bowing their heads to pay respect to our beginnings, I felt a great appreciation for our Hindu civilization. From the look on Ramu's face, he did too.

Before we started back to the Guest House, I told Ramesh I wanted to enter the large classical temple at the back of Dasaswamedh Ghat, the *mandir* dedicated to Ganga Mata. Inside a woman from the city here told me that to truly honor Shiva's Night one had to give up a great personal desire and carry Ganga water on a pilgrimage to Rameshwaram near the very southern tip of India.

As we walked back to Rashmi, I told Ramesh, "I have at last properly sent Shiva out of this vale of sorrow and back to the sacred mountains of the north with his father."

When we strolled on our way back to the guest house through the Vishwanath Gali about which I had heard such fabulous stories, Ramesh wondered whether I wanted to buy a set of the wonderful, golden earrings of Sati on display there.

"No, that is something I can forbear," I said. "Instead I hope you will let me carry the rest of the Ganga *pani* you have taken down to Rameshwaram, from which I can bring back some sand to offer at Vishwanath Temple to thank Lord Shiva for what I have learned today...."

*   *   *

Shashi began her pilgrimage directly from Varanasi, taking Priya's return ticket to Patna while she returned with Ramesh and the children in the SUV. Shashi then continued on through Patna to Kolkata and Chennai by train. At the outset, her pilgrimage spun out in reverse of her husband's life intermingled with that of her son Shiva – Varanasi, Patna, Bhagalpur, and Kolkata – as her steps in the Holy City of Kashi had proceeded through Lord Shiva's life after Mohan's cremation.

Then, from the Tamil Nadu capital of Chennai, she traveled mostly by bus inland to Madurai and from there on to Manapam, the small town at the end of the Indian mainland from which she was to cross onto the island of Rameshwaram, where at its center was located the temple that was her destination. From the beach nearest this Temple of Ramanathaswamy where the second most important of Shiva's *jyotirlinga* landed at the time of Creation, Shashi would gather the jar of sand she would bring back to Vishwanath's golden spire in Varanasi to fulfill her vow.

So at the Ramanathaswamy Temple, she circumambulated the 1212 delicately carved pillars and bathed in each of the sacred 22 tanks, from which she gained wisdom among other virtues and the eternal love of her husband. Before leaving the temple, Shashi delivered her Ganges water inside to the *shivalinga* Hanuman had brought back from the Himalayas. Then she paid obeisance to a *lingam* outside which Sita had fashioned from the local sand at the time of the *Ramayana*. Finally, before collecting her Ramanathaswamy sand to carry back, she swam out to visit the nearby Kali temple in the placid waters of the Bay of Bengal.

Prior to starting back to the north, Shashi traveled out to the eastern tip of the island where the seas meet at Land's End less than thirty kilometers from a peninsula reaching west out of Sri Lanka. It was here Rama and Hanuman rescued Sita from the clutches of Brahma's demon descendant Ravana in the *Ramayana*. And there in honor of the ablutions Rama made upon his return from this victory at nearby Rama's Bridge, Shashi stepped out toward the first of the boulders Hanuman's army used to cross the sea to rescue Sita. Only after taking these initial final steps east did Shashi turn around and begin her long journey back to Kashi.

This time she walked the length of Rameshwaram Island with hardly a stop, past the fishing boats that reaped the great harvest of lobster and shrimp and through the mantra-chanting *sadhus* who built their own sand *lingams* outside the Ramalingeshwara Temple complex around the sacred *jyotirlinga*, halting briefly at the Gandhamadhana Parvatam built around the marble footsteps of Rama himself. But then, always within easy reach of the water on either side of the long and narrow island, she continued on under the sheltering coconut trees with boughs spreading in the breeze, created by the windmills standing above the lapping of ubiquitous salt waves, pausing only to appreciate the house of India's first Muslim President APJ Abdul Kalam.

This time too she walked across the two kilometers of the busy Indira Gandhi Bridge that was initially built by the British to accommodate a narrow-gauge rail line but was re-dedicated in 1988 by her son Rajiv Gandhi to honor his mother, just a few years before he was assassinated not far away by the Tamil Tigers who were once so powerful in these parts. By the town of Mandapam at the edge of the mainland again, however, she realized she was exhausted, having slept only a few hours at Dhanushkodi Beach close by Lands End across from the straits that separated not only India and Sri Lanka but the turbulent seas of the Gulf of Mannar from the serene, green water of the Bay of Bengal.

So in this town of Mandapam she began looking for a more-protected place to spend the night, and, lo and behold, she came upon an *anganwadi* in the first settlement on the highway beyond the small city. Familiar from her volunteer work for the Association of College Women in Patna with the walled courtyards around which these help centers were invariably established, she departed the road and entered its closed patio. At its far end was a door into the adjacent building that stood open in the approaching dusk.

The lady and children in the one tent in the courtyard were battening down its hatches for the night, so Shashi proceeded directly to the open door, from which she saw three women around forty years of age, she guessed, gathered about a desk in the office inside. "Excuse me, *Srimatiya*," she said, edging into the office. "I am a Ramanathaswamy pilgrim from North India, and I was wondering if I might spend the night in the courtyard here. I have walked the entire length of the island today, and quite frankly I don't know if I can go on."

The youngest of the ladies, who was dressed in a light-blue *salwar kameez* and seated behind the desk, looked intently at Shashi then smiled. "My name is Kamala Bachari, and I am the Anganwadi for this Child Development Center," she said in English. "What are you called, *ji*?"

"I am Shashi Verma from Patna, Bihar," she replied with a slight smile. "I know next to no Tamil, and I must admit I did not expect anyone to speak English here."

"You are lucky, Srimati Verma, to have happened upon this particular children's center," said the youngest of the other two ladies, who was seated on the right side of the woman behind the desk. "Kamala is the only English-speaking Anganwadi in the villages surrounding Ramanathapuram. My name is Jaya Srinivasan," she added, standing in a gray *kurta* with *paijama* and stepping forward to extend her hand toward Shashi, "and I am Kamala's Makhyasevika or first-line supervisor."

"Actually you are doubly lucky," the oldest woman said, also standing and coming toward Shashi in a light-green *sari*. "I am Poonam Gounder, the Development Projects Officer for these two ladies, and we just happened to have a work meeting here this evening. Otherwise this Anganwadi would be so filled with children at this time that we wouldn't have time to think."

"I don't want to disturb what I'm sure is an important meeting," Shashi said, backing toward the door half a step. "I am familiar with Anganwadis and the critical work you do."

"How do you know the Child Development Centers?" Kamala asked as she assessed Shashi's dusty but expensive pink, silk *sari*. "I doubt that you have used our services before."

"I used to volunteer for the Associated Women of Patna College," Shashi explained. "We tried to facilitate the growth of Anganwadi in the villages that grew around the city there because of families moving to the capital to look for work. But as you may know, the Government of Bihar hasn't been very supportive of rural children's health programs, so we didn't make much progress developing these *anganwadiya* there."

"How do you happen to be taking a pilgrimage to Ramanathaswamy at, if you will pardon me, your advanced age, Srimati?" Ms. Gounder asked, sitting back down. "Patna is almost a continent away."

"I just cremated my husband in Varanasi," Shashi said as she stepped forward again. "Ten years ago our son Shiva passed away unexpectedly, so after my husband's cremation I paid honor to Lord Shiva in the Vishwanath Golden Temple there with my youngest son Ramesh." She paused to catch her breath and swept her eyes over all three women. "I made a vow to bring sacred Ganges water out to the Temple in Rameshwaram and take sand from it back to Kashi."

She observed the faces of the ladies facing her. "I felt it would be the best way to thank the two fine men I have lost and miss so deeply."

"That's a wonderful sentiment, Srimati Verma," the Projects Officer said. "But surely you realize there is a better way to remember them."

"What do you mean?"

"I mean by doing good for others in their stead, you will be giving them a better chance in their next life," Poonam said.

"But I was hoping that fulfilling my vow to Lord Shiva would release them from being reborn," Shashi said turning up her palms. "That as a result He would take them out of this world of illusion and give them a home up on Mount Kailash."

"You don't really believe that, do you?" Jaya said from the other side of the desk. "I would hesitate to say this to most Hindus, but I can see you are an educated woman."

"I am old enough to have learned that education and a spiritual life are not incompatible," Shashi said with authority. "So I do, in fact, believe that if I fulfill my pilgrimage vow, my husband and son who have gone on will have it better in the next stage of their existence." She paused a moment then asked, "You don't categorically reject this idea, do you, Ms. Gounder?"

"Of course, anything is possible," the Projects Officer said. "But I think that if we achieve the goals of this Child Development Office for instance, there will clearly be a better chance that the children around here will have a more fulfilling life."

"So what are the goals of this Anganwadi then?" Shashi followed up.

The middle-aged woman on the far side of the desk read from a piece of paper she lifted. "Here is the fundamental charge the Integrated Child Development Services Act imposes on every *anganwadi*. First, by providing proper inoculation against disease for both child and mother, a proper foundation for improved child development will be laid, and second, we give complete pre-natal and post-natal care for them to insure that this foundation is firm."

"In building on this base we have established, our obligations are well known," Kamala, the child-care worker behind the desk, continued as she turned to a placard on the wall in back. "To begin, we purposefully involve the client community in choosing the specific direction for administering our remaining resources. I, for example, was born and raised in this very village," she said, pointing her forefinger to the ground. "So my mother tongue is the very particular dialect of Tamil spoken around Mandapam."

"That makes sense," Shashi observed."

"Next we surveyed the community to find out what specific aspects of child development were desired here," Kamala went on as she fixed her eyes on Shashi. "In making that assessment, we pay special attention, of course, to what the community mothers want from us."

Shashi indicated her understanding by nodding, while Jaya and Poonam smiled in approval.

"At this center here, we first of all provide pre-school care and activities for all the toddlers before they go to school and then for the half-day they are not there when they first start school," Kamala said. "This service, of course, enables the mother to augment her education or supplement family income by working outside the family."

"You do not require mothers to work out of the home as a condition of allowing their children to be eligible for services here, do you?" Shashi asked.

"Certainly not. We only want to provide the mothers with alternative ways to give better opportunities to their children," Jaya said, emphasizing her point with her forefinger. "Very importantly, for example, we make available a wide range of learning about health and nutrition, and we also provide a midday meal to the kids and some bulk foods for the mothers to take home."

When Shashi said nothing in response, Poonam picked up the narrative," In addition, we teach mothers about proper breastfeeding techniques and," she paused while lifting her eyes to Shashi's again before continuing, "family planning for those who are interested."

"Have the fathers objected at all to circulating information to their wives about contraception?" Shashi said tentatively.

"It's been surprisingly rare," Poonam said. ""When the veils of ignorance are lifted, it turns out most fathers would rather provide more to fewer children than little or nothing to too many of them."

"Really," said Shashi, hiding her surprise by looking around at the other posters on the office walls.

"Absolutely," Jaya underscored the point. "When knowledge about birth control becomes common, the average man does not want to keep his wife in ignorance and completely dependent on him. He wants a partner in caring for the family, certainly as much as a woman wants to share in the responsibility of raising her family's standard of living."

"What she's saying," Kamala added, "is that most men do not want a woman just plopping themselves on him when they get the chance to."

I felt an uneasy spasm in my stomach on hearing these last words as if I fully understood Mohan for the first time now. "Yes, perhaps," I ventured, "there are other things I can do for Mohan and Shiva after I get this Rameshwaram sand back to Vishwanath at Kashi...."

*   *   *

Shashi stayed on at the Anganwadi outside Mandapam for several weeks, helping Kamala care for the children, teaching their mothers and learning herself much that science and common sense had revealed that would make life better for their families and themselves. On her way back to Varanasi, she got off the train at Patna Junction and found her way on foot for the first time to the house on Seventh Road.

When she knocked on the front door there, it was Priya who answered it. "*Namaskar, Mataji*," she said, then stooped to touch her mother-in-law's feet before stepping back and offering her admittance. "What a lovely surprise." Her beaming face betrayed no duplicity. "We've been expecting you would be finishing your pilgrimage for some time, but we thought you would call first when you got to town."

"No, Priya *bahu*," I said, smiling. "I have been trying to behave like an ordinary pilgrim in India, not an Indian-American in need of special comforts. I wanted to inconvenience you less this visit."

"You were no inconvenience the last time, Sasuma," she said as I passed into the house. "Ramesh is up at the orchards in Madhubani. It's Friday, and he finds the weekends up there restful, he says, just like your husband used to find them."

Yes, Mohan used to love it there," I said, remembering fondly those times when we went up there as a family until Tara began finding reasons not to go along. "I haven't been back there for years," I explained. "I think I'd find it too sad now that my father and husband are gone."

Priya nodded sympathetically. "I can imagine."

"Ramesh doesn't stay up there all weekend, does he?" I asked, cocking my ears to hear if the children were home. "Since my sister went to live with her son in Darbhanga, there's really no one he could stay with around Maniarwa anymore."

"Oh, Ramesh is his father's son. He's very good friends with his orchard manager in Khajauli," she said, turning around to see what I was looking at down the hall. "Besides he's built a little shelter right next to the trees. But, no, he usually comes back after a day. This time, though, the kids and I are going to go up there and meet him Sunday morning," she added. "I've taken a few days out of the office next week, and we're going to go over and see the Baag Taraag among other things."

"You're kidding," I said as she started for the kitchen. "I remember when I went there the first time after I graduated from college." I reached out to catch her hand and hold her in the room. "You don't need to go and make me tea, though, Priya."

"Don't you need some refreshment after your trip?" she said.

"No. I'm a pilgrim, remember." I thought back over the last few months. "I don't know when I've had tea just like that."

Priya turned back from the kitchen and sat down on the couch, and I took a seat in the easy chair across from it. "You will stay the rest of the night, won't you, Ma?"

"Of course," I answered, pleased that she had asked. "But I think I'll go on to Varanasi tomorrow." Then an idea occurred to me. "Then maybe I'll come over and meet you at Khajauli. I wanted to see Maniarwa before Mohan died," I explained, "and it's on the way coming back from over there, isn't it?"

"I think so," Priya said, getting up to retrieve her cell phone from her purse next to the door. "But first you must call Najib. When he found out that you had cremated Mohan before he even knew he died, he was very upset." She punched a number into the phone. "He told Ramesh he wants to go to Varanasi and pay his respects to him when you return there with the sand."

"*Are, Bap*," I said, smacking my forehead and feeling guilty. "I never thought of Naju when I was here before the cremation. Things were moving so fast it just didn't occur to me to call him." I paused and realized that I didn't even know Najib was still alive. "How is he anyway?"

"He seems fine," she said, handing me the phone. "Go ahead and talk to him now. He might even drive you over to Varanasi and up to Khajauli when you're done there...."

*   *   *

Najib did all he could to facilitate Shashi's fulfillment of her vow. He drove her to Varanasi and helped her offer the Rameshwaram sand to the *shivlinga* in the Vishwanath Golden Temple. From there, they decided to go to Maniarwa, where Naj would return Shashi, through Kushinagar, the town straight north near the Nepali border in which the Lord Buddha passed on to the next world. Once there in Kushinagar, they were so close to Lumbini, Buddha's birthplace across the frontier in Nepal, they went on to further honor the Verma men by meeting Arash, who happened to be celebrating Gautama's birth there, before they turned west toward Maniarwa.

From Lumbini, they returned back to India from Dibni on the bank of the Burhi Gandak where they passed the simple bamboo shrine laden with flowers which marked the spot where Mohan had actually died. There the two pilgrims, the deceased monk's dutiful widow and his best friend, laid marigolds and a cluster of his beloved lychees on his memorial and anointed them with the purest of Ganga water they had carried from Kashi. Then they proceeded on toward home through the equally holy ground of Paschim Champaran District, where Mahatma Gandhi had almost a century earlier begun his *satyagraha* movement against the British indigo planters.

They stayed the next night in Motihari in rooms of the Dak Bungalow, which had once been the residence of George Orwell's father during his tenure as the Raj's District Magistrate there in 1904, and got up early the next morning to drive onto to the home of Shashi's niece in Maniarwa, where she would meet Ramesh's family before Najib turned south to return to complete his circuit to Patna. But when Najib stopped for tea in Sitamarhi, the two pilgrims learned of a temple in the nearby village of Punaura, which marked the miraculous conception of the Goddess Sita in a vessel unearthed by her father King Janaka when he was plowing a field so long ago to honor the god of rain Lord Indra, and they decided to visit that last landmark.

There for the first time in years Shashi heard the lyrical lilt of her native Maithili. Under an ancient paakar tree, near where Sita was said to have rested the night when she came from the seat of her father's Kingdom of Janakpur to visit her birthplace, they met a woman devotee seeking alms in its shade. This tattered woman told them of how the adjacent Shivghar District had separated from Sitamarhi a decade and a half earlier because the celebration and commerce of the pilgrimages honoring Sita in Sitamarhi District had become completely dominated by men to the exclusion of women.

Both Shashi and Najib had thought that such a situation was ironic in the homeland of Sita and decided to drive the several hours to Shivghar Town to spend the last night of their pilgrimage there. By sunset, they were pulling into its small district headquarters and quickly found an inn in the center of town. In the inn, they were greeted by another elderly woman, who explained that she was tending the place because most of her family were several miles to the east on the banks of the Baghmati River, where the beginning of the local Chaiti Maiya festival was being celebrated.

"What is this Chaiti Maiya Puja?" Shashi asked her hostess while she was warming them a small meal on the fire. "I have never heard of it before."

"It's an ancient festival special to this place," the old lady said, turning to look at Shashi. "It is sort of a Chhath, which was celebrated two times a year before the Vedas were written, today at the beginning of each year and then during the harvest season. The name *Chhath* comes from the number six, because the harvest always begins on the sixth day of the month of Kartika."

"So where does Chaiti Maiya come in?" Shashi asked

"It is the modern name for the Goddess Usha," the lady said as she stirred the curry. "The festival celebrates the bounty of life on this Earth that is made possible by the sun and the rain, both of which are worshipped during the ceremonies." She glanced at Shashi again. "It is said the King Surya Patra Karna of Ang Desh was the first to give thanks to the warmth of the sun and the coolness of water from the seat of his Kingdom at old Bhagalpur. His wife was Usha or

Chaiti Maiya, and she is able to remove a person's troubles in this world." She paused. "In other words, she can liberate anyone who worships properly during this life on earth."

The lady looked outside into the deepening darkness. "Traditionally at Chaiti Maiya water and milk are offered to the sunset," she continued as she began to dish rice and curry onto silver *thali* for the visitors "But since the festival is closely associated with dawn of our life here in the east, the rising sun is the most important.

"Tomorrow is the last day of Chaiti Maiya," she said, bringing the plates to the Shashi and Najib. "If you go east tomorrow morning to the Baghmati at the point where there is a mound on its bank, you will see the close of the rite. There women devotees will make the final offering that allows them to break their fast which they are performing today."

"You know, I haven't actually eaten anything yet today," Shashi said, sliding her plate on the table back toward the woman. "I think I will keep this fast till then too."

"Don't bother about fasting now," the old innkeeper said as she extended her hand toward the food she had prepared for Shashi. "You've missed the first three days of the Chaiti Chhath already anyway. You can begin your observances at the harvest rites in six months."

"No," Shashi said resolutely." I want to start now, imperfect as I am. My friend Najib here can eat what you have made for me if you can't."

"He is a Muslim?' the woman, apparently recognizing the origin of his name, asked.

"Yes. He is my late husband's best friend," Shashi said quickly. "He missed Mohan's cremation at Kashi, but he has just taken me back there to deliver to the Vishwanath *shivlinga* the sand I had brought back from Rameshwaram after Mohan's cremation."

"*Are, Bap,*" the woman said, bending over to retrieve my plate. "We have many Muslims who worship the sun and rain on Chhath…."

Early the next morning, Shashi and Najib descended from their rooms and set out to greet and worship the rising sun at Deekli, where the women celebrants honored the dawn with the rice *kheer* and wheat *chebua* they had carefully prepared. Then Shashi followed the thousands of *vratta* women into the waters of the Baghmati to complete the ritual.

Later Najib and she partook of the *chebua, kheer,* and bananas that were left over to break the fast of the observers. While they were savoring the delicious treats from the traditional banana leaves on which they ate, a Western man dressed in a *dhoti* seated himself across from them.

"I know you," he said, smiling at Shashi. "We met several years ago at the Ganapati Temple in New York. My name at birth was Alan Findhorst but I am now Harihara Pashipati, and we were attending the same seminar on Dharmic Universalism."

"You did look familiar," Shashi said as she reached out to shake his extended hand. "I am Shashi Verma, and this is Najib Khan, my late husband Mohan's best friend. We have just come from Varanasi where my family had cremated him."

"I'm so sorry," Harihara said, putting his hands together and dipping his head. "So how do you happen to be at Deekli?"

"We are headed to the east, to my native village in Madhubani District," she answered, "where Naj will drop me off with my family and he will go back to his home in Patna." She studied the thin American man a moment and asked, "What about you? How do you happen to be at this out-of-the-way place?"

"We didn't just happen to be here," he said, turning to motion over another Western man in rich purple and gold robes whom Shashi also recognized from her Dharmic seminar a few years back in New York. "Guru Rishiji found this area some time ago. We here have been establishing an ashram in Shivghar Town for the last half year."

"You mean there's a Sanatan Ashram in that little town we stayed last night?' Shashi said, thinking that she could not help but believe that she had been drawn here because of it. "Do you think we could find rooms there for tonight?"

Harihari said something quietly to the man in the rich robes as he came toward our circle.

"Most assuredly," said Rishiji as he seated himself next to Harihara. "I think it is more than mere chance that has brought you to us. You know the circumstances of the founding of this new Shivghar Dsitrict, don't you?"

"It's the reason we came here," Najib said. "Shashi and I were both intrigued by the idea that a district like this devoted to Lord Shiva would be more hospitable to women than the District which is the birthplace of Sita just a few kilometers away."

"Indeed," Rishiji said, nodding in agreement. "And you too, Najib, do you as a Muslim also believe in the freedom of the fairer sex?"

"Of course he does," Shashi interjected brusquely. "As my late husband's dearest friend, he would believe in nothing less."

"And the two of you came here together?" Rishiji inquired, shaking off the restraining arm of Harihara Pashupati. "Have you also lost your wife, Najib?"

"As a matter of fact he has not," Shashi said as she felt the anger rise to her face. "But, anyway, since both of us are almost ninety years of age, neither one of us would have a desire to remarry, Rishiji."

"No, I suppose not," the Guru said, dropping his eyes and thinking. "So it may be, Mrs. Verma, that you are, in fact, the sort of person we are looking for in our Sanatan Ashram here in Shivghar."

"What do you mean?" I asked, uncertain if he thought me available now that he realized I was not attached in a physical way to Najib. "I hope you don't think that all ashrams in North Bihar have to have a *dasin* as they might have had fifty years ago."

"Certainly not," Rishiji said with force. "I understand you have been to our society in New York City and know we don't tolerate such immorality. What we're looking for here is a woman to direct an ashram for people who want to become modern Dharmis. Shivghar is a model district created for the modern Indian woman who wants to live a rural existence." He paused here and scrutinized me closely. "It is the perfect place to show that a female can be in charge of a form of communal life that is beyond the anachronisms of both capitalism and socialism. In other words, a society that is true to the dictates of the *puranas* but which has been tweaked to fit the demands of modern global civilization...."

Chapter Twelve

Shashi decided that fate had given her a perfect opportunity at Shivghar. During the years that Mohan had lived as a Buddhist monk of the Forest Tradition in India, her commitment to the Universal Sanatan Dharmi Society as the hope for the Hinduism of the future had become more resolute. Now there was a chance to help its beliefs become a reality. So she nominally became the executive of the Shivghar Sanatan Ashram and Harihara the collective's administrator. Both he, as a former American Peace Corps Volunteer doing dairy work in Motihari during the early-Seventies, and Shashi would reside permanently in the Ashram , while Guru Rishiji would remain in the U.S. but visit on an as-needed basis to give critical direction when problems came up.

One such problem arose in the middle of 2014 after Shashi had been the SSA Director for almost five years. Rishiji had come to India on the Society's Concorde via a direct flight from the Society's new headquarters in Kansas City to the Indira Gandhi Airport in Delhi, which was the nearest location to the Ashram with runways big enough to handle the plane. The Guru with Ambien had gotten a good 8 hours of sleep on the flight to India and had chartered a private Lear jet that got him into Muzaffarpur before the time he had left from Kansas City, almost exactly on the opposite side of the planet.

On the hour and a half drive to Shivghar in the Ashram's Hummer that still got him on site a few minutes short of a day since he had left home in the middle of the U.S., Shashi, who had gone along to pick him up at the airport, explained to him in detail the problem that had required his presence. "If it was up to me, I wouldn't have bothered you, Guruji," Shashi said from the passenger's seat, where she sat across from the driver Kishore Sinha. "I would have just gone ahead and authorized the purchase of a desktop computer. But Harihara insisted that you would want the last word on this decision, so I agreed in the interest of accord."

"You recognize, Shashi, that all our facilities – even in the United States – are completely computer-free, don't you?" Guruji said, smiling benevolently from the beige leather of the spacious back seat. "There is a reason for that, you know."

"I understand that a principal tenet of the Sanatan Society is the avoidance of consumerism, Guruji," she replied obediently. "But one computer in the administrator's office would free up many Dharmi hours for more productive tasks in the fields. It seemed like an easy decision, Sri Rishi," she added, dipping her head to him while bringing her palms together before her chest.

"You forget the danger of the Internet, Srimati," Guruji said, returning his eyes from looking out the one-way side window to fix upon mine. "Once we have a computer, the Dharmis' children will be clamoring to get on the web. Even the driver here," he went on, "would not object to them doing so, would you?"

"Not at all, sahib" Kishore snapped to out of his afternoon heat haze to affirm.

"See what I mean?" Guruji said to me. "We would have no way to keep the children from whatever filth they could find on the Internet."

"But there is no Internet cable anywhere in Shivghar as far as I know," I argued I now knew in vain.

"But eventually there will be. There is no way to stop it from getting here sooner or later," he said calmly. "Look at this man – Sneadham's his name, isn't it? - who stole the secrets from the CIA," he declared by way of example. Besides," he leaned forward and whispered to me, "I know Harihara wants it, and," he dropped his voice even lower and held up his hand to shield his next words from Kishore in case he understood more English than he let on, "I going to admit this only to you – I don't really trust him…."

We made it through Banti on the divided National highway 26, and when Kishore then pushed the accelerator all the way down, I turned back around to face forward and buckled my seat belt with blue knuckles. At Nehsi in Champaran, Kishore slowed down a bit, and I asked Rishi if he wanted to stop and get some tea.

He shook his head and waved us on. Kishore pressed the accelerator again till we reached Brakla, where we turned north and almost immediately crossed the Chota Gandak.

It was not much longer before we passed into our district, and a short time later, we entered Shivghar Town on the narrow and winding Highway 102. As the road turned east, we came upon the gate to the Ashram.

Kishore sounded the horn, and the peep hole was opened to ascertain that the huge, electrified, iron door could be rolled back safely. In just seconds, we were in front of the office, where Harihara greeted us.

"*Aap kaisee hai,* Guruji?" Harihara salaamed the Rishi. "*Sab thik hai aapna safar ke douran?*"

"It went according to clockwork," the Guru said, getting out of the car as Kishore held the door and helped the Guru descend to the ground. "I could use a spot of tea now, though, Hari, if you don't mind," he said, wiping his brow. "It's bloody hot here."

We went inside where Harihara switched on an overhead *punkah* and nodded to a *baira*, who turned around and disappeared through the back door in front of which he had been standing.

Guruji, who was adorned in the same gold and purple robes he always wore, looked at Hari and lifted his palm up to the ceiling fan. "A bit higher, Hari," he said, moving his eyes over to the switch. "Everything's hot and up to date in Kansas City, but it's nowhere near as humid as here. If I had to spend more time in Shivghar," he went on, "I'd probably break down and let you air-condition a few rooms." For some reason, the Guru insisted on calling Harihara *Hari*

Harihara returned his smile and walked back over to turn up the speed of the fan. "Well, in that case, will you authorize a bare-bones Mac for the office here?" He turned and spread out his hand to the side room opposite the door through which the *baira* had disappeared. There we saw the prim, middle-aged Kunju, who was the Ashram's clerk, in a green sari sitting behind a desk nearly surrounded by old file cabinets.

"Before we get to that, Hari," the Guru said, looking toward the door through which the peon promptly returned with a fully loaded tray, "I trust we can have a bite to eat, and if it's not too hot outside when we're done," he removed the orange silk scarf that had been hanging around his neck and used it to wipe off the perspiration which had gathered there, "I was hoping we might even get a look at the fields."

"Of course, Guru," Harihara said and then turned to me. "Are they still weeding the maize and *gehu* this afternoon, Shashi?"

"I expect so," I said, meeting the Guru's eyes which I felt were upon me. "A number of our best *kisan* happen to be pregnant now, but there should still be some Dharmis working when the sun gets lower…."

In another hour, the Guru, Harihara, and I started alongside the paddy field behind the office for the lentils, corn, and wheat that were planted beyond it all the way to the ashram's back wall, which was lined with neem trees. Although there were few pigeon peas grown in this western edge of Mithila, this acreage of cash crops always reminded me of our old family plot my father worked so long outside of Maniarwa

"It looks like there will be a good harvest this year," the Guru observed as we reached the deep green rows of maize that were already above our heads.

"I think so," I said, reaching out my hand to brush the strong but supple stalks. "The monsoon has been late this year, but the irrigation system has done very well."

We began to pass a group of mostly women fieldworkers on their haunches pulling the weeds from the narrow, hand-dug canal several rows back from us. "How many Dharmi are at the Ashram now, Hari?" Guru asked. "The last time I looked, there were 24 Americans. Remind me how many Indians were here at last count?"

"Not quite as many," Harihara answered, shrugging his shoulders. "Two left last week. One because his mother died in Dumma Kishore. The other because her husband from Kezva came and got her."

"So now including the 3 with child, that means we have 19 Shivgharis living in the ashram at this point?" I asked no one in particular.

"No, it's much more than that," Harihara said. "There are at least half again that many staff like Kunju and the *baira* in the office here. You're right, though," he added, "we now have only 19 residents from the District. But like we Dharmi say," he said, smiling, "it's quality over quantity in the Sanatan."

"Yes, quality is important," Guruji agreed. "I didn't spend seven years getting a doctorate at the University of Missouri for nothing." Turning to me, he asked, "Are our evening English classes still well attended, Shashi?"

"Regularly by over ninety-five percent of the Indian Dharmi," I said. "and—"

"A hundred percent of the Americans usually attend the Hindi sessions," Harihara offered proudly. "For me, teaching those conversation classes are the best part of my day."

"And what about the Veda classes?" Guruji asked.

"Not as well attended," Harihara said, and I shook my head in dismay with him. "Both the locals and the *videsi* say they've already learned most of the Puranas."

"That's unacceptable," the Guru declared. "The Sanatan is the eternal way. What the Vedas teach us is the thing we hold most dear in our Society."

"We're trying," I said, catching up to the Rishi to walk alongside of him. "Alan – I mean Harihara – excuses anyone who goes to Vedic instruction from some chores the next day."

"But we still can't get most of the Shivgharis to go," Harihara said from behind us. "The Americans will sit through anything to avoid washing dishes, but the Indians are proud and stubborn. They say they've grown up with the Vedas, and we can't teach them anything new."

"We're going to have to do something about this," the Guru said, bringing down his palm to slap the front of his thigh for emphasis. "The essence of the Guru's Sanatan Dharmi Society is the eternal and true Indian way. We call it Sanatan Dharm instead, but it is the true Hindu religion the Vedas spawned."

"In other words, you mean the Hinduism the Aryans brought to India and developed here," I said. "You don't say that, but—"

"No, how many times have I told you, it is not the same thing as modern Hinduism," Guruji declared as he came to a halt. "The Hinduism in India now is Vedantism as degraded by a thousand years of Muslim and Christian rule. What I teach – the religious history I have made – is the eternal law of the *Puranas* before that degradation."

The Guru started to walk again toward the cornfield, and Harihara and I exchanged glances and followed him.

"This cornfield we are coming to, "Rishiji began again, "is the property of the GSDS and no one else. We accept Jains and Buddhists, Muslims and Christians, Native Americans and anyone else here as long as they accept the primacy, the truth, the eternality of the original Vedas as modified for these times by the GSDS," he proclaimed. "No one else can claim this land."

"You mean the Vedas modernized as you see fit, Guruji," I said as he came to another stop alongside the first cornstalk we reached. There the Guru stooped down to caress it where it emerged from the dark soil. "Or not modernized as the case might be," I continued, "like the computer Harihara wanted to help in the Ashram administration but you don't."

The Guru looked angrily up at me. "You were not supposed to say anything about that outside the office," he said, pausing for effect without straightening up. "As I indicated to Hari when we first got here," he went on, "we will talk about that in due time. Right now I wanted to give you a lesson about this hardy plant that the natives of our America domesticated there. The Aztecs of Mexico, to be specific, just about the time the Spaniards arrived there."

He was more gentle in beginning this lesson, and Harihara and I looked at each other again as we squatted down so we could see the Guru's eyes as he bent over. "Hey, you're pretty good at that," he said to Harihara. "I never could get the hang of squatting like that, but each of us is good at some things and not others," he added, looking deeply into my eyes. "As you know, the first tenet of GSDS as with every religion is that it is guided by a *true* guru. By virtue of my religious studies and capacity for visions, I am uniquely qualified to be that *rishi* for our Guru's Sanatan Dharmi Society."

Harihara and I both dropped our eyes and nodded.

"Now back to this corn plant," the Guru continued. "See this tassel," which he lovingly clasped, "that the Aztecs under the guidance of the Spaniards learned to nurture for the wild fruit within. Corn has become one of the most important – perhaps *the* most important – food in the world."

He looked up at us listening carefully to him and went on, "And see how it flourishes next to the paddy here in India. It is not so tasty for human consumption, but corn is wonderful nourishment for animals," he spoke slowly for this to sink in. "In fact, you Hari are trying to develop a strain of maize on this very farm that the sacred cow might grow to love, and—"

"I know, Rishiji," Harihara said, "and Native-American corn may make each of the five products of the cow better at accomplishing their tasks for us humans who worship Mata Gai."

"Precisely," Guru said. "And the corn-fed milk will make us smarter, and—"

"And the corn-produced dung will better chase away the cold of the night here beneath the mountains," Harihara continued to recite, "and its urine better to shield us from the mosquitoes." I watched Guru's facial muscles tighten at the interruption. "Except that I don't think it will," he said. "I was a dairy volunteer here in India before I worked with poultry, and I don't think we'll ever get any better milk or *ghee* or cheese out of cows by feeding them corn."

The Guru's stony silence was deafening.

"So like you say, Guruji, some things – like the Vedas with the Qur'an – can't be mixed or blended," Harihara concluded. "And we can't mix and blend corn and cows either," I added softly. "So you, or any guru, is not always righ—"

"I see you have been talking about this," the Guru cried, moving his eyes between the two of us. "You know that the GSDS credo does not permit such sacrilege. Its truth extends into every field of human endeavor, every aspect of human concern, and cannot be contradicted."

"But it is fundamental to Hinduism that no single human being is infallible," I said quietly. "Even you."

"Have you been doing the mantra," Guru demanded of me, "every night when you meditate?" His eyes shifted wildly to Harihara. "Have you been eating the *egg* which you Peace Corps people made so popular here in Shivghar?" Then back to me, he said, "Have you two been having sex outside of marriage?"

Both of us shook our heads slowly. "No, of course not."

"Of course not," I repeated partially to mask the smile that wanted to erupt in the wrinkles of my ninety-year old face.

Rishi stood up and looked over at the dozen eyes of the fieldworkers that peered at us through the corn rows. "I think we better finish this in the office," he said, starting back the way we had come. "Or better yet," he amended the thought while he chuckled bitterly, "maybe we should take a *chilam* or two together on the patio before we do."

We also rose and followed him while I said, "No can do, Rishi. We strictly abstain from *ganja* at the Ashram."

Nonetheless, we were seated in wicker chairs around the low, matching table outside the office a quarter of an hour later as Alan – Harihara, I mean – and I watched Guru draw deeply on an American Spirit he had retrieved from a brown package in his bag. "I can't believe I'm hearing this," he said. "You want to sell the Ashram?"

Both Alan and I nodded. "And we think we should split the proceeds half and half between the global office in Kansas City and among the people here," I said as I watched Rishi's face grow redder.

"And we'll split our half pro rata among all those who have worked these last years here," Alan said. "To each according to the number of minor children dependent upon him, her or them."

"So you've become a socialist, Hari?" Rishi demanded, shaking his head in dismay. "And you had specifically agreed with our principle of the eternal over the material, and, moreover, you were the one to suggest that our Manifesto sanctify all rights in private property."

"Which also demands the protection of all rights of inheritance," Alan added. "How does that square with the 'abolition of all income not earned by work' contained in its language?"

"What's inconsistent about that?" Rishi demanded. "Remember, our manifesto also favors decentralizing all national banking systems and shifting the means of communication and transportation into family-based local institutions."

"And it also urges that the first resort against crime be 'based in the individual person, his family, and his local community'," Alan said. "That, in itself, causes us some concern."

"Especially in a country like India where there is some history of communal violence," I added. "In the end, it seems that GSDS has taken on a radically extremist political agenda."

Rishi was silent for a minute. "Okay," he finally said, throwing his hands up. "I can see that we're going to have to part ways. How many weeks of severance pay do you want?"

"I don't think you've been listening to us," Alan said quietly. "We want the Ashram to be sold, and half the proceeds to come to GSDS personnel living here."

"You can have a third," the Guru said. "And I'm being generous. No one here has invested a cent of their own in this place."

"Half," I replied. "Haven't you heard of the concept of sweat equity?"

"Forty percent," Guru said. "We're still paying off the balance on this land."

"Fifty percent," I said. "You forget all of us Dharmis paid for you to fly over to Delhi in a Concorde...."

*   *   *

With the approximately million rupees, Alan and I each got out of the early 2015 sale of the Ashram after all the other distributions from the proceeds, the two of us set our sights on some acreage right on the district boundary line on the road south of Shivghar town near the confluence of the Baghmati and Chota Gandak rivers. The Friday after we deposited the money in the First Shivghar Bank, we caught a bus to Darbhanga and then headed up north on the train to talk to Ramesh, who was working on his lychee orchards at Khajauli for the weekend.

From Khajauli Station, it was a ten-minute *tonga* ride to the hut Mohan had finally built on the near side of the orchards for the nights he wanted to spend on the land. Ramesh had clearly improved and added to the structure, but when we finally arrived, there was only the faintest light of a lantern turned down to show that we were expected. So I called out, "Hello, Ramu, Priya, anybody here?"

"Ma," Ramu's muffled voice came from within. "Is that you?"

"It is," I answered. "Is there room at the inn?"

"Are you alone?" Ramesh said, as I heard a *charpoy* creak inside as he got up.

"Alan came with me as I told you he would," I said. "Our money came through from the sale of the ashram today, and we've located some land in southern Shivghar that looks perfect for what we want to do."

Ramesh pulled back the door and came out into the dim light of the verandah, where he lifted the lantern off the pole on which it hung. "Well, let's hear about it tomorrow," he said smiling while he turned up the flame a bit, and his features emerged from the shadows. "Everything always sounds more promising in the light of day."

"Sounds good to me," I said, seating myself on a bench by the outside table.

"You mind sleeping out here?" Ramu said to Alan, indicating a mat rolled-up and leaning against the wall of the hut. "We've got a narrow *charpoy* for Ma inside, but that's all the extra sleeping accommodations we have here."

"No problem," Alan said, removing his pack and setting it on the bench next to me. "I've got my trusty sleeping bag with me as always."

"Come on in then, Ma," Ramesh said, getting up to pull back the door, but he stopped before he went inside. "We'll see you in the morning, Alan. Make sure you turn off the lantern before you get settled in."

I was tired from the long journey and quickly fell into a deep sleep in the fresh air of my Mithila homeland once again….

The next morning I awoke to the sounds of Ramu and Priya bustling about the fire pit to prepare the morning tea. I heard my friend introduce himself as "Alan Findhorst" as I wiped the sleep from my eyes, and then my son asked him, "So what exactly is your plan for the land over in Shivghar?"

"Your mother wants to set up an *anganwadi* there for certain," Alan answered. "Other than that we're not entirely sure what we want to do. We're only clear on how we want to do it differently than what the GSDS did in its ashram in Shivghar town," he added. "We're here in part to have you help us figure it out."

"That's what I understand," Ramesh said, chuckling as I emerged into the sunlight rubbing my eyes. "Ma has come a long way since my father died. She's told me how much she wants to change things that she had accepted so easily when she lived in India before."

My breast swelled with pride. Since Shiva's death, I had realized how much I had harmed my children by my many sessions away from home at the Institute, and I was determined to be here a long time for them now. "Ramu's absolutely correct," I said, smiling at Priya stoking the fire as I walked over to join the men. "When I think about how shallow and selfish I was as a young mother I realize I have a lot to make up for."

"Oh, you weren't that bad, Mother," Ramesh said, sliding over on the bench to make room for me. "You were always good to us when you were at home, and you wouldn't be the person you are today without going through all the troubles you had."

I thought a moment and saw that he had a point. "You're right, Ramu," I said. "But when I remember how good Najib was to me when we wandered into Shivghar the first time, I cringe when I think of how I was so ashamed that my poor old dad's father may have had some Muslim blood. At first I even tried to hide that part of his background from Mohan."

"It's ironic, isn't it," Ramesh said, gazing off into the rows of full, lush lychee trees to reflect, "that Pita would probably have married you sooner if he had known that one of Grandpa's ancestors had been a low-caste convert to Islam."

"I didn't know that," Priya said as she pumped water into the kettle for the tea before turning to me. "If I had, I wouldn't have been so nervous around you. I'm sure Ram told you right away my mother was a Shudra."

"Which is one reason I fell in love with you," Ramesh said and laughed. "I never could stand those stout Brahmin girls who powdered their faces so much they looked like ghosts washed over."

"I agree," Alan endorsed the sentiment. "For those with European roots who've come to America, the bronzed skin of those who've grown up in the sun here is like coming back to our own humble roots."

I looked at Alan with surprise. "You see why I've partnered with this man on this cooperative idea," I said to Ramesh and Priya. "Alan's about as far away from a caste-ridden Brit or Brahmin as a human being can be. And it's not an act," I added. "A lot of things I found objectionable about the Sanatan Dharmi operation he initially pointed out to me."

Priya began serving her signature *alu* and lentil curry onto tin plates. "I guess I better get the *puri* warming," Ramesh said, getting up and walking over to open and feed the simple, clay oven. "So what exactly is it you wanted to talk with me about concerning your open fields, your *Maidan* in Sivghar District?"

"What a perfect name for what we want to accomplish at Tajiani," I had to say. "Maybe you want to get involve—"

"Maybe we should call it Mata's Tajiani Maidan," Alan offered over my words.

"One of the things I was interested in doing there is cultivating lychees," I lifted my voice slightly to say. "It's not far from Muzaffarpur, and everyone agrees the lychees from there are the most delicious in the world."

"And the soil at Tajiani is even better than Muzaffarpur's," Alan excitedly added.

"And milligram for milligram, the lychee is one of the most healthy and nutritious foods in the world," Priya authoritatively declared.

"What a coincidence," Ramu said, directing his attention back to the oven. "We're going to have some lychee salsa we've concocted to put on our breakfast *puri* when I get them out to you."

The meal turned out to be one of the most savory I've ever had, causing me to remember the time Mohan secretly made the food for our picnic lunch outside Islampur so many years ago. "Besides helping us with growing lychees," I said to my son, wiping the sweet and tart sauce off my plate with the last morsel of *puri*, "you might want to take a more active role in what we will call the Maidan, that is if Alan agrees."

"To what?" Alan said, smiling. "Of course, I'd love to have Ramesh get involved at Tajiani, and the Maidan is a perfect name for our cooperative."

"You're pushing fifty now, Ramu," I went on to convince him to join us. "Your kids are doing well on their own, so you don't want to stay too long in the overseer role with Ram like Mohan did with you."

"Oh, I don't know," Ramesh replied straightforwardly. ""Dad wasn't much older than I am now when he started taking me over to Bihar Bus terminal on the weekends. And bringing me up to these orchards too," he added wistfully as he looked out into the morning dew lifting from the trees. "But, seriously, I thought you'd never ask," he said, throwing us a wide grin. "Three," he said, looking from me to Alan, "is a much better number than two anyway."

"And four rounds out three exquisitely," I offered, turning to Ramu's still-winsome wife. "You're about ready to counsel some happy people again, aren't you, Priya? Hopefully we're going to have a lot of them who'll still need a little help at the Maidan, you know."

"Yeah, I might just like to do that," she said, nodding slowly after pondering the idea for a second. "But I don't want to get involved any further than some counseling," she continued, "and perhaps help in the orchard," she grinned, "besides making my special salsa."

"What do you mean *your* special salsa?" Ramu said, laughing. "I thought we came up with it together."

"So we're settled then," said Alan, summing up. "For the leadership and management of the Maidan, we'll just be three then." He paused a moment, then went on enthusiastically. "Mataji at the top, and Ramesh and I as co-directors just below her. The place will be in the center of Bihar after all, and a woman really should be the face of the Tajiani ki Maidan to the rest of the state."

"Are you certain that's what you want?" I asked, and the others waved their heads in unequivocal agreement. "Okay, but one thing is for sure," I continued. "We will be guided by the most hallowed Hindu principles of tolerance for those who follow other forms of spirituality. I don't know exactly how we'll work it out, but we won't turn anyone away who sincerely wants to join us there because of their faith or lack of a religion. And we won't allow anyone to pressure someone else to change their preferred expression of their spirituality."

"Sounds like a good first principle," Ramesh said, and Alan and Priya nodded in agreement.

We all sat there in silence for some time to appreciate the enormity of what we had decided.

"I've got a lot of things I should make up for in my life," I said finally. "I've hurt many people, but I do not think I would be here proposing these specifics to make our dream a reality unless I had taken the path I have. Because if I hadn't taken the path I have, I would not now ready to correct myself and align with the powers of the universe...."

*   *   *

Ramesh and Priya contributed a third, equal share of the down payment, and Alan and I made an offer to the elderly *zamindar* on the land at the confluence along the Shivghar District border. When it was accepted, Ramu and Priya turned the basic operation of their land sales, bus routes, Madhubani district orchards, and counseling offices in Patna over to their son, son-in-law, and/or workers and established their principal residence at Tajiani ki Maidan as did Alan and myself.

Ramesh and Alan dug into the preparation of a large, prime orchard of Sahi lychee trees there, though Ramu continued to travel the state lining up donations for our cooperative and markets for all its products. I too, as the face of the Maidan, had to travel widely at first recruiting cooperants and all those who wanted to contribute to our social and spiritual experiment. Alan as a result fell into the position of administering the day to day functioning of the Maidan's village and *bighas*, and Priya spent an increasing amount of her time at the cooperative, being available to resolve problems of our cooperants and those others who temporarily sought love and care there. Soon her skill too became critical to the Maidan's survival.

One day in the middle of the month of Phalguna during the cooperative's third year of existence, a young couple from Shivghar town sought sanctuary with us just as the paddy was turning green and the lentils beginning to sprout and the first buds on the lychee trees bursting forth into the warm breezes rolling down the mountains and over the plain. The young bride

Saida had been promised by her family to the scion of an old *zamindari* family in Shivghar but had fallen in love with a low-caste Hindu boy named Navin who had gone to secondary school with her. When they ran off to Kolkata to get married, neither of the families wanted them to come home, so they appealed to us for admittance to the Maidan, which we immediately granted.

The problem quickly became that neither of their families could let the matter go at that. In the following two weeks that the couple had been living at the Maidan, I had received several delegations from Navin's joint family demanding that I expel the "Muslim harlot" and one from Saida's family asking that I return her to it so she could be instructed in the duties of a Muslim woman. In either case, it seemed to me that Saida's life would be in danger.

Indeed, that proved to be true. In the communal tension that the government of the Bharatiya Sangh Hindutva had initially brought into North Bihar and, indeed, all over India, alternating crowds of Hindus and then Muslims and then the other again starting gathering at our front gate, demanding that Saida be released to them, until finally a radical BSH activist shot Saida while she was helping harvest a field just beyond the fence separating the Maidan from the road leading past its front gate.

Fortunately the shot only grazed her shoulder, but the incident only whetted the appetite for violence of the most extreme BSH cadres and incensed the local Muslim community. As a result, both groups now came daily to demonstrate in front of our gate, and everyone came to realize that if something was not done, it was only a matter of time before the cooperative would be engulfed in communal strife.

Finally, one day when both groups were being particularly virulent to each other, Alan and Ramesh sought me out at the *anganwadi* wing of the Maidan's main building, where Saida,

Priya, and I would provide child care and counseling through an ayurvedic medicine class to the small children of the cooperative and most of their mothers. "Shashi, Ramesh and I have just come from the front gate, and we can no longer control the situation there," Alan cried breathlessly when they reached me in the classroom. "Besides that, on our way in here just now, we passed Saida directing the games of the kids on the playground, and I could see that her arm has become so infected that we are going to have to take her to a physician in Shivghar town."

"She refuses to go," I said to both the men as I looked toward the sound of the commotion that was coming from our front gate. "She doesn't want to leave the Maidan, and under the circumstances, I can't say that I blame her."

"Maybe we can kill two birds with one stone," my ever-practical son Ramesh said. "We'll take her to town in the Wagoneer, and both of Muslims and Hindus chanting outside will be brought to their senses when they realize how badly Saida is hurt."

"He certainly is his father's son," Priya said to me as she joined us from her office down the hall. "Only a son of Mohan could be at once so pragmatic yet so trusting. It'd be dangerous even for an armored car to try and ease its way through that crowd outside now."

I thought for a moment. "But we may not have a choice," I said to the others as the noise from the protesters rose to a crescendo again. "Clearly the treatment of Saida's infection is beyond my skill, and we can't just let her die here." My eyes fixed on Priya as I went on, "And if we don't do something about those people outside, they're going to eventually come in here and harm her enough to kill her."

"Ma's right," Ramesh said, looking at his wife. "I say we have to try to get the Wagoneer through the demonstrators to Shivghar."

"But I'll talk to them first," I offered. "We'll all go outside the gate, and I'll try and speak to the protesters before we try and bring the Jeep through."

"It's too risky for Shashi," Alan said after pondering my suggestion. "I say Ramesh and I try and calm the crowd down first, and Shashi and Priya can bring Saida through in the vehicle while we're talking to them."

"No way," Priya said, holding up her hands. "I'll drive, but only after Shashi talks to the protesters. She's the only one who can communicate with both the Hindus and Muslims."

"We'll all go out front first," I said. "We'll surround Saida to protect her, and the crowd will see from her arm that we have to get through." I paused to make sure that everyone agreed. "Then Priya'll go back inside to bring out the Jeep, and we'll all get in and leave."

"Okay, let's do it," Alan said, starting for the garage beyond the other side of the building. "I'll bring the Jeep over to this side of the gate and meet you there."

"Priya, will you and Ramesh go to talk to Saida while I dismiss my class," I said, starting back toward the classroom. "I'll join you on the playground in a minute."

"I happened to have Navin waiting in my office right now," Priya said, turning to go back down the hall. "He was concerned about what's happening outside, and I'll see if he'll help us convince Saida to go along with this plan," she continued. "Ramesh, can you get Saida to bring her kids into the courtyard, and I'll meet you there."

A few minutes later, we had convinced Saida we had to try to get her to Shivghar, and the four of us left the courtyard to find Alan leaning against the Jeep behind the closed gate. Ramesh dug his keys out of his pocket as he walked past him to the gate, which was rattling on its hinges from the hands and *lathis* beating on it from the outside. "Alright, *bhai*, we're coming out," he hollered, and as he unlocked the huge padlock holding the gate shut, the battering stopped.

When Ramesh and I emerged through the narrow passageway he had cracked in the gate, the crowd edged back a meter or so to give us room. Inside Alan beckoned to the *chowkidar*, who came forward to close the gate again after Priya and he also slipped out of it to take positions on either side of Saida.

"We have to take this injured woman to the hospital in Shivghar," Ramesh announced over the quieting protesters as he nodded his head toward Saida, who had come to stand behind Shashi and him. "She's going to die of blood poisoning if we don't get her some antibiotics quickly, and if that happens, then things will never be the same for any of us."

"We don't want things to stay like they are now," screamed a portly Hindu lady in a yellow sari on the left side of the crowd facing the group which had come out from inside the Maidan. "That Saida knew she should have stayed away from my son, and she deserves what she got."

"You can't mean that, Srimati," I said, stepping forward. "I've talked to your son Navin, and he loves her and—"

"She's nothing but a *dasin* of this Maidan who has bewitched him," Navin's mother cried out as she spit at Saida, and the people behind roared their approval. "We're honest Yadav people, and no Yadav in his right mind would marry a *vaish*, especially a Muslim *vaish*."

"If you had bothered to talk to them, you'd see you are wrong," I said, as the Muslims on the other side of the crowd in front of me started to stir again. "They're deeply in love, and Saida's as a fine a lady as you and me."

"No, she isn't, not anymore," shouted the old man in a green *lungi* in front of the Muslims. "My wife died when she was born, and she was a good daughter to me until she met that Navin. I want her back now," he cried, stamping his foot, "or she can die for all I care."

"You can't possibly want that for your own flesh and blood," I uttered in astonishment. "I've had a child die myself, and it's worse than losing your own life!"

"Well, my son is as good as dead if we don't get that Saida away from him," Srimati Nautal shouted. "I don't want him to go on living if he lives with her!"

"Don't you realize how selfish you're being," I said with emphasis. "I used to be like you." I looked hard at Navin's mother. "I thought my sons should always be mine no matter what wives they chose, and then in part because I was so selfish and mean to the woman my son Shiva loved, he took his own life." The crowd stilled considerably. "To accept my responsibility for that act is the worst thing I've ever had to go through, for I'll never be able to undo the results of my selfishness. I'll never be able to bring my son back...."

My voice broke here, and I had to compose myself. "I don't wish that on any mother, Srimati Nautal," I whispered. "I certainly don't wish it on you."

The crowd now was completely still.

"I don't care what you say," Saida's *bap* suddenly screamed from the other side. "These Hindus never let us forget that they think they're better than us. I've heard it every day I've been alive!"

"But hasn't Saida always shown you she's as good as any woman?" I said calmly to the girl's father. "Don't you know that she's a beautiful creature," I continued, moving my hands slowly over the whole crowd to include every person I was facing. "Don't all of you really know that in your heart of hearts?"

"No, I don't," Saida's furious father suddenly screamed and threw the stone he had hidden in his right hand at her. "You should all die!"

The rock sped past my temple and – *plunk* -- smashed into the forehead of his daughter, who collapsed to the ground.

Horrified, most of the protesters evaporated. I dropped to my knees over Saida, while Priya ran inside for some gauze and alcohol. Alan quickly opened the gate all the way to let the *chowkidar* edge the Jeep outside, while Ramesh dashed inside for a stretcher. The old Muslim man and Hindu woman who had mobilized the protests stood frozen in their fear. "*Aiii, nahii,*" Saida's father wailed.

The men lifted Saida onto the stretcher and carried her around to the back of the Wagoneer where they opened the tailgate, lifted the back window, and carefully laid out the stretcher inside. Alan and Ramesh climbed in the rear compartment to attend to the girl while Priya and I jumped in the front seat, and we wound slowly around this distraught old man and woman and the few other stragglers….

The lingering cry of "*aiii, nahii*" followed us as we pulled onto the road and started north through the last of the protesters fleeing on either side up the road….

I watched to the rear from the front seat as Alan and Ramesh staunched the girl's blood flow. What a way to disperse an unruly crowd, I thought, beginning to pray. Please, God, don't let her die, I silently implored from the bottom of my soul. Not for me, I cried, but for her…and the tiny creature she carries….

                    *   *   *

Saida did not die, though the female of the twins she carried did not survive the delivery. Her robust three year old son Shyam, however, did live to cavort in the playground outside the Maidan *anganwadi.* His father Navin, being skilled at repairing almost any machine from a pump to a printer like so many of the scheduled castes, became the Maidan's facility manager, and in the following several years the cooperative's unusual philosophy and organizational structure made it a place of refuge for Indians of all stripes and a spot to stop for foreigners seeking to find hope in North Bihar.

The acreage of the Tajiani ki Maidan at the confluence of the rivers tripled to over a thousand *bighas*, and the number of permanent residents there grew many times to almost five thousand. But one of these residents who would not be there long was the nominal head of the Maidan's directorate, Shashi Verma, who was rapidly closing in on a full century upon this planet peopled by humankind that was called Earth. Shashi prepared for her imminent passage to the beyond by an increasingly concentrated study of the supramental yoga perfected by the early freedom fighter Sri Aurobindo, and cooperative compatriots contributed to the coming transition by holding a renaming ceremony for her on the occasion of her 99th birthday, the day after Shashi completed her ninth annual celebration of the Chaiti Maiya in Shivghar District.

The Master of the Ceremony was Saida Nautal, the little Muslim girl Shashi had taken in and saved several years before. "Sri and Srimatiya," Saida began to the assembled thousands in the open-air theatre behind the Maidan's administrative center, "there is no task in life possible that could give me greater pleasure than facilitating this honoring of the extraordinary human being who has led this institution since its founding, the lady we have all come to know as our mother, Shashi Chaudry Verma. I met Mother Shashi a little over three years ago after my husband Navin and I had run away to Kolkata to get married and had come back to our home in Shivghar town a few kilometers up the road."

The crowd of primarily cooperants and neighbors gave a rousing show of pride in their homeland, and when it had subsided, Saida continued "But, as most of you know, Navin is a Hindu, and I am a Muslim, and neither of our families welcomed us back then with open arms. Fully sixty years after the father of our country, Mahatma Gandhi, was assassinated for dreaming that all peoples could live together as equals in Independent India, it was unthinkable for an Indian Muslim and Hindu to marry, no matter how much they loved each other, or how good they are for each other, as Navin and I have proven to be since Mother Shashi took us in here at the Maidan."

An even greater cheering from the growing mass of the audience erupted, and Saida's remarks were brought to a slightly longer halt this time.

"So today as our Maidan Mother enters her hundredth year on Earth, we have gathered here to honor her life," another burst of applause was deafening this time, "and celebrate her next one," Saida said when she could finally be heard again. "Somehow, as a practicing Muslim of India, I have come to hope and believe that the best of us from every creed will be born again on this lovely planet spinning around through the universe," The crowd erupted here again with a rousing *"Errrraaaaah"* that cast out a sound and a gust of wind shaking the trees atop the great Himalayas in the north and roiling the sacred waters of the Ganga to the south. "So I expect our Mother will soon be back with us in a form where she will be able in her new beginning to help us here at the Maidan achieve our basic goals of beauty, truth, and love for all...."

"Errrrrraaaaaaah...."

"But now, from the Indian who, perhaps, more than any other person alive, knows the story of our Mother's life, is her natural son and co-director here at the Maidan, Ramesh *bhai*."

Ramesh came forward to a polite greeting that rolled over the rich, black fields that surrounded the platform upon which he stood to face the multitudes. "My mother – our Mother Shashi – was born on November 15, 1923, not much more than a hundred kilometers due east of here in Madhubani District in the heart of ancient Mithila, where Sitaji and so many other great Indians among us were born. As with millions in Mata Bharat today, she had to leave our beautiful countryside," he said, moving his hand along the horizon from banyans to eucalyptus demarking the bountiful green *bighas* cut by the deep blue runnels of water rippling down from the mountains to the north, "to make a living, then married a classmate she met at Patna College, and bore and raised five children for him in our state capital there on the other side of the Ganga.

"Her husband, my father, Mohan Verma was, as I understand it, a wonderful speaker, who at their senior-class meeting in 1943 convinced a crowd of about this size not to aid the Nazis to help us gain independence from the British and in the process won the heart of my mother forever. Just as importantly, he was a kind and hard-working man, and after he came back from fighting in World War II, they were married, and he long toiled throughout Bihar invigorating and diversifying its land, transportation system, and agriculture for a good half century. Then my parents retired to America to help raise the children of my youngest sister Reva, who was like so many women by the end of the 20th century a working mother there."

The crowd was mostly silent as Ramesh spoke, most of them clearly unfamiliar with this part of Mataji's life, although Reva and their family smiled broadly at the rendition of the American chapter of her story. "My father had a harder time adjusting to America than my mother did, and after a number of years there, he converted to Buddhism, became a monk, and was dispatched to help resolve some important temple business in Bodh Gaya. Unfortunately not long after he was finished with this task, he was accidentally killed on the road as he was walking toward the place where Buddha was born not so far away from here in Nepal. Thus my father finished his life in his beloved India, and it is entirely possible that he passed through this very place on his final journey." Tara and Gopal and their spouses and progeny also listened attentively to their youngest sibling on the portion of the elevated platform behind him.

"His death was a great shock, following upon the unexpected demise of my older brother Shiva not many years before, and my mother came back here immediately to cremate my father at Varanasi. From there, both for my father and brother Shiva as well as herself, she made her first pilgrimage, carrying holy Ganga *pani* from Kashi to exchange for sand from the Shivalinga at Rameshwaram in Tamil Nadu, which tradition required that she bring the sand back to the Vishwanath Golden Temple in Kashi.

"After this return trip to Kashi, my mother, accompanied by the best friend of my father began another pilgrimage, and most of you know it ultimately landed Mother in this place where we are honoring her today." At this point he looked back at Naj and his wife Mira who stood next to his friend Arash Narriman behind him on the stage.

"The two of them started this second pilgrimage at Kushinagar at the northern edge of U.P. where the Buddha died and continued on into Nepal as far as Lumbini where Lord Buddha had been born as Siddartha Gautama. From there, they turned east to lay some flowers at the very spot my father was killed, and re-entered India at Dibni in Paschim Champaran, intending to continue on to Mahubani District to drop Mother off to meet me at her native village.

"After the place my father was killed, they passed through Motihari, where the Mahatma more than a century ago started his *satyagraha* movement against the English that resulted in them finally leaving our country in 1947, and into Sitamarhi, where Sita had been miraculously born thousands of years ago. It was in Sitamarhi that my mother learned of this remarkable Shivghar district, which had separated from Sitamarhi because women could not get a fair chance at life in the homeland of the Goddess Sita," Ramesh finished and caught his breath while Shashi looked smilingly on from amidst her friends and other children behind.

"At Shivghar town, Ma met people from the Global Sanatan Dharmi Society, with which she was familiar from her time studying how to revitalize Hinduism in America, and she decided to stay on at their ashram in the District, where she worked closely with the third director of our Maidan, our good friend and cooperant Alan Findhorst." Ramesh turned back to acknowledge the tall, sandy-haired man standing next to Shashi. "After several years there, they had some disagreements with the Sanatan Dharmis about administration of the ashram, and when it was dissolved four years ago, my Mother and Alan recruited my wife Priya," Ramesh looked back to acknowledge her on the other side of Shashi, "and myself to join them in this endeavor we named Tajiani ki Maidan here." Ramesh came to a halt again as the crowd lifted a cheer now.

"You have heard Saida tell the story behind the first crisis in the Maidan's life our Mother guided us through, and I am going to allow Mataji to tell you why this cooperative is such a unique and special place now," Ramesh moved into his concluding remarks. "But first I want to tell you about an award we here at the Maidan have unanimously decided to bestow on her." The murmur of the still-growing audience grew to a buzz the volume of a billion cicadas in full harmony deep on a summer's night. "We have decided to rechristen the little girl Shashi Verma as Mata Naveena, a more fitting name for a woman of the stature she has achieved." The crowd of Hindus, Muslims, Buddhists, Parsis, Sikhs, and Christians raised the pitch of its hum uncertainly now. "In doing so, we pay honor to another woman of substance, who also had an adopted name and who did so much to help the poor, the unwanted, and unloved of India during the second half of the 20th Century. But as similar as these two women are, our Mother, to be renamed Mata Naveena for her new birth today, is different from Mother Teresa in several important respects."

The crowd lowered its pitch but cranked up its volume in anticipation here. "First, she is an Indian," Ramesh said, "born, bred, and returned home to her beloved North Bihar. Second, her new name *Naveena* in Sanskrit means 'new', one who loves solitude yet still is kind and pleasant to others, but one whose greatest desire is to become spiritual.

"Thirdly, our Mata Naveena, just as Mother Teresa, suffered great doubt in her life, but unlike her predecessor, she did not suffer it during the process of achieving saintliness. Instead our Naveena suffered doubt before she began to grow. The soul of our Mata was forged by the greatest insults and injuries life can inflict upon a human being, and her response was not to give up and escape this existence, but to get better, trust again, love more, and do more for each one of us in this world.

"Lastly, *Naveena* also has the connotation of 'birth', and for our Mata Naveena, this day surely signifies her rebirth into the bigger person she has become in this life, and what I as an observant Hindu know with certainty will be another birth into her next life here in India, where she will certainly do for all of us here unimaginable good for the benefit of mankind," Ramesh finished, stepping back and extending his hand to his mother. "Srimatiya and Sri, please welcome our Mother, Mata Naveena."

The cheering was tumultuous as Mata Naveena came forward. She bowed her head and folded her hands before her chest and started to speak, *"Namaste aur shukriya.* I cannot begin to express how wonderful it is to be honored with this wonderful new name and have it bestowed upon me personally by my own child, my youngest, Ramesh."

The guests behind her including Arash, Naj and his wife, and the rest of her family smiled and clapped politely as the crowd emitted a gentle approval from the mouths of their beatific faces. "It makes me feel that a part of my life before I came here to the Maidan, that part which was fraught with problems and my weakness and mistakes, was not all in vain. I have beautiful children," she stepped back and acknowledged each of the four of them behind her, "all of whom chose wonderful life mates and produced beautiful children themselves, and some of whom," and she stepped back even further to point to several of the younger women on the stage who held toddlers, "have even given me the gift of great-grandchildren."

"Yes," she went on, turning to face the audience again and smiling broadly, a gesture reciprocated by Didi, whose mischievous eyes twinkled from the first row, and by her husband Varun at her side, who joyfully uttered *"kaisa sundar hai"* as he lovingly glanced at his wife. "I am old now and will not be on this Earth that much longer." A smattering of the crowd ventured "no's" that lingered over the mass of heads assembled before her as she continued. "But what a wonderful last few years of my life have spun out here in the Tajiani ki Maidan. While neither it nor I are perfect, we have a lovely community here – we have chosen to call it a cooperative – and we are most proud of the fact that while we have people of all faiths living here, very few of them who have come have later chosen to leave our community." The crowd clapped in approval, as Shyam on its left flank reverently hummed the tune of his favorite *raag.* "We have proven that we Indians can work and play together productively, that we can live together in peace over the long haul."

The crowd roared in affirmation at this point, and Kavitha from the coop kitchen knew with certainty from the second row that her Mata would always be there to envelope her in an embrace that would dissipate any fear of the future.

"One of the reasons for the Maidan's staying power is the hard work we have done here over the last four years. When we began, we had three main objectives. The first, of course, was to provide a place of refuge for the ostracized people of North Bihar like Saida and Navin as Mother Teresa did for the unfortunates in Kolkata. In this we have been very successful, as these folks have been transformed into healthy and productive citizens within the cooperative, or they have been trained to go back into the society outside and find useful work out there." Slender Rashid, who had pulled a rickshaw till he had dropped off some passengers at the Maidan gate and entered himself to find a home there nurturing his cherished *urad* in the dark earth again, cheered gleefully in the truth of this claim of universal usefulness at the cooperative

"Secondly, when I took my first pilgrimage, I happened upon a children's health center in South India popularly called an *anganwadi*, where I stayed on and worked for an extended period, providing health and educational care to mothers and their young children. Here in the Maidan, we have not only replicated these services and expanded them to provide health care and employment training beyond women and children to include as recipients the men of the family, but we also have established accredited primary and secondary schools in the cooperative that will bring all our children to the point of being able to take care of themselves anyplace at any time.

"Thirdly, from the fields of our cooperative, we not only fully feed our cooperants, but with our fine lychee orchards my son Ramesh has developed here and the excellent dairy and poultry programs Alan has started and trained a number of our members to perpetuate, we now provide healthy and desirable foodstuffs to the surrounding markets and generate enough income for the cooperative to buy the necessaries that we cannot produce ourselves. Beyond this, we have improved new strains of paddy, lentils, pulse, and other vegetables here, which we hope in the future to expand beyond production for our own sustenance to becoming cash crops also." At this point, wizened widow Jyotila in the crowd's third phalange cuddled her orphan charge Prashant from the nursery to give him constant tactile reminder that his recently departed older sister would never be far away.

"Lastly, Alan as Maidan manager has walked a fine line in sufficiently automating its administration that has become a model operation that is serving as a basis for further vocational training for the children of our cooperative. Already we are seeing the development of some of the fine, problem-solving minds that have made Indian software products a beacon in the field for the entire world and that have raised the standard of living for more than a half billion of our Indian people to the level of any country on the planet."

This remark touched off a roar of nationalistic pride in the audience including old Srilal in its fourth file, whose self-respect warmed his *anahata* chakra, while Mata Naveena leaned back and waited for the noise to subside. After perhaps a quarter minute, she began again amidst a remnant smattering of applause, "But, of course, there remains much to do. Nearly half of our Indian people still are mired in conditions of unacceptable impoverishment of material and mind, and when I go on to the next world, this cooperative will continue to attack these conditions that still plague hundreds of millions of us in this country.

"Not only will the Maidan continue to give a better life to the thousands who will find a home here, the material and social relations we evolve on this *busti* and *bighas* will serve as a beacon for the rest of those left behind in India and, indeed, all over the world." She came to a pause as the approbation of those listening rose again. "But before I leave you today, I want to confess something to you, an experience which I had as a small child that came back to me in a dream I had last night."

A silence descended over the audience as it became acutely alert, especially Ramesh, who had an inkling of what his mother was about to say. He waited in trepidation for the words that would next issue from her mouth.

"The dream was very vivid and accurate as I now remember one of the earliest memories of my life. *A small girl of no more than four was enjoying her first experience of the city. Her parents had brought her and an older brother and sister from a small village not far from this place, a village in the shadow of these same great peaks we can see to the north from here on a clear day. The family was going over to Kashi, and while they waited in front of the railway station for a rickshaw or* tonga *to take them to the house of her father's sister there, a horribly disabled beggar came up to them to ask for alms.*" High on the shoulders of her father in the middle of the audience, little Marisa clutched the crude cross around her neck and listened carefully to the sort of *sapana* that would still often plague her early morning hours until her vast extended family in the Maidan surrounded her with its customary attentions before the sun rises.

"*The* bhikhari *was grotesque,*" Mata Naveena continued. "*His body was twisted, and he had to pull himself along on a rough trolley with his least deformed arm. He had no teeth, and though he could speak, his words were slurred and shrill, and her father had to lean in close to him in order to understand what the beggar was saying.*

"Suddenly her father broke onto a smile and said something while he searched in his bag for some coins. 'Why are you talking to this man, Dada?' the little girl cried, jealous that her father was not waiting upon her every wish as he usually did when he was with her. 'He is so ugly, and he smells. He doesn't even have any teeth, and you can't even understand him.'

"Her mother shushed the little girl."

"And my father went on and gave the man some coins back then so long ago.

"'Where did you learn to act like this?' my mother scolded me 'We didn't teach you to treat people this way—'

I awoke this morning with an awful shame."

The crowd was transfixed by the telling of this dream, and Mata Naveena herself stopped a moment and gazed into the multitudes. "I have always believed that a child is born perfectly innocent into this life, without evil following him from the previous one." She paused again, looking into the crowd for a sign.

Then she started again. "A few years after that trip to Kashi, I was subjected to some terrible abuse from someone outside my home, and I did not like the person I became afterwards. I always thought that the shock of that abuse had molded me to be fearful and selfish. Surely it did contribute to the type of person I was as a young woman – and I assure you I was not a very nice person until I was forced to grow beyond it when my son Shiva took his own life.

"But last night, this dream brought back to me how self-centered and thoughtless I was even before I suffered that abuse," she said, tears forming in the corners of her eyes. "As just a little girl, I had treated that beggar man inhumanely. I had done so long before the shock of the abuse I later suffered began to shape me."

She stopped again and then slowly, softly began to beg her brothers and sisters before her for forgiveness. "So none of us is without *pāp*, without bad that we have done for no good reason. Each one of us has done something shameful, something we must be forgiven for."

Mata and the people around her were still and silent for a long while.

Finally she began again one last time. "Soon I will leave this world. I am a Hindu and believe I will come back to it again, for I know I have not been pardoned for all the bad I have done in this life. I have become a better person since my child died, but there is still much that I must atone for.

"For the last several years since I have been here in the Maidan, I have started to study yoga so I would know how to best rise out of this world. I have studied the Integral Yoga of Sri Aurobindo and the Chinese discipline called the *Secret of the Golden Flower*.

"I do not now seek to escape this world when I join with the Godhead. I will die for myself and for everything else in this world now and to come. And I seek to join Brahma and return to bring his goodness to continue helping every living thing here on Earth to get better.

"Soon I will die..., but I will be back. Hopefully I will return to this very Maidan, maybe with some new ideas about how we can...."

SPRING AGAIN

Chapter Thirteen

The next morning Mata Naveena got up with the sun and went out into the fields to purge herself as she had been taught to do at the time she was a little girl. When she had emptied herself, she walked over to sit beneath an ancient banyan tree.

She straightened her back, folded her legs, and laid her hands upon her thighs. She softened her breath and thought only of the whisper of air she took in through her nose, and then she released her breath to gently brush the scattered white hairs above her upper lip.

She became utterly still and released her will completely. She did not think of what she wanted to do for the world when she came back, and she did not even pray that she would be able to do it.

And, in time, she lifted up....

HINDI/HINDUSTANI-ENGLISH GLOSSARY

aap – you (formal) as in *"Aap kaisa hai?"* or "How are you?"

aaj - today

aaj kal – the day before yesterday or the day after tomorrow, or idiom for at present

aarti – Hindu ceremony, the lamp with which to conduct it

achaa – good

abhii - now

adivasi – tribal

alu – potato(es)

Amma – Mom

anahata (chakra) – heart, the fourth yogic channel in the body

anganwadi – childhood development center of the its director

arthavaca – Parsi priest

aur – and

babu – title for a respected man, a clerk

bahnoi – sister's husband

bahu – daughter-in-law

bahut – very, much, very much

baira – waiter, servant, boy

baraa – big, older

beta – son

beti - daughter

bhagat – devotee

bhai - brother

bhang – marijuana prepared as an Indian beverage

bhati or *bhatiji* – niece

bhikhari – beggar

bigha – a measure of land in South Asia from 1/3 to 1 acre

bilkul – absolutely

bindi – a colored dot between the eyes to show a woman is married

Brahmin- the highest Hindu caste, a priest

cammac – spoon

chacha – father's brother

chappals – sandals

chappati – flat and round piece of bread individually cooked

chatai – want as in *"Kya chatai hai?"* or "What do you want?"

chebua – wheat preparation

chini- sugar as in *"Chini chate hai?"* or "Do you want some sugar?"

Chup rahoo! – "Be quiet!" or "Shut up!"

chota – small, younger

chowkidar – watchman, guard

Dada – a form of "father"

dasin – a woman who attended Hindu priests in a temple or monastery

daya – compassion, selfless

devi – goddess

dhanyavad – thank you (Hindi

dhoti – cloth loosely wrapped and tied around waist usually worn by Hindu men

dost – friend

dudh – milk

gai – cow

Gannesh – Hindu god in the form of an elephant symbolizing beginnings, success, learning

ganja – marijuana

gehu – wheat

ghar – home

ha – yes as in *"Ji ha!"* or "Yes, sir!"

hai – are, am

halva – sweet usually made from semolina and dry fruit

hamara(e) – our

harijan – untouchable

jaiiyee – please go

jaldi – quickly, soon

    Jaldi milengee – See you soon

jelabi – a fried pretzel-shaped sweet usually eaten at breakfast

ji – an honorific appended to names or forms of address as in "Mataji"

Ji ha! – certainly

jyotirlinga/shivlinga – twelve celestial bolts flung down by Shiva onto India

kab (kabhii) – when

    kabhii nahii – never

kacca – raw, unripe, unmetalled

kaisa(i) – how

kal – yesterday or tomorrow

kasam (qasam) – oath or vow

kayastha – a caste of scribes, traditionally keepers of records

kisan - agriculturalist

Kooi baat nahii. – literally "not any talk" meaning "It makes no difference"

Kshatriya – the caste of warriors or leaders

kya – what as in *"Kya hota hai?"* or "What's going on?"

lassi – a yoghurt drink

lathi – a big stick or pole used as a club

lingam (linga) – a sacred sculpted penis

lungi – a hanging cloth wrapped worn like a long skirt usually by Muslim men

maidan – an large, grassy open space

mama – mother's brother

mandir – Hindu temple

masala – a mixture of spices often particular to each chef

Mata Gaai – Mother Cow

mausa – husband of mother's sister, more generally the husband of any aunt or cousin

mausi – mother's sister

mera (i) – my, mine

milengee – We will meet

mithai – sweets

    mithas - sweetness

Mithila – area of northern Bihar and adjoining Nepal speaking the language Maithili

murgi – chicken

musselman – Muslim

nahii – no

nam – name

namaskar (namaste) – hello

nathaa – a Hindu priest's upper garment

pakka – hard, strong, firm

paisa – the smallest denomination of Indian money, penny

pandit – a Hindu priest, teacher, master, or learned one

pani – water

pāp – gratuitous bad act

punkah – overhead fan

purana – old, an old Hindu tale with a moral

puri – a delicate Indian bread similar to a croissant

qasam – oath or vow in Urdu transliteration

rasgulla – a ball of soft cheese soaked in syrup

roti – bread

sab – all, everything as in *"Sab thik hai"* or "All is well", "Everything okay?"

sabzi – vegetables

sadhu – a Hindu mendicant holy man

safar ke douran – journey

sahad – one who tries to help

sahib/sahub – sir

sali – sister-in-law

salwar kameez – a Indian woman's long loose-fitting blouse and pants

samajhna – to understand as in *"Samajhta hai?"* or "Do you understand?"

sapana - dream

sasuma – mother-in-law

satyagraha – literally "insist on truth" or the term for Gandhi's non-violent resistance movement against the British colonial occupation of India

shukriya – thank you in Urdu

sidhee – straight

srimati – Mrs.

stupa – Buddhist temple

sundar – beautiful, terrific

svagat – welcome

tabla – a small Indian drum

teesri(a) – third

tirthyatra – Hindu pilgrimage to a sacred site

tonga – a two-wheeled cart usually pulled by a horse

tu – very informal and familiar you

tum – a slightly more informal form of address for you

urad – an Indian black bean or lentil

vaish – slang for a bad woman

vesya – prostitute

videsi – foreigners

vrata – Hindu religious practice to carry out certain obligations to receive divine blessing for a specific desire(s)

    vratta – one who performs this practice

waalah – one who is or does something as in, for example, *"rickshaw-waalah"*

Yadav – a cowherd caste

zamindar – a large landowner